BEBE'S BY GOLLY

Wow!

ALSO BY YOLANDA JOE

He Say, She Say
Falling Leaves of Ivy

BEBE'S BY GOLLY

Wow!

YOLANDA JOE

DOUBLEDAY New York London Toronto Sydney Auckland

PUBLISHED BY DOUBLEDAY
a division of Bantam Doubleday Dell Publishing Group, Inc.
1540 Broadway, New York, New York 10036

DOUBLEDAY and the portrayal of an anchor with a dolphin
are trademarks of Doubleday, a division of
Bantam Doubleday Dell Publishing Group, Inc.

Library of Congress Cataloging-in-Publication Data
Joe, Yolanda.
Bebe's by golly wow / by Yolanda Joe. — 1st ed.
p.   cm.
I. Title.
PS3560.0242B4   1998
813'.54—dc21   98-11248
CIP

ISBN 0-385-49255-3

While working on this novel I had the devastating experience of losing the grandmother who raised me and my father, both in the same week. The experience showed me how important it is to build your faith over the years so that you can draw on it in trying times. Despite all troubles, there is no fault in God. So I dedicate this book:

To My Grandmother: Bernice Barnett,
whom I was blessed to have for a long time and . . .

To My Dad: John Joe,
whom I was blessed to have for a little while . . .
You are loved and you are missed.

Blessed are they that mourn, for they shall be comforted.
Matthew 5:4

Be of good courage, and He shall strengthen your heart, all you who hope in the Lord. Psalm 31:24

Acknowledgments

To my family and friends who love and encourage me in my work, I say thank you. Kudos and kisses to both my agent Victoria Sanders and my editor Janet Hill. Hugs and high fives to the behind-the-scene folks at Doubleday . . . from the art department to publicity to sales. A big shout out of "You go, girls!" to all the book clubs that have supported my work. And finally thanks and praises be to God for allowing me to create and be happy doing it.

BEBE'S BY GOLLY

Wow!

THE PEOPLE

Beatrice Mae Thomas

Bebe

I'm Bebe. The Be. I'm a lot like the bumblebee, only personified. I'm black and yellow too. Black is my race and yellow is my skin color. I fly high naturally, too. And I like to flit around looking for something sweet to get into. I've got a sexy buzzzzz sound when I'm happy and I sting something fa-fa-fierce when I'm mad. And come to think of it, when I rub my legs together I can make honey, too. The Be. Just like that BUT times two. Be-be!

Now whatEVER somebody it was that said, "God don't like ugly and ain't stuck on pretty," was obviously somewhere in between, and trying to give herself some props. I'm leaning on the pretty side myself, but I'm not mad at God for not being stuck on me.

Who wants God to eyeball everything you do? Shoot, not-tah-I! When I get to heaven, I'm going to have enough explaining to do as it is. And EVERYBODY knows that you absolutely cannot lie your way into heaven. THANK GOODNESS, too! That means I ain't gotta worry about seeing none of my ex-boyfriends there. Those Negroes? Please! When their mamas told them to stop lying they thought she just meant get up outta bed!

One ex-boyfriend stands out in my mind. Sergio. He and I took a road trip to Hotlanta, Georgia. On the way back, we stopped at a little inn located in some small town. It was a cute, pink and blue frame house with a birch swing. There was a barn, too, with a red-feathered rooster for an alarm clock and a group of plump, sassy hens laying eggs for our country breakfast. The inn had ten rooms. Each room had a skylight. At night, newborn speckles of light would lie dozing on the burnt coloring of the seamless sky. The bed had a mattress that was partially stuffed with hay. Hey now, rural yet romantic.

My man Sergio started loving me at my toes, kissing each one with tenderness. They curled in appreciation. He licked the inside of my thighs, and I stroked the back of his neck and he stroked my insides with easy, long soul-clapping thrusts. The soft sensuality of our good loving made us grip each other with our hands and our hearts.

The next morning while Sergio slept, I tiptoed down to the kitchen, deciding to bring breakfast to him in bed just like he liked. The old cook was a bowlegged brother, crispy brown in color, just like the bacon he was frying. "Sergio sure knows how to train his women," he said. "They all come down here like clockwork to get his breakfast."

Come to find out, Sergio had taken road trips before, and this was not a special place just for me. In fact, Sergio had taken some other woman down there two weeks before, when he told me he was on a business trip. As I stood in the kitchen, I decided I was going to give him the business! I took Sergio his breakfast—two eggs over easy—right on top of his head!

We broke up after that but Sergio kept trying to get back together. So one night I got a little tipsy and I started playing my "old school" records. (And I've got a ba-ba-baaad record collection, chile!) As I sat back and got comfortable I let some of the songs inspire me to write Sergio a final, parting note. I used nothing but great duets to make my point. I wrote:

Baby, I was searching for an ENDLESS LOVE, and before I knew it THEN CAME YOU. Our lovemaking was full of FIRE AND DESIRE. So I began to BUILD MY WHOLE WORLD AROUND YOU. I forgot about everyone else and told you that YOU'RE ALL I NEED TO GET BY. But IT TAKES TWO. You had others on your heart and in your mind. I even told you, "I'M GONNA MAKE YOU LOVE ME." But you made sure I failed. AIN'T NOTHING LIKE THE REAL THING, which we obviously didn't have. I thought we could be SOLID AS A ROCK. Sorry, MY MISTAKE.

But all jokes aside, I'm a straight-up person with easy rules: treat yourself and the people you care about well, and God will take care of the rest.

I'm an only child. I was drug up here from the South when I was a little girl but SOUTH *side* of Chicago is what is in my soul. My parents are gone but they remain in my heart. I've got cool aunts and cousins, and a best friend named Sandy who is family-sister-girl to me. Good job, good health, and good-looking. Now I just need a good man. I often wonder, will I ever find him?

Isaac Sizemore

Isaac

I'm a simple man with simple tastes. But simple does not mean that I am not selective. I believe in choices and choosing well. I'm a godly man who knows when to THANK his Maker, when NOT to challenge Him and when to HELP Him out.

When it comes to music, I prefer the brothers—as in Isley, Johnson, and the Jackson Five. I also like Marvin Gaye, the Chilites, K-C & the Sunshine Band, the Stylistics, the Four Tops, and Diana "I Can Give Diva Lessons" Ross.

I'm forty and five years old. I'm the child of parents who were part of the great migration from the South to the North. That means there's one degree of separation between me and a society that could have totally crushed my ideals. I experienced the "Shout It Out Sixties" and the "Reconstruction Seventies." I have scars from the "Holding Pattern Eighties" and the "Backlash Nineties."

I like Spike; adore Mike; think Colin is rolling and Tiger can't get much higher. I like collard greens, pinto beans, sports teams, sweet dreams, and women who say what they mean.

I'm a fireman and ever since I was a little boy I've loved fire. Ancient civilizations worshiped fire because they thought it was a spirit given as a gift by the gods. The Scandinavians believed in Thor, the god of thunder (brah man was supposed to have hit his hammer against a piece of flint and created fire). The North American Indians believe buffalo from the land of the gods ran across the plains and the sparks from their hooves created fire. The Greeks say Prometheus stole fire to give to man so he would be master of all the animals and elements of earth. To me, a fireman is an alias for "master of the spirit." Fire is a spirit. It's an unruly, fleeting, consuming, hot-hot, devastating spirit. Every day I try to master the spirit and hope never to experience the day when it masters me.

I am also a father. My daughter Dashay is a handful; just a headache for her old man who wants her to grow up slow, smart, and steady. She, however, wants to be grown before her time. I'm not gonna let her!

I dream ambitious dreams. I hope when I am awake. I wish for luck and prepare for opportunities. I fight my problems and I embrace my good times. I've got less money than Bill Gates but more money than the brother offering to wash my car windows for a buck.

My temper, my hook shot, and my barbecue grill are all quite nasty. I've got too much pride and too much debt from helping others. I'm divorced by force, think love is from above, like my books long and my brewskis in a short glass.

I believe in both meaningful conversation and talking shit although I'm not always sure I know the difference when I'm hearing it or speaking it.

There are unanswered questions in my life: about my ex-wife and what happened to us. Also, I've got a good friend who gambles like a fool with a bunch of shady characters; I wonder if I'll be able to save him or will his funky habit destroy our friendship?

All questions are answered in time, although we may or may not like the answers we get. But that's life, all a brah can do is wish everyone good things and hope they wish nothing but good things back.

Dashay Sizemore

Dash

Beat Box:
Boom da-ka boom, da-ka boom-boom-yeah!
Boom da-ka boom, da-ka boom-boom-yeah!

My name is Dash, this is my song.
I'm thirteen years old, ain't been here long.
I rap, rhyme and like to sing,
I dream of long braids and fine gold rings.
I'm kinda cute, or so the boys say,
But Daddy's watching, can't give 'em no play,
I jam with lyrics and in math too,
A straight-A student, I'm still real cool.
My best friend Tasha, she's on the one,
We talk and rap, have lots of fun,
No 40's, drugs, or boys with gats
'Cause we ain't down with no stuff like that!
Got Daddy's color, hair, and his eyes,
Slim like my mama, who left with no good-byes.
Uncle Lucius, yeah, he lives upstairs,

WOW!

Tells funny stories, and really does care.
I guess that's all, I got to go.
You've peeked in my world, so now you know.
I'm not being rude, ain't trying to joke
But, like the cartoon says, "Tha-tha-that's all, folks!"

Sandra Mae Atkins

Sandy

What does life teach us about ourselves?

My late father used to ask me that question all the time when I was a teenager growing up in our working middle-class neighborhood on the South Side of Chicago.

I'd like to think that life teaches us about our strengths and weaknesses. My strengths are my loyalty and dedication that I have for friends like Bebe and for family, like my mother, who is happily retired in Arizona. I love music and literature. My keen business sense, my calm professional manner, and my tigress aggression have all contributed to the success I've had at the jazz station where I work.

My weaknesses? Wow, that's a tough call. Ohhhh-kay, let me see . . . I fall in love too fast, too often, and with the wrong person like my ex-boyfriend T.J. I'm kinda insecure about my looks—I'm always wondering, Am I too dark and too skinny? I also worry that I won't achieve all my goals and all my dreams.

If I had a crystal ball, I would see the trouble that lay ahead for me on my job; trouble that would make me question myself. But where can I buy a crystal ball, huh? Every working woman could use one, because working in corporate America can give a sister the flux on a regular basis.

W O W !

Since my father's not around anymore, I have to ask myself the question: What does life teach us about ourselves?

Well, I'd say that in my twenty-five years I've learned that life is never dull. As a young black woman I know I have to step lively, push harder, pray louder, and hug myself and others tighter so I can get the most out of life.

THE STORY

Bebe

Like a fine liqueur on the rocks, I'm straight up expensive—sweet on the lips—intoxicating in small doses—hard to put down—and good to the last drop. Why have I not found a brother who will savor me the way he savors a good drink? I'm not bashing, I'm bothering. I'm bothering to let them know that I need their attention on a positive tip.

I'm neither perfect nor hopelessly flawed. I'm a regular sister. And there are way too many nice, single, working black women out here looking for love. I'm in my forties and if I have to stay single, I'm not going to cry . . . at least not in public. But privately I will long for the sweet love, nurturing, and companionship that I wish I could-a, would-a, should-a, shared with someone. I think emotional ties between people, men and women, friends and family, are key.

At night I say a prayer, a special one I made up myself. I believe praying is like investing in the Dow Jones—you have to put stock in it, be consistent, be patient, and in time the payoff is big.

My prayer is this: "Dear God, send me a good man to share my life with. Let him be a Christian, a family-oriented man, and a head of household just like the box says on the income tax form. May he be pleasing in Your sight and in mine. And please, GOD, let me know him when I see him. Amen."

The reason I'm on this man subject is that I'm getting ready for a hot date tonight with a new guy named Isaac. It's going to kill me to say it but I've got to . . . I'm nervous. Yes, me the Be. The confident Be. Maybe I'm nervous because I took myself out of the mix for so long after my last fling with Duke, who knocked me for such a loop that I went on a self-imposed sex sabbatical. But then, a couple of weeks ago, I met Isaac. . . .

How'd we meet? Well, I don't want to brag, but ah, I'm a recent college graduate! Yep, and at my graduation I did a very dignified stroll across the stage (to much applause, thank you) and got my B.A. in business. It was a hell of a lot of work, I'm here to tell ya! But I did it! I took classes at night and during the day worked full time at the bank as a supervisor. My best girlfriend Sandy cheered me on all the way. She's the one who encouraged me to go get my degree in the first place.

Anyway, we were in the hallway after graduation. Ah, let's see—me, my aunt and uncle, and my cousins from out of town, Sandy—and this man stepped up and touched me on the shoulders in an ever so nice way and turned me around to him. You didn't hear it from me, maybe you read about it in *Jet,* but the man was fine. Not that that matters but, Lord Jesus above, it takes a load off a girl's eyes, heart, and mind.

Anyway, he said, "Hi, my name is Isaac Sizemore."

I immediately liked his looks and his voice, too. Isaac is around six-four, broad-shouldered, barrel-chested, the color of a perfectly browned steak, with thinning hair, and a sexy little gap in the middle of his two front teeth. He told me his friend's daughter was graduating and then he asked me if I would like to go out sometime. And I knew right then and there, exclamation point, my sabbatical was over.

It doesn't pay to rest too much anyway. You'll lose your edge, understand? Today you need to be ever more sharp to deal with these men out here. That's because they come at you in all sorts of crazy ways.

We exchanged phone numbers and I knew he was going to call but I didn't know when. Finally, several days later, Isaac called, then we set the date for tonight. I had to put both my hormones and my nerves on ice. But I've been wondering all week if Isaac has been as nervous as I've been.

Isaac

I'm a nervous brah man about my date tonight. But I had to ask this woman out. I knew I wanted to talk to her as soon as I saw her cross that stage like she constructed it plank and nail. Her head was back . . . legs fully extended in full strut . . . hips swaying . . . attitude sashaying . . . stop, grab the diploma, strike a pose. Lady, lady, I laughed to myself!

Yes, this was a woman I wanted to get to know and my mind was made up. My grandpa, God rest his soul, said I was headstrong to a fault. Grandpa said, "Boy, know when to quit. Know when to let go. You'll grab ahold ta something and sink wit' it before you let it go. Stubbbbbb-orn!"

That's what he always said. And it made me feel bad. Stubborn was a negative word and I didn't want to think there was anything negative about me. There was enough prejudice against a black man as it was. So I looked up "stubborn" in the thesaurus and found a word I liked better. "Tenacious." I've always felt that I have tenacity. And my tenacity said, "Get that woman to let you take her out no matter what!"

Now the date is set for tonight. I just took a shower here in the firehouse and I'm getting ready. The rest of the guys are downstairs watching the tube. I like to watch old reruns. You know, the classics,

"Good Times," "The Andy Griffith Show," "What's Happening," "Big Valley," "Batman," and "Gunsmoke." I don't care too much for these new shows. Oh, yeah, and I love "Soul Train." It's the hippest trip in America and my all-time favorite show.

I'm standing in front of the narrow mirror tacked onto the back of the door. I've got my peppermint-striped beach towel wrapped around my waist and my flipflops on. Breathe in. Breathe out. Am I getting fat? Everybody's always talking about exercise. Sit-ups. Push-ups. I just like to get up in the morning. But I better take a good look here. Women can be mean when it comes to a man's body. What did Diana Ross say? "I want muscles." Women, including Bebe, I bet, want muscles.

That's her name, Bebe. I like that name. It makes your lips pucker and your throat pop when you say it. Be-be. It's an old-fashioned, Southern name, but stylish, too. And it fits her. I don't even know her that well, yet I sense the name suits her.

I like my name, Isaac. It's a strong, solid name from the Bible, picked for me by my grandpa. It has longevity, power, and a little mud on it from old crazy-butt Ike Turner and his punk woman-beating ways. That's why I don't let anyone call me Ike. I'm Isaac, period.

Okay, I'm all dressed now and with my silk multicolored party shirt, I could be on "Soul Train." I'm sporting a pair of dark blue slacks and my shoes are all shined. Let's check the mirror. Brah looks good. Now all I have to do is get my wallet, keys, and the address to that new club. I put it right in my wallet just behind—what! Three singles! I had a fifty-dollar bill! Where'd it go?

Who would take it? Did I really have to ask myself that? I started running downstairs. There was going to be some humbugging in the firehouse tonight and I knew just who to get after, too!

Bebe

Check-check-check it out. I needed to be cleaner than Clorox for my date tonight. So I had to have a new dress, but getting it was some drama for your mama, let me tell you.

I've got plenty of clothes in my closet but when I go out on a first date with someone I like to wear something new. Something fresh. Anything. A hat. A blouse. Pants. Skirt. Something new. Call me picky. Call me extravagant. But like the comic says, "Call me what ya wanna, but you WON'T call me broke." THE BE knows how to shop. All you have to do is go to a designer outlet store. More power for the dollar y'all! You get the same stuff that is in ————'s and ———— and ————.

My homette Sandy? My best girlfriend? She doesn't believe in that. She'd rather go empty her wallet for a new dress or sweater just so she can say she bought it at one of those high ass places! Please! As long as you look good and the merchandise is quality, what's the point?

I drug Sandy, lips poked out, attitude flaring, all the way down to the store with me. She'd been moping around ever since she broke up with her boyfriend, T.J. But I knew she needed to get out. We got to the store and I picked up a flier that said, SALE: RED DOT ITEMS TAKE EXTRA 50% OFF.

Sandy said, "I don't like this, Be."

"What?" I said. "Girl, stop being so bourgeois!"

Sandy can get so uppity sometimes! She just rolled her eyes at me and tried to hang back. I hooked my elbow around that skinny little arm of hers, pushed forward, and sang: "Onward, Christian Shoppers, marching as to war . . ."

We got inside and women were everywhere. Fat. Skinny. Black. White. Tall. Short. Shapely. Flat as a board. Some of everybody was up in this store, do you hear? That's why I love shopping—there's something for everyone. Me and Sandy don't look nothing alike: I'm tall, light-skinned, short unruly hair, and very shipshape—hips, butt, and legs for life. That's me. Sandy? She's dark-skinned, got good hair, and ain't stout nowhere. Girlfriend makes a stick look fat. But we can go up in a store and both come out happy. So, like I was saying, we were inside this store and everybody and their grandma was there for this sale! Clothes were flying everywhere. Folks was trippin' looking for that booyawh buy! We went to the dress section to look around. Sandy pulled out a dress and said, "This is cute, huh?"

I looked at it and said, "Naw, I had a fallin' out with those two heifers."

Sandy said, "What?"

I pointed to the label. "Polly and Ester!"

We both went back to the racks. I spied this feisty number. It was fitted at the top, strong flair in the hips, and came back in and would hit me just above the knee. I couldn't sit in it but I sho' could shake in it! It was money green too! It looked like me. It spoke to me, saying, "We both are fine so let's get together, huh?"

I reached for it and when I cleared the rack another hand palmed the other side of the hanger. There was this woman standing there who must have been five nine and about a buck seventy-five out of uniform—cause she sure had to be playing football for somebody somewhere. I mean for real, she was a big girl with big hair. And I mean big, blond hair. Big and wild like a nest had fallen on top of her head. Her skin was bleach white and she had vampire brown eyes.

This woman gave me an evil look and said in a nasty tone, "Is there a problem?"

I looked her dead in the eye. "Not if you let go."

She couldn't possibly fit in that dress! Not with Slim Fast, Nutra Sweet, or Richard Simmons himself fighting to keep a spoon out of her mouth. But don't you know she snatched the dress right out of my hand?

Sandy leaned over my left shoulder and teased, "Girl, if you can take her I'll set up a match against Mike Tyson!"

That reminded me, I needed a pair of ear muffs.

I let Drusilla the Biscuit Eater have the dress. I pretended to go back to the rack but I was really watching Miss Dru and my dress go into the fitting room with about five other items. With every step she took with those thunder thighs, I heard the baseline from that old cut, "Ain't Gonna Bump No More With No Big Fat Woman!"

I saw her go in the fitting room and after about five minutes she came out in the dress and stood in the waiting area. God! She looked like Newt Gingrich in a leprechaun outfit! She looked terrible. Miss Dru walked back inside to try on more dresses. After a few minutes she hung *my dress* on the outside of the door. I tipped over there, took the dress, and made my own Taco Bell commercial as I made a run for the border!

So, that's how I got this dress! I'm standing in front of my bedroom mirror. It's one of those old-fashioned, oval mirrors with wood trim, and I'm looking too fine, chile. My hips are luxurious. Impressive. Weighty. They are curvy-curvy cute. But the brothers on the corner would use words like booming. "Boo-yawy! Baby got back!" But God gave me what I got and a little bit of the Be goes a long way.

WOW!

When he called to set up our date, I told Isaac that I liked to dance and he said, "Great, me too!" He said that after his shift we would go out dancing. I'm looking at myself in this dress. Isaac is a fireman. So I know he can put out a fire, but what I wanna know is, can he start one?

Isaac

Someone had started some "sh" and I intended to finish it out with the "it." And I knew exactly who that someone was: L.A.

I reached the television room downstairs and about five of the guys were sitting around watching the news. L.A. was sitting on the blue velvet recliner in the south corner of the room. L.A. is twenty-six years old and like a little brother to me. That's why I don't mind kicking his butt in public. I grabbed his neck and jerked him up, "L.A.!"

"Is-eye, why you tripping?!"

That's L.A.'s nickname for me, Is-eye. "Where's my money?" I said.

L.A. is skinny. I mean, he's so skinny his pockets meet in the back. He's pecan brown with a 'fro. And he has sloping eyelids and large brown eyes. "L.A., I said, where's my money?"

Cliff said, "Isaac, L.A. lost it while you were upstairs sleeping. Adam cleaned us all out in five-card stud!"

Cliff is a veteran fireman with the most years logged in. He's short, stout, with big black bug eyes. "We're all tapped out," he said. "Ain't got squat! Adam broke luck and broke camp with all our money."

L.A. started griping. "I borrowed it, Is-eye. I couldn't hit a hand, man. You understand, being a card player yo'self! You know, you my boy!"

L.A. was all up in my Fruit of the Looms. I shouted at him, "L.A., I was supposed to use that money for my date! What am I going to do now?"

I let go of him because I was disappointed. I was going to have to cancel my date with Bebe because I was flat broke now.

Bobo stood up in the corner and stretched. Bobo is half black and half Mexican. He has ink-black, slick hair, a very neat goatee, and a thin mustache. Add his burnt red coloring to all that, and Bobo has a period look from the Civil War. Bobo talks very fast, pronounces his words hard, and never seems to take a breath until after several thoughts.

Bobo said, "I-thought-that-was-your-party-shirt-you-had-on! Isaac, hey-your-girl-ain't-gonna-have-that!   She's-not-gonna-stand-for-that-two-timing-Esse!"

"Shut up, Bobo," I said.

L.A. smiled. "Not to worry. Not to worry. I got you covered Is-eye!"

Everybody else groaned.

"Naw," L.A. said, "I got this pass I saved to a club where my cousin works downtown. He'll hook you up with free drinks, too. It's cool, but you gotta hurry because the pass expires in about two hours."

"Hey, be quiet!" Cliff yelled, "We're trying to watch 'Jeopardy.'"

I grabbed the pass out of L.A.'s hand and said, "Just give it to me. She's expecting to go to that new club, the After Set. This will have to do, though. But hey, L.A., I still want my fifty dollars, okay?"

"You know a Negro like me!" L.A. said and started laughing, happy I wasn't going to kick his butt.

"L.A.! You big mouth you!" Cliff shouted. "I missed the end!"

L.A. laughed. "Chill, Cliff! Hey, Is-eye. We'll get our own show. A black man's version—call it, "'In Jeopardy'!"

Everybody else laughed. L.A. likes to joke his way out of trouble. Take my hard-earned fifty dollars? Ha-ha, my behind!

"Yeah," L.A. went on, "we'll get Bryant Gumbel to host it."

He had an audience now. L.A. grabbed the latest issue of *Ebony Man* magazine. He rolled up the magazine and held it like a microphone. L.A. can do voices. He can do just about anybody. He started going off, sounding just like Bryant Gumbel.

"Welcome to the new black man's game show, 'In Jeopardy' . . ."

Then L.A. started walking around the room, doing Gumbel. "The category is Ghetto. For a hundred dollars, a yellow substance made in blocks that constipates."

All the guys just looked at one another.

"Egggh! Time! What is government cheese!"

Bobo said, "L.A. is loco!"

"Ghetto for two hundred dollars! During trial of the century, lawyer who put on a skullcap and looked like a preemie baby."

Cliff yelled out, "Johnnie Cochran!"

"Right you are! Two hundred dollars in food stamps for Clifford!"

I cracked a smile but I didn't want to.

A couple of the guys were giving each other high fives. "Ghetto for three hundred dollars. Child actor who talks like Mike Tyson and has hair like Don King. Eggh! Who is Buckwheat!"

L.A. came over to me and threw his arm around my shoulder. I folded my arms across my chest and tried to look mean but he was funny.

"Final question for four hundred dollars. Longest-running TV show that features butt popping, hip swinging, lip synching, and whistle blowing. Answer?"

I smiled and said, "What is 'Soul Train'!"

L.A. hugged me and I decided not to kill him. "I'd better get my fifty dollars, okay?"

L.A. howled, "Is-eye! You know a Negro like me!"

All the guys moaned together at once, "Uh-huhhhhhh!"

I looked at the pass L.A. gave me. I was looking forward to my date but now I was really getting nervous because none of my plans seemed to be going well. I grabbed my jacket and rushed out to pick up Bebe. I got to my car, a 1996 Lincoln Town—black and shining. I'd gotten it washed and waxed for my date. It was clean! I got in and cranked the engine. Nothing. I cranked it again. Nothing. I got out and popped the hood. I checked the battery. It was as dry as a right-wing Republican at an N-double A-C-P meeting.

L.A. came out and looked over my shoulder at the battery. "Damn, Is-eye," he said. "You need to clean off those cables and jump it off. I got a tool kit inside."

"I can't wait that long!" I said. "This is not my night!"

L.A. reached in his pocket and tossed me his keys, "Take my car—it's clean, not as new as yours, but it's in mint condition."

I stood there trying to think.

"You're already late—you'd better break!" L.A. said.

I got in his car, a 1987 Monte Carlo. It was an old model but it was in mint condition. L.A. kept his wheels in shape. I took the pair of dice off the rearview mirror and tossed them to L.A.

"Aww, man!" he said catching them. "These are good luck! You ain't gonna get no leg now!"

I cranked it up and the car turned right over. I sped off to pick up Bebe. Hopefully my luck was changing. Maybe she wouldn't notice that I was a little late, huh?

Bebe

Has Timex stopped tickin'? Rolex stopped rollin'? Pulsar lost its pulse? What's the deal? The man is forty minutes late. FORTY: like the number of acres we were supposed to have, but did not get; like the number of the posse ridin' with Ali Baba.

Finally, after twenty MORE minutes, Isaac rang the bell. I looked out the window and buzzed him up. He looked cute even though his shirt was a little too loud, but I admired him for wearing it. A lot of men aren't comfortable wearing bright colors. They think it's sissy or soft. They're scared to be bold. But help me, Lord, Isaac had no fear with that shirt. It had light blue, gold, red, pink, and white in it. He could have been one of the Fifth Dimension lost in the Age of Aquarius in that shirt. But he did look cute.

"Hi, Bebe. I'm sorry I'm late," Isaac said. "Let's go."

Ain't that nothin'? First he comes tipping over here an hour late and now he was trying to put a rush job on me! I just stared at his butt. Isaac got nervous as a convict on death row. He started looking up, looking down; swinging his arms back and forth, slapping his palms together. "Can I show you my place?" I said, hoping he'd relax.

"Nope," Isaac said, moving to my closet. "I'm just anxious to get to the club so we don't miss out on all that great dance music."

Did he like my dress? Isaac didn't say anything about how I looked, and I know I looked good. Why was he so nervous? As soon as I slipped on my coat, Isaac grabbed my elbow and steered me toward the door.

I said, "Is there a fire somewhere?"

"Ah-huh, excuse me?" Isaac grunted.

"Never mind," I said and just shrugged. I'd hoped that he'd be more exciting than this.

Anyway, we got outside and Isaac has a nice car. It's a late-model Monte Carlo but it's in mint condition. He opened the door for me. A gentleman, I thought, and I liked that. He seemed like he was starting to relax a little. We began to chat. Isaac asked me if I was still excited about getting my degree. And ya know this, I truly am. I told him that my best friend Sandy and I were going to pick out a frame and mounting for my diploma. Then I glanced over and noticed that the gas gauge was on E.

"Better get some gas," I said.

Isaac dropped his eyes and shook his head like he was surprised. Boyfriend didn't know whether or not he had gas? We drove his batmobile into the gas station and I heard him tell the woman on the intercom, "Two dollars, unleaded."

"Two dollars!" I said out loud to myself in the car. "Brother sure knows how to pimp a car off some gas." But was sister-girl me about to offer gas money? No, indeedy! I'd rather put my money between my knees and pee on it than to give it away to a man I ain't married to.

I watched Isaac pump the gas for a second, then I checked my purse for a tissue to blow my nose. I had a little sniffle I'd been trying to shake for a week. I checked the glove compartment. Guess what? There were a bunch of little pieces of paper, torn off with phone numbers on them. "Get with slips," I call them. It looked like Isaac was trying to "get with" a chick named Candy and Lulu and so on.

Even though I thought he was a nice guy, I guess Isaac is a play-boy. Sister-girl me don't have time for that stuff. Chile, things were looking pretty weak. Anyway, we got to the club but it wasn't the club I was expecting to go to. I'd heard about the new "old school" spot, the After Set, and I really wanted to check it out. Isaac drove up to this place I've never heard of called the Trap, and there was a line outside of the place. And the people looked young, too.

He said, "Change of plans, hope you don't mind."

Too late now, I thought. What was I going to say? We were already there. I thought it was kind of tacky of him to change places at the last minute like that and not say a mumbling word. But chile, chile, the BE wanted to get out in America and see what she could see!

So I just said, "Okay, let's try it—if we don't like it, can we go to the After Set?"

"You'll like this place," Isaac said, displaying a dazzling smile. "I've got pull here. Watch how I get around that line."

And you know what? He did. We walked right by everybody. I heard people mumbling some sho' nuff ugly stuff, too. Now even the masses should know better than to try and play me. They were cuss-ing us under their breath. Shoot, that was attitude ammo for me! I put a Diva Ross look on my face. I even put a little pah-pow in my normal milkshake step and sashayed into that club. Maybe with some added V.I.P. treatment, it would be a nice club anyway.

But when we got inside the club, my jaw dropped faster than a prostitute drops her panties. I turned and looked at Isaac, and said, "What is this?"

Isaac

I didn't even know.

Brah man was shocked, embarrassed, and speechless. I had serious egg on my face: scrambled brow, poached eyes, and a hard-boiled mouth.

This club was way wild! It was dark. The only light was a strobe that rotated and pulsed like the emergency lights on top of my fire truck. The music sounded like it was a 45 record stuck on a deep scratch in the middle of James Brown screaming "Hey-humpf" while some crack addict sampled an erratic drum beat underneath. Every-one in there, EXCEPT US, looked like they were in college, *maybe*.

I was gonna kill L.A.—slow and painful! I imagined how they would do it back in the days of Zeus—like tying L.A.'s skinny butt to a tree and letting the buzzards eat him.

Bebe was just staring at me, so I said the only thing a brah man could say.

Bebe

"Wanna dance?" Isaac asked me, trying his best to look sappy-eyed. I had to admit the boy was cuddly-dudley cute even though his taste in night life was obviously suspect.

But let me tell you about this club, which could easily double for a penitentiary/freak show. There were posters hanging from the ceiling showing people in various sex positions. There were ropes painted wild colors, like lime and fuchsia, hanging from the lights.

The D.J.? The D.J. was in a cage, behind bars—yes, they had locked his butt up. With the music he was playing, they should have thrown away the key. The music was all boom-boom-boom! All these folks were out on the floor bumping and grinding on each other. Not the respectable way like we did in the seventies—hips on hips, eyes closed, trying to cop a legitimate feel. That was serious business. These young folks? They needed blue-lights-in-the-basement lessons. They were palming butt and running their hands up and down each other from kneecap to nipple.

"Wanna dance?" Isaac asked again, holding out his hand.

So I came up with a plan. After a dance or two I would get Isaac to take me to the other club. We got out on the floor and the D.J. faded in a mix. I got excited—this song had lyrics! But it only had one refrain, "Do. Do. Do . . . the . . . nah-stay!" Isaac and me? We

32

were doing a side-to-side two-step. There was no room for anything else. But who cared? I mean, who wants to jam to "Do-do-the-nah-stay!"

Suddenly, Isaac's pager went off. "Excuse me," he said and led me off the floor. Isaac headed for the phones, which were near the front door. I sat at the bar for a few minutes and a young dude in a black cat suit—yes! a black cat suit—came up to me and leaned in my ear, whispering, "Let me lick you up and down till you say stop."

I looked at Sir Freaky Deke and he stuck out his tongue and there was a ring in it. Gross! Gross! Gross! Just what I needed, to be hit on by a Dennis Rodman wannabe! This guy had more nerve than a trauma center.

So I just boogied—as in toward the door. This place was definitely not for me. I'm old school, and I thought Isaac was, too. I headed straight for Isaac to tell him I was ready to go quick and in a hip-hop hurry. When I got closer to him, I realized that he was yelling into the phone.

"I mean it! It's none of your business where I am or who I'm with. You don't tell me what to do! C'mon, baby, look-look-look, don't start crying. I'm sorry I yelled, I'm having a bad night. I'll be home sooner than you know it—"

Here Isaac was out with me and he had the woman he was living with on the phone. How stank! Boy, had I read him wrong! I eased past him and got my coat and left. I would cab it home. Wait until I call Sandy and tell her about this mess.

Sandy

If I were a plant, I'd be impatiens.

Impatiens flower irregularly and that's just what I do. I flower irregularly in matters of love. I recently broke up with my boyfriend, T.J., and once again I got broadsided after letting my heart roll out into traffic without checking all the warning signs. I got nailed. And I didn't have any insurance at the time. T.J. and I, we simply faded.

It was some ugly mess that led up to the end but I-I don't want to go through all that—I even managed some vengeance thanks to a little scheming by Bebe—but it's just that I had high hopes for us. But there was too much betrayal and certainly too much drama. And still, because he's so fine and seemed as if he were making some strides toward change, every now and again, I think about maybe giving him a call.

But we just faded . . . to black.

T.J. called me a couple of times after we broke up. We went to dinner once. It just wasn't the same. I haven't heard from him and he hasn't heard from me in a while. On nights much like tonight, when I lie awake, thinking about his creamy, dark skin and the way his body fit with mine and the passionate love we made, *I get fitful*. But I know he's got a ways to go before he can satisfy me in ALL WAYS. T.J. is AMID—a man in development—and I just don't want to be a proces-

34

sor. I want to be a receiver. I don't want anyone who is not ready anymore.

I made my mind up to forget about T.J. and get some sleep. But my best friend Bebe called me and woke me up. She was not a bit happy. And when Bebe gets angry, it's something terrifying to behold. She called up and said, "Homette, I just had a terrible date!"

Now I was there when Isaac? (Is that his name?) Yeah, Isaac, asked Bebe for her phone number. And this Isaac guy was nice looking, well spoken, and later Bebe told me that he was a fireman. I know Bebe. We've been friends for years and I think it's kind of rare that someone in her twenties like me and someone in her forties like Bebe are as tight as we are. We've got different opinions on things—like men. Bebe's old school and she doesn't cut men too much slack at all. I know how demanding and critical she can be of men. Bebe will give a sister the benefit of the doubt, but a man? Bebe won't cut them any slack at all. And that's not fair. People are people—she'd been asked out on a date by a nice man and she was already blowing him off. Why?

"Okay," I said. "What did he do?"

"Why'd you say it like that—all smart and stuff, like it was my fault I had a bad time?" Bebe said.

"Girl, look," I said, "it's too late at night for drama. You know I've got to go to work tomorrow and meet with the new partners at the radio station. As head of sales, I have to be sharp."

"I know but I thought I could call my girl and vent a bit."

I wasn't trying to blow her off. I wasn't. "Be, let's start over, okay?"

"I don't know if I wanna start over," she said and I could tell Bebe was pouting.

Drama queen! "Bebe, tell me what happened, please." I didn't mind catering to her, really. I sat up in bed. Bebe told me about Isaac being late, about the two dollars' worth of gas, the "get with" slips, the whacked-out club, and his phone conversation that sent her over the edge.

Then I heard a siren humming behind her voice.

"Is that a siren?"

"Yeah, must be some mess going on somewhere," Bebe said.

"It's getting awful loud," I noticed.

"Yeah," Bebe said. "Sounds like it's really close. On this block."

"Go look out the window," I suggested. And I heard Bebe moving around.

Then Bebe said, "It's Isaac! He's hanging out of the window of a fire truck running the lights and the siren!"

I fell back on the bed in surprise.

Bebe was impressed. She said, "I'll be doggone. Check this boy out. Where'd he ever get an idea for a crazy stunt like that?"

Isaac

I'm a brah man of ideas. Like a drop of sudden yet needed rain, the idea came to me that drastic situations call for drastic actions.

After I got off the phone with Dash, I looked around for Bebe. She disappeared! She just left without saying a word! Then the guard at the door told me she came over by the phone, looked funny, got her coat, and broke for the door.

I'd made a big mistake. By L.A. losing my money, my car not starting, being late, the wild club, and all that—it made me nervous. I haven't been dating at all recently. I'm rusty. I drove back to the fire station totally upset and I decided that I just wasn't willing to let it go like that. Bebe looked too good in that green dress and I never even told her so. That dress reflected her beautiful, full body and she gave off such a warm, natural energy that I was a little overwhelmed at first and that made me even more nervous.

I started back home, then I started thinking about Prometheus, who stole fire from the gods of Olympus to give to man. He wanted man to have something special, so he went out and got it. Brah Prometheus was aggressive. That's what I needed—to be *aggressive*. As soon as I saw that fire truck, I knew what I had to do. I revved it up and took it out.

The closer I got to her building the more determined I became. I turned the corner and hit the horn and lights. I drove right up the side drive to Bebe's three flat building. She stayed on the second floor. I got on the horn, "Bebe!"

I saw her at the window with the phone in her hand. When I shouted her name, she stepped back. I shouted it again, "Bebe!"

Some of the people in her building were looking out of their windows too. I said on the horn, "Don't be alarmed. There is no fire. Repeat. There is no fire. This is a personal emergency here and I won't leave until I talk to Miss Bebe Thomas."

I heard someone raise their window and yell, "You're crazy!"

Bebe came to the front door in her robe, shivering. "What are you trying to do? Make my neighbors hate me? Get me kicked out of this building? What?"

"Just let me explain about tonight, that's all," I said, determined not to give up.

"Go home!" someone yelled.

"Let him in already!" someone else shouted.

Bebe looked like she was stuck between mad and interested. She finally waved me over. I shut down the truck, hopped out, and followed her upstairs.

"You're crazy, you know that?" she said, shutting the door behind us.

"Yeah, I am. Remember, I'm a fireman. You run away from a fire and I run into a fire. So I've got to be a little crazy, but nice crazy." And I gave her my best smile. Brah was getting the old confidence back.

"Well, get ta gabbin'," Bebe said and she crossed her arms in front of her. She had on a silk, royal blue robe and matching slippers. Her hair was still pinned up from our earlier date.

"I wanted to explain why I acted so strange tonight." Bebe looked more interested and even offered me a seat on the couch and a drink.

I accepted the seat. "One of my friends at the firehouse, L.A., he's a wild guy, a young brah, he borrowed fifty dollars from me without asking."

Bebe smiled. "Whoo-wee, friends will take liberties, won't they?"

"Yeah, but he's a good guy. Anyway, he lost it in a poker game . . ." And I went on with the rest of the story about my car, borrowing L.A.'s car, the pass, and I made it to my phone conversation.

Bebe was relaxed on the couch, had fixed herself a rum and Coke, and was looking awful sexy sitting there.

"Bebe," I said slowly, "I know you overheard my conversation on the phone."

"Uh-huh," she said and mashed her lips together like she was about to hear a huge lie. But she wasn't.

"I was wrong for not telling you about Dash—"

"Look, Isaac," she said, "we ain't got to have no drama. I let you in to explain but I really don't want to hear about you not loving this woman and only living with her because of finances or some sob story like that. I don't know if y'all married, divorced, or just shacking up but I'm not for any man trying to get with this one over here and that one over there. No multiple relationships. I ain't a sharer. I'm too old for playing games, no hard feelings, huh?"

I laughed! I couldn't help it. I grabbed Bebe by her wrists and said, "I'm laughing because you're right and wrong at the same time. You're right. You should have a man's undivided attention. But you're wrong about Dash. Dash is not my woman or my wife. Dash is Dashay, my thirteen-year-old daughter!"

Bebe looked very embarrassed. I pulled out my wallet and showed her a picture that Dash and I had taken last year at the big food festival, Taste of Chicago, in Grant Park.

"Aww," Bebe said.

Dash and I had on matching Chicago Bulls T-shirts and she and I both were slurping on snow cones and had red juice running down our chins and hands.

Bebe laughed. "She's so cute! And she looks like you, too, has your eyes. Yeassss, cute, but where is her mother?"

Straightforward, wasn't she? But I told Bebe the truth. "I wish I knew."

Dash

Ththw! Ththw! It's one-thirty and Daddy is still out? He's too old to be out runnin' 'round and what not. Ththw! Old people don't even need to be tryin' to get busy with each other. Suppose he has a stroke or something?

And why does he need to find somebody? He's got me to look out for him, don't he? I know how to fix his favorite foods and I laugh at his stale jokes and what not. I listen to his dusty old records when he makes me and I don't even try to dis him about it either.

I paged him because I wanted to know where he was at and what not. He didn't even tell me that he was gonna be steppin' out. I was worried . . . and he just started getting on me. I was worried. Daddy thought I started crying because he was yelling at me, but nah-uh. I was worried . . . and scared.

I was scared that he might go and not come back. Like Mama. I don't know why I thought that because Daddy is not like that. He's a different person from Mama. He's happy. Daddy likes to feel happy. But Mama, she never seemed to let herself feel happy. She had a happy block.

When I was seven, Mama and Daddy broke up and we went to live by ourselves. And Mama didn't hardly want to let Daddy see me on the weekends. On some of the days when I knew he was supposed to come and get me, she'd pack up that old Volkswagen and drive to my grandma's house in Milwaukee. And I'd cry because I knew Daddy would be ringing the bell and ringing the bell and nobody would answer and there would be no note or anything. I knew he would be sad. The court fight was ugly but get off of that, let's get off that—except to say, Mama needed me and that's why I had told the judge I wanted her. I wasn't turning down Daddy, I was trying to boost up Mama. Mama was never satisfied and I was thinking like, hey, if I picked her instead of him that Mama would feel satisfied and that would help her be happy. But I wasn't enough to satisfy her. I wasn't. How do I know? Because if I was, she would still be here instead of . . . where . . . ever.

She left. Mama just pulled up. I woke up one morning and she was gone. It was a week before my tenth birthday. She had packed her things and left. Mama was outta there. And I was alone. And it took two days before I called Daddy. I stayed out of school for two days. I sat by the window in our apartment, watched the snow fall, crossed my fingers and my toes, and ate Lucky Charms cereal twice a day with and without milk. Now I know that was crazy-stupid. But I wanted my mama. I knew she would come back. She wouldn't just leave me. I didn't care what her note said. I still have the note—it's hidden away. I never showed it to anyone, not even Daddy. I knew then how Daddy must have felt ringing the doorbell while me and Mama were on the way to Milwaukee, and it messed me up inside.

Every now and then I get a postcard from Mama. I got three. She's out seeing the world. At least that's what she writes on the back of the postcards. "Hi, Dash, I'm seeing the world. Love, Mama." I got three postcards—Brazil, London, and Amsterdam—and they're taped to my dresser mirror. When I look in the mirror I see myself and part of Mama too. That makes me feel hopeful.

For now, it's just me and Daddy and I want him to love me and be satisfied with us, together. We're all each other has and we get along real cool and stuff. I don't need nobody else tryin' to bum-rush in on what we got.

I don't know who this chick is he's startin' to see. But, uh, I hope that she don't think she can just come in and start taking over and what not. I, Dashay Sizemore, ain't havin' it!

Bebe

Deep-deep-too-deep, chile. Can you imagine someone, a loved one, just up and disappearing on you? Poof? Like Al-la-kah-zam, I'm outta here, ma'am?! Like David Copperfield or some-magic-making-somebody does in those Vegas shows 'cept this woman didn't ever come back? I got a quick, stabbing pain in my stomach as Isaac told me the story. My heart went out to Isaac and his little girl 'cause I can bet that was some sho' nuff hurtful stuff.

Isaac told me that his ex-wife, Alicia, divorced him about five years ago, and that she always dreamed about far-off, exotic places. Isaac said that he never could seem to please her. Even after they took a trip to the Bahamas and Hawaii. He said that Alicia's family lives in Milwaukee and that they said she used to daydream as a child about seeing the world.

"Alicia," Isaac said, "just didn't seem pleased with anything, anybody, or any part of herself."

Isaac said she left him first, then a couple years later she left Dash, too, disappearing to see the world. And Alicia went *poof* real nasty-like, too. Isaac said the first time she left him, he had come home one day from the firehouse and everything in their home was gone EXCEPT his stereo console with the eight-track player and tapes.

"You still had a stereo console with an eight-track?"

"Yep." Isaac smiled. "And I still do. I keep it working. I'm very handy. It's going to be a collector's item one day. Dash thinks I'm crazy."

Dash is just about right! An eight-track player! The thought of the old schooldays and those eight-tracks made my insides commence to giggling, so I decided to switch the subject. I'd had enough of this sad stuff. Isaac and I sat back and talked about eight-tracks, back-seat car dates, bell bottoms, and rent parties. And we laughed so easily with one another.

That made me think, what do we have here? I was enjoying this man I was swapping stories with on my "come hither" couch. Boy-friend made me tense when he first arrived, but now everything was cooling on out on a friendly, soothing tip. We were talking with ease-as-you-please. And that's the sho' nuff good foot you wanna get on when stepping into a new relationship.

We started talking about music. Isaac liked Diana Ross, the Isley Brothers, the Jackson Five, the O'jays, and Marvin Gaye. I told him my favorites were Patti "put the mike down" Labelle, Chaka Khan—with or without Rufus—and Luther "weight loss" Vandross. I asked him again if he'd like a drink and he opted for a pop and I went out in the kitchen to get him one.

When I came back in the living room, Isaac had turned the head of the torch lamp toward the wall and that had the effect of dimming the room. He also had turned on the stereo and tuned into "Night Moods," the old slow-cut radio program. A favorite jam of mine hap-pened to be playing and it was a damn good song. Isaac took the glass of pop out of my hand, set it on the table, and asked, "May I have this dance?"

The Stylistics were crooning "Betcha By Golly Wow." Hey-hey, summer of '72! That song is the all-time slow jam of the century and I don't care what anybody says, that song is it!

Howdy hormones! We had a good old-fashioned bump and grind going. Then Isaac broke back, two-stepped holding both my hands, then pulled me in, turned me, stopped short, reversed back out, two-stepped back in, and resumed the slow bump and grind again. This boy was dancing his butt off! Then he started singing in my ear and he had a nice voice. It was one of those deep "get some" voices, if ya get my meanin'. But Isaac was going falsetto to keep up with the lead; though truth be told, with the right hand on the Bible, can't nobody really keep up with the lead on "Betcha By Golly Wow," but Isaac was fetchin' top marks for effort.

I wanted Isaac but I was afraid to say so. When the record was over, Isaac reached back and turned down the volume and kept humming the song. Dude kinda sneaky, huh? He pulled me back in and said, "Bebe, I have to get home. But when can I see you again?"

And I wanted to say, Don't leave! Don't go! But I said softly in his ear, "Yes, yes, you can see me again. When?"

And we decided on Sunday brunch. Saturday was Isaac's day with Dash. I understood and thought about how far off Sunday was as Isaac left. I went to the window and waved good-bye and laughed to myself. 'Cause boyfriend, boyfriend Isaac? He looked some kinda crazy backing that fire truck out. I don't want to be a party pooper ('cause I love the idea), but would a fireman get fired for pulling a stunt like that?

Isaac

Brah man's interest is really piqued. The date started strange, almost got a little buck wild at the club, but turned out pretty cool. Bebe could be a lot of fun. I need some fun and I need someone. I just hope I don't get tense. Sometimes I get a bit tense. I know it's because of Alicia. She left me with a bit of fear, a bit of careful-careful if you want to break it down like that. That girl busted up my heart, but good. That kind of action will make you kind of leery of letting someone get too close. I've done that before; gotten close and got scared and broken it off. And there's Dash to consider. That's touchy-touchy. But brah man is no fool; I know I can't go through life like a quarterback getting blitzed. I may have to take a few hits to get that touchdown.

I must be getting old thinking about this stuff so early in the game. When brah man was just a young rooster, I just worried about getting into the henhouse, if you catch my drift. Yeah, that was the deal.

Bebe. Be-be. She is a pistol. I see that she's going to keep me on my toes. That just might be nice to have someone keeping me on my toes for a change, hmmm?

Bebe

Sugar pie honey bunch, what's gonna be the deal with you? Isaac is long gone but boyfriend got me stuck on expectations. See, there are two kinds of expectations. To the left, y'all, is what you think is due you. To the right, y'all, is what you think will happen to you. My expectations of love relationships are about as high up as the street curb. And that's bad to say but I'm being Girl Scout honest, cross-my-heart-hope-ta-choke-on-some-thin-mints. I think it's 'cause of the way I saw my parents play emotional bumper cars when I grew up.

See, my mother loved my father. She loved his dirty drawers and I know that he loved her. Ba-ba-but, y'all, on the low end, Daddy NEEDED her more than he LOVED her. See what I'm talkin' 'bout? Daddy needed her to take care of him and he needed her to be that stable factor for him. But, like, Daddy loved the streets more than he loved her and, well, me.

Daddy would get paid and head straight for the streets and party his butt off and then he'd come home broke, looking for some of the money Mama had earned on her little job. *Whoooo! Ghetto kaboom,* because that, my friends, would blow up the whole house!

I remember one time when I was eleven or twelve, Daddy came home after spending all his money at a bar and playing dominoes and he wanted to pimp the money in Ma's little stash. He tried to snatch her jar and she grabbed his arm. Daddy tried to throw Mama over his shoulder and she was screaming, "Leave my money alone!"

And do you know that Daddy was steady trying to open that jar with Mama hanging onto his neck, her feet up, weight down, looking helpless as she tried to bulldog his runaway spirit? I remember Daddy yelled, "Everything in here is mine!"

He took and smashed the jar on the floor and tossed Mama off his back like she was a hand-me-down shirt. She hit the floor, boom! rolled over into the corner, and he grabbed a handful of bills before she could run over, arms whirling windmill fashion. Daddy took two slaps before knocking her down.

Now that would piss me off. Who! Watching it made me mad as a trapped bear then. I can feel my eyes burning now, just as if the tears were again falling from my eyes. But Mama forgave him and took up for him with a fierce regularity, chile.

"Your daddy isn't a bad man, naw. He loves us, just has some bad habits that need breaking. Only Jesus can break 'em cause I've tried and tried. I love your daddy more than life," she said. "I understand him. That's what women have to endure sometime to make life work for them. Marriage is first. Keeping the marriage together is a woman's first mission, it's in the Bible."

Now, ya know I checked the Bible, don't you? Where does it say a woman has to put up with some trifling mess in marriage? John-chapter-where? First Corinthians-verse-who? Song of Solomon-show-me?

Now, let me check my memory banks, and telling the glorified truth, I think that's the only outright lie my mama ever told me. And, chile, the Be don't think Mama knew it was a lie at all. No-no-no. I believe my mama thought that was true. But call me an old soul in a young body, sister-girl me knew better even then. I knew that what I had seen that night, the nights before, were not what I wanted, what

49

Mama wanted, or what God wanted. Mama just accepted it. But me? *Simon says sister don't think so.* I think a woman should only accept goodness and, if it doesn't go that way, she should get ta going the other way.

Hey, ask me to cluck and strut and call me chicken but I hate a struggle. But, sister-girl me ain't no wimp. I can work through a struggle but I hate every gosh darn minute of it. Some people get off on a struggle, rise to the occasion—it brings out the best in them. Brings out the nasty in me because I'm mad as a stung bear that I've got to struggle. I want good times, all the time. Now I'm not "Cinderella looking for a shoehorn." I know that life doesn't work out magically like that, particularly in ways of love. But I know I'm due better. And this Isaac? This Isaac could be what's due me, could be my "Betcha By Golly Wow" but I don't wanna organize a parade for him just yet. No, not yet. I think I'll wait.

Sandy

I called Bebe up on the phone and started playing around as usual. "Beeeeeee! Girl, call the doctor."

"Sandy! What's wrong?" she said.

"Girl, we so fine it's killing me!"

Then together we sang, " 'Fine, fine as blackberry wine fresh off a California grapevine . . .' "

Bebe then proceeded to tell me about what happened last night after Isaac came back to her house. Bebe is crazy! Bebe doesn't know how to let a good thing happen! Isaac and that fire truck?! I think that is so imaginative and romantic.

Bebe said, "Yeah, he's got potential."

I said knowingly, "Umm-huh, yeah, right. You can't fool me. Bebe, you just don't want to admit you're kind of excited. But listen, I have to run to this Saturday meeting. Talk to you later, 'bye."

I hurried and got dressed and headed down to work at J-108. I'm in charge of sales at the jazz radio station. It's a family-owned station and it's a good place to work. My boss, Harvey, is a good guy. He finalized selling forty-five percent of the company to Standard Electric, an appliance chain, for a nice hefty chunk of change. I led a small team that put together the overall company profile. Harvey had put a lot of faith in me and I put the project together like a puzzle.

But I didn't get to give the presentation because of some B.S. with my ex-boyfriend T.J. and a snake coworker. But God is real and works everything out.

Anyway, this meeting was to introduce key staffers to the new part owners. When I arrived, everyone was standing around chatting, munching on bagels and cream cheese, Danish, fresh fruit, coffee, and the like. I bumped into a man I'd never seen before. "Sorry," I said with a smile.

He smiled back and said, "Hi, I'm Richard Belder."

"And I'm Sandra Atkins."

"Atkins-Atkins," Richard said. He was short, fat, and very sloppy-looking in his clothes. But confidence? Oh yes, full of it! Richard exuded confidence with a tilt of the head and a flat-foot, toes-out stance. "You're in sales, right?"

"Right, how'd you know?"

"Harvey has said good things about you," Richard answered and then he tweaked the few fuzzy brown hairs remaining on the top of his head. "He said that you put together the proposal that helped sell our company on buying into the station. We at S.E. were leaning toward another radio property at first."

"Yes, I worked very hard on that proposal. But I knew how important it was to us, a station growing in the market, to have the extra muscle that a company like S.E. could give us."

"That's good vision on your part. I think there are a lot of changes that could be made for J-108. Right now it's run like a Mom and Pop operation. It does need that corporate kick!"

What nerve! What did Standard Electric know about broadcasting? Making a radio wasn't the same as doing radio!

"Well," I said, "I'm sure the two companies can learn from each other." Luckily, it was time for the meeting to begin.

We all sat around the conference table. There was Harvey, of course, at the head. To his right, he introduced the vice-president of finance for S.E., then S.E.'s marketing director, and finally Richard Belder, associate sales director with S.E.

Harvey then warmly introduced us: the community affairs director, the programming director, and me, head of sales. Harvey also introduced Diana, his executive secretary.

The vice-president of finance for S.E. was Alan Krantz. He stood up and gave what was the equivalent of a pep rally—talked about how J-108 was the first step in a new direction for S.E. Krantz then said that S.E. had a presence in everything it did.

Finally he sat down and Harvey got up and started flying low so he could drop a bombshell right on my head.

"As Alan said so eloquently, S.E. is the kind of company that wants to make its presence felt, not in a heavy-handed way but in a helping way," Harvey said. "That's why we will have a new addition to the J-108 family. Richard Belder, associate sales director for S.E., will join us here as executive sales consultant. . . ."

Boom! My vision blurred but I looked straight ahead. I didn't want to exchange eye contact with any of my colleagues because I knew they were staring at me. Corporate curiosity. They wanted to see if I'd been in on the decision. I cracked a faint, pleasant smile and hoped it seemed real.

How could Harvey just bring someone in and not tell me? And this guy of all people, who was obviously a jerk. Didn't I work like a dog for J-108? I had brought in big accounts. I put together the presentation that helped Harvey seal the deal with S.E. Yet I couldn't be in on the plan to bring in Richard Belder? As soon as the meeting was over I went to my office and paced back and forth because I was mad as hell. I kept thinking, I should tell Harvey's butt off. Right?

Bebe

Wrong! I'm glad my homette called me first! She was like, "Bebe, girl, Harvey just disrespected me in front of a roomful of people! I'm going to go right into his office and tell his butt off!"

"Slow your roll, now," I told her. "You can't go in there and tell that white man off! You do that and you'll be standing in the grocery line wearing 'Pay Less' shoes and using food stamps!"

"But, Bebe, I work like a dog! And Harvey, he plays me like that?"

I know how the girl feels, on the real tip. It's happened to me before, too. So I just reminded her what all working sisters know. Hear what I'm saying?

I told Sandy, "Homette, you know how they do us on these jobs. We work twice as hard, twice as long, and don't get no dap! Huh? We're overworked, underpaid, dissed, and played. I ain't saying don't say anything, no. But be cool with it, baby girl, and see what's up. Maybe he has some kind of excuse or reason."

"All right," Sandy said, calming down. "I'll wait a bit before going to Harvey's office to talk to him."

"Cool," I said, then asked, "But what are you going to say?"

Sandy

I said, "Harvey, I want to talk to you about the meeting. It's very important."

"Sure, Sandy," Harvey said with a smile, closing the door behind me. "I was very pleased with how it went, you?"

"Well," I said, "to be perfectly honest, Harvey, I was disappointed."

"Why?" Harvey said as he sat down behind his huge oak desk.

"Harvey, we've worked together a long time so I'll get right to the point. How would you feel if you found out someone was coming into your department without your knowledge?"

"Sandy, he's just a consultant," Harvey said and he began drumming on the desk with the tips of his fingers.

"But, Harvey," I said, "he's going to be looking over everyone's shoulder. I mean, did you consider me at all?"

"Consider you? Look, Sandy," Harvey said, "this is my radio station. My father started it. My family has run it for years. I don't have to get your permission to do anything."

Harvey just changed right before my eyes. He had always leaned on me when it came to company sales matters but now Harvey was showing me a tough face, a blunt role that I'd never seen before.

"I didn't mean it like that—" and that's as far as I got.

"Think, Sandy. S.E. now owns part of this station; if you bought in, wouldn't you want a pair of eyes and ears around? Huh? And it was just a last-minute thing. I see no harm in it. In fact, Belder seems like a sharp guy. His brother also works for S.E., ranks just below the CEO of the company. His knowledge will help boost our sales. We'd be stupid not to take advantage of his expertise. It's not costing you a thing. You still have your title and your salary and my confidence. But don't ever question me about how I run what's mine. Understand?"

Of course. Who doesn't understand a slap in the face?

Dash

Saturday is me and Daddy's day to hang out. I can't hardly wait and stuff. I made us some pancakes, with strawberries and sausage, and I was jamming with that skillet and jamming listening to L. L. Cool J., Mary J. Blige, and Bone-Thugs-N-Harmony. Daddy lets me play my music loud on Saturday morning. The rest of the week, I have to hold it down when he's around. But hey, when Daddy goes to work, I kick up the box. Then I can blast my music as loud as I want to, and what not, because Uncle Lucius is hard of hearing.

Uncle Lucius is my great-uncle. He lives on the second floor of our house and has a separate entrance and what not. He's suppose to watch me while Daddy is away. Uncle Lucius is bugged! He wears those old man clothes, cause you know he's an old man, and he tells funny jokes. He cracks on people all the time. Signifying, he calls it.

Uncle Lucius likes to play card games like Tonk and Poker. He taught me how to play Pitty Pat and Go Fish. He likes me to come upstairs and hang out with him and play cards. Sometimes we play on Friday nights, waiting for Daddy to get off. Then he'll come home, come upstairs, and play, too. It's like an early start to our Saturday hang-out days. Usually our Saturday hang-out days are spent at the skating rink just like today; we spent the afternoon at the rink. I love to skate. Daddy likes to skate, too, because he says it keeps him in shape, plus, they play a lot of old songs at the rink and the old songs got a better skating beat. We hold hands and bop from side to side, rolling with the music and what not. Other kids get jealous 'cause they parents drop them off and break. The other kids, they say stuff like, "Your daddy is straight, Dash. Wish my daddy was cool like that."

Uh-huh, I know he's cool and I wouldn't trade him for nothing. But I-I still miss Mama. But it's like I'm okay with it, sort of.

No teary eyes, few words to say.
My mother pulled up, she went away
To exotic places around the globe,
New things to see, new trails and roads;
But not forever, it's a temporary thing.
She'll be back, the doorbell will ring,
And I'll be mad, but glad to see
My mother finally back home with me.

Isaac

I was an excited brah when I picked up Bebe for Sunday brunch. My Thunderbird was waxed down and I was clean in my Sunday suit—no tie, open collar, because I wanted to be sporty casual. I slipped on my trench coat. I felt good and I looked good.

Bebe has flair. She had on a bad royal blue hat, wide brim broke down over her left eye. Her two-piece royal blue dress was knit with gold buttons. She had a shawl, speckled blue, resting on her shoulders. A good-looking woman is the most beautiful thing a man can lay his eyes on.

"Bebe," I said, "you look very pretty."

And oh, she just smiled! Bebe didn't want to, I could tell, but she just couldn't help it. I could tell that Bebe liked to play the defensive. I could tell how she held back a hair, not in a bad way, but in a cautious way. This lady had been hurt before, and I believe often.

We went down to the House of Blues at Marina City in downtown Chicago. The House of Blues is always rocking; every day of the week there is a hot group to be heard. But the thing I like about H-B is that it specializes in a gospel brunch. Each Sunday one of the hottest gospel acts on the scene is showcased. There is a buffet of pancakes, sausage links, fried chicken, roast beef, shrimp, collards, macaroni and cheese, green beans, potato salad, pasta salad, tossed salad, lemon cake, peach cobbler, orange juice, and punch.

The place was packed with beautiful black people. God, when we get dressed and get out with a positive attitude and flow, there's nothing better. The place just felt good. Couples jockeyed for the best seats near the stage swaddled in communion-red drapes where the choir would sing. We got a good spot and went over and got our plates.

"Who's the featured choir today?" Bebe asked.

I wasn't sure.

Bebe said, "I like the Winans. Bebe, Cece, D-E-F-G . . . on down the line it's a truckload of 'em and they all can sing."

The choir this weekend was Reverend Watson's New Day Full Gospel Pentecostal Choir.

Bebe leaned over and asked, "Why do choirs have such long names nowadays? It's like, the more names they have, the better they think they sound? Here's a name. How about the Old Testament Inspirational Got a New Attitude African Methodist Ain't Run Out of Breath Yet Mass Choir?"

We both laughed. But Reverend Watson's New Day Full Gospel Pentecostal Choir jammed. Everyone in the entire place was standing up, clapping, and rocking. "Go, girl!" Bebe shouted at the soloist and waved her hand in the air. She brushed up against me and I hugged her. She smiled and dropped her eyes down, then back up at the choir. Before we knew it, it was time to go. As I helped Bebe on with her shawl, I started staring at a woman in the choir.

"Say, I think I know that sister right there," I said to Bebe. "I think she used to work at the dime store in my old neighborhood."

"That's more than ten cents a minute worth of attention you giving her," Bebe said with a sly look on her face. "An old flame?"

That made me laugh a bit, "No, just an old friend from the neighborhood. C'mon."

"Yeah," Bebe teased, "well, if I see a tear jump up there in them eyes I'll know what's up for real."

Bebe and I walked over and I was right. Gina and I hugged and I introduced her to Bebe. She introduced us to her husband, who was sitting in the audience. And ain't the world tiny? I'd met the brother before at the Million Man March! We exchanged phone numbers and promised to keep in touch.

"You went to the Million Man March?" Bebe asked as we decided to take a little walk over to Michigan Avenue in a lame effort to step off some of the calories we had just piled on. We held hands.

"Yes," I answered. "I went."

"Me and my homette Sandy watched it on television. It looked absolutely powerful!"

"It was! It was great!"

"Yeah, but I heard that some brothers didn't go because it was Farrakhan's thing, you know? What do you think about that?"

So I told her straight, "All good men serve and worship God. There is only one God, one supreme good supernatural power. People just call him by different names. Jesus Christ, I say. Allah, Farrakhan says. Same God. Religion itself is man's interpretation of God's laws. Farrakhan interprets his way. I interpret my way. I don't have to agree with anyone else's view, just respect their right to have and believe in that view. So, no, I wasn't following Farrakhan. I wasn't into the messenger, I was tapped into the message. That message was so good, Bebe, that it couldn't have come from anywhere but God.

"The message was saying that African-American men want to be righteous, need to be righteous, and a lot of us are righteous. The message was brotherhood, unity, atonement, peace, and family values. The Million Man March was all that. Now what could be wrong with it? The Million Man March was like a big family gathering. We felt a kinship, a—a brotherhood, Bebe. I hadn't felt that good since my daughter Dash was born. In a funny kind of way, it was like birth too. It was a new feeling, a new spirit, and new goals being let loose on the world."

"Ummm, Isaac, you make it sound so wonderful. The media seemed like it was trying to downplay it, though," Bebe said.

I agreed. "Yeah, I think so. This wasn't the image the media had of us. That's all I can figure. They wanted to show African-American men as criminals. They said we were all in jail. But there we were. They said we had no direction. But there we were. They said we didn't care. But there we were. They said we had no focus. But there we were. They said we wouldn't come. But there we were."

"One million beautiful black men!" Bebe said with a little spin on it that made it sound like a hallelujah shout. "And I can count!"

I smiled. "You know what, Bebe? There was this man there, crying while he sat on a park bench. He was old and sick. Teeth, gone. Ears, knotted up and short. Face, as ashy as burnt coals. Tears, gumming up his eyelashes. About fifteen of us had gathered round him and were asking why he was crying. We huddled around him and said we'd comfort him if he'd only tell us how."

"What? What'd he say?" Bebe asked in a very anxious voice.

"Bebe, the man said that he was crying because he was happy. That old man said he'd grown up in an orphanage, worked the coal mines as a kid, ran the streets as a policy man, and was a bum on the street now. He said he told anyone who would listen that he was going to hitch a ride from Pittsburgh to D.C. for the march. That old man said that everybody laughed at him. But he said he got a ride, food, a place to stay, and got to hear a great message too. That old man said that in all his seventy-three years on earth he'd seen good in the world but that it had never touched him until right then. Bebe, we each took turns hugging that old man. It was no fake, high-five, hug stuff. No! It was an all-encompassing embrace. We were hugging him; he was hugging us; we were hugging each other; we were hugging our past; we were hugging our future. Lady, lady, I tell you that it doesn't get much better than that."

Bebe

Hey now, chile! Isn't this a first? It's the first time that I've been attracted to a man primarily because of his mind. Isaac is a thinker and he is very clear on what he believes and is so silky smooth about relating that to other folks. Boyfriend has a sharp mind and I think that is going on!

We talked while sitting outside there for what? About an hour? The time flew by before we knew it. Then we went back to my place and I asked Isaac in to take the chill off his bones. I needed a little warming up myself if ya get my meaning.

You see, my body started to crave a man's touch. Some women don't like to admit publicly that they have strong physical desires. Only at a hen party, spoken in whispered tones or hearty laughs with a cutting of the eyes, is that kind of conversation okay.

I have a portable fireplace, it's round and black, and jumps off fast. Isaac got it up and going in a hurry. It knocked the chill off the room. It had gotten cold and cloudy outside and Isaac closed the blinds and that let the glow of the fire light up the room.

Aww, do that now, I thought to myself as Isaac scurried around. You take one step, sister-girl me will take two. I opened us a bottle of wine and it was chilling between us as we settled down on some pillows on the floor. Now, the funny thing? All this time while we were, ah, let's say, setting the tone? We both knew where we were headed and what we wanted, but check it out, like, there was no verbal thing needed. Aww no now, for real, we were on the instinct tip. We were just as comfy just going about the business of getting into this romantic thing. Neither of us said a mumblin' word. We both knew we wanted this afternoon lovemaking.

There's something about the smell of a fire and the crackling of a fire that turns folks on. It's just a fact. Like, someone might say, why is the sun in the sky? It ain't no Lucy and Ricky thing so don't try to 'splain! Accept it, enjoy it, and push on. So the fire was working me, this instinct thing we had going was working me, and I was just waiting on boyfriend Isaac to start working me. Little did my man know, a little bit of me goes a long ole way.

Isaac got ta running on my face with the back of his hand. His touch, the wine, and the fire mellowed me all the way out. The next thing I knew, we both had our clothes off and it was time to get down.

My anticipation was high. I had high hopes for deep, sensitive, good loving. My self-imposed sex sabbatical was about to come to a much-needed end. Yes, yeah-yes, my thoughts and emotions were prickly pert and reat to go. Anticipation-*anticipation*. But I got my hopes busted. Isaac's foreplay was too quick and not sensual enough. I mean, I know he was trying but it just didn't do it for me. For such a thoughtful guy, he wasn't thorough about his loving. He had what I call the Rough Rider syndrome! Boyfriend Isaac moved in too fast, too hard, and pooped out too quick.

Isaac was moving like someone was chasing him. Where was the race? Pimp to the finish line, baby. That's what I wanted to say—but sssh!—I knew not to. He just rushed on through but was grunting and groaning and moaning like it was the end of the world. And making more faces than a kid with Play-Doh! Women know what I'm talking about. That look like he's peering down over a fence while suckin' on a peppermint, then the look like he just swallowed a sour ball, and the look like there's a contest to see who can touch their top lip against the tip of their nose and your man is winning. Those faces? And then it was over and Isaac looked so pleased and happy and satisfied and I just gave a smile.

"That was real good," Isaac said and he was beaming.

"Ummm-huh," I said and hugged him to me. Isaac is a good man. I'm sure it'll be better for me next time for sure.

Isaac

Pow! Brah hasn't lost his touch. I was a little afraid that I might have. It's been a while. But it's true, it is like riding a bike. You never forget. Bebe's body felt soft and plush beneath my body. She's got big curves and big legs and that lets a man roll around and get comfortable.

I knew that I missed sex. And even though most men won't admit it, you can go without it. But I don't recommend it. A brah won't die or dry up or lose his balls like L.A. would have you believe. I needed that sex and it felt so good to me because it has been awhile because I don't rush into dating or making love with just any somebody. The reasons are twofold; one, life is too hard to just roll in and out of people's lives haphazardly so a man should choose carefully and go into it seriously.

Secondly, Dash. Dash was hurt very badly when her mother abandoned her. She has this fear about losing me too. I love her. I love Dash and she knows that but she has a fear about other people horning in on our relationship. She's crazy about L.A. 'cause he likes that hip-hop rap stuff and wears an earring and those big, loose clothes when he's off duty. But when other people come around us, she clings to me and demands much if not all of my attention. That has, well, made it difficult to develop a full relationship with a woman. Dash is fragile. The few women that I have dated wanted to, well, kind of push her aside. They would say, "Your daughter doesn't like me." Things like that, which makes me uncomfortable, and so I eventually just let the relationship go. But Bebe, I sense, might be different. She might be able to deal with Dash and put in the effort it would take to build a solid relationship. I'm going to get her and Dash together and see how that goes.

Dash

Me and my posse were heading to the movies and I was broke. I went to Daddy and said, "Yo, D. I need some benjamins." He looked at me all crazy. How come parents can't be more hip? I had to translate, "Benjamins—money. Like the song says Daddy, it's all about the benjamins." Daddy just rolled his eyes and came across with the cash and told me to be back early so I could meet this Bebe woman. She somebody he's been trying to hang out with. Up until now, I wasn't trying to meet her because I really didn't give a care. When Daddy would say, "I'm going to bring her by . . ." I'd break for Tasha's house up the street. What I wanna meet her for?

But this time Daddy had that "I ain't playin' " look on his face and said, "Come back early from the movies to meet Bebe."

I didn't wanna push it, so we went to the first show and what not. But we didn't even get to see the whole show because fools was up in there talkin' back to the screen and what not. Mental. Then the same mentals that was holding def dialogue with Denzel on screen started arguing with some retards in the back of the theater. Next thing we know, everybody is throwing popcorn and candy but I wasn't throwing my stuff, dawg, you know how much that popcorn cost? I got on the down low behind the seats and watched those fools. Mental.

They turned the whole theater out. So we got back WAY early and what not. We were coming up the back stairs and, through the window, who do we see sitting in the kitchen eatin' up some stuff? Daddy's new friend Bebe. Now I'd talked to her on the phone a couple of times and she was all frantic like, like, "Can't wait to meet you and you sound so cute."

Duh? Cute as in like stop suckin' up to me. I was like, yeah, right. I know these chicks are trying to get with my daddy and trying to get me to like them and what not. I got a mama and she'll be back one day. I don't need a stand-in until then and that's it straight up. Anyway Daddy was at the sink bustin' suds and Bebe was sitting at the table eating MY sweet potato pie. I mean, she was throwing down!

"That's your daddy's new girlfriend?" Kendra asked. She's really short and we call her Midget behind her back and when we want to shut her up.

"Midget," I said, "my daddy doesn't have a girlfriend, she's just an acquaintance."

Soon as I said that, he came over to get her plate after she ate the last of MY sweet potato pie. And what did Bebe do? She fed him the last piece of her crust and then he kissed her.

"Yeah, they acquainted all right!" Tasha said and giggled.

I was so embarrassed, here Daddy was swapping slob with this chick and what not! Strike two!

"Dawg, Dash, she all up in your daddy stuff!" Tasha said, laughing. Then she started working her hips. "Bet they doin' it."

"They are not!" I said defensively.

"Old people don't really do it, do they?" Melody asked. Excuse her. Melody is not as mature as the rest of us but we let her hang with us anyway 'cause she's Tasha's second cousin on her stepfather's side.

"Yeah!" Tasha huffed. "Old people do it. They just can't do it as long or as much."

Kendra spoke up. "Well, she's kinda cute . . ."

"In an ancient sort of way!" I said. She was being all tacky eating the last of the pie and kissing on my daddy all in the kitchen and what not.

"Well, she's got good posture," Kendra said. She was always looking for the bright side—her mama was an evangelist.

"She better, with that big lead head, 'cause if she tilt, she'll fall over!" I said, and me and Melody slapped high five. "I don't like her already!"

"How do you know?" Kendra asked in a tone like she was opening the doors of the church. "You don't really know her yet!"

"Shut up, Midget!" I said. "I don't gotta like everybody and I don't have to have a reason why!"

Then Melody said something on the straight and narrow, "Yeah, sometimes people try to move in on your family and stuff changes. You'd better watch out, Dash."

Tasha nodded her head, agreeing. "What are you going to do?"

"I'm not letting some big-headed woman come pushing in here." I told my friends. Then we all high-fived, though Kendra's was a little weak, and then we said our hangout line: "All for one, one for all . . . Tupac lives!"

They left and I put my key in the door and turned the lock as loud as I could. I wanted to make sure they weren't feeling on each other or something gross like that.

Daddy was like, "Hi, Dash." Then he gave me a hug and I kissed him and rolled my eyes at her. Daddy said, "This is Bebe. Bebe . . . Dash."

I said, "Ummmh!"

Bebe grinned.

"Are those your real teeth?" I asked very nice-nice.

"Dash!" Daddy said and he squeezed my shoulder.

I smiled nice-nice, "Oh, I was just asking because I saw this show on A&E and they were explaining how easy it is to cap teeth and the caps are usually BIG like that! I was just wondering."

"No, honey," Bebe said and smiled wider, "these are all mine."

"Sit down, Dash," Daddy said, turning back to the sink. "I'll pop us some popcorn and we can play Tonk or something."

"Sorry, I'm sick," and I gave Ms. Sweet Potato Pie Head an evil look and I worked my neck but Daddy didn't see. I said, "Real sick to my stomach."

She didn't say anything and Daddy turned around and looked a little concerned.

Bebe spoke up then. "Maybe she needs castor oil?" She said it in a voice sweet but deadly and she stared at me like nah!

Maybe I went a little tooooooooo far?!

Bebe

Chile, Miss Dashay is just like castor oil—so nasty you can only take her in small doses. I'd had a little dose of Miss Dashay and I was thinking pig Latin—Dashay X-nay! Her attitude is a mess. You know those Iowa babies born seven at one time? If Dash was one of them babies, the rest would-a tried to move. And those parents would sho' nuff need every last one of them free Pampers 'cause Dash's attitude is sho' nuff shitty.

But I'm real. I tell the truth. Dash is a cute girl. She has got flawless skin, which is rare for a teenager. I remember my skin was wrecked for a while there and I thought I would die! Dash, she's got nice smooth and glowing skin. And she's got large eyes, soft, doelike. I couldn't tell how she's built up because she had on those big-ass clothes that the kids wear now. You know those Bozo bloomers that they have hanging all off their butts. Who told them that was cute? Huh? There go them crazy designers again, drawing up some bullshit to sell to folks. But that's the style, hey, what can you do!

Maybe we'll grow on each other. I'm gonna give it a sister-girl try. I'm going to be the mature one. She's just a motherless kid. So sister-girl me is just gonna be sweet as bread pudding. That'll work, huh?

Dash

.

Bebe-smeebe! Schmooze my daddy, trying to get with my daddy! Please! I went to my room, opened up some Jolly Ranchers, which Daddy calls wine candy, and tried to bring my taste buds back to life from that castor oil! Yuck! Then I watched "The Beverly Hillbillies" and wrote me a little Bebe smack rap.

Come listen to a story about Bebe's big head,
Round as melon, heavy as lead.
One day she was over just ah eating up our food
And Daddy didn't care that the chick was really rude.
    Tacky that is, low grade, not all that!
Well, next thing ya know, old Bebe's got a man.
Teen folks said "Dash, girl, take a stand,"
Said "Break it up is what you oughta do,"
So I made up my mind to be really crude.
    Sabotage that is, no fun, give her a hard time. Yeah.

Bebe

Like Miles plays the horn, like Mike plays ball, like Mahr-tin plays crazy. Isaac is playing me.

I called him three times, left messages on his answering machine, and gave Dash a message—though she might be trippin' with her humbugging self.

I even called the firehouse and his boys there said, "Just missed him!"

I am missing him! That's the damn point! He gotta give me some more time. Okay, okay, dig it. I invited Isaac over to watch a rerun of the "Motown 25 Special" with me. That is one of my favorite shows of all time. I love me some Tito. Tito is a manly man—bass voice and guitar. My man Tito kept both his Negro 'fro and nose! I wanted Isaac to watch "Motown 25" with me but did he show? Was Michael moonwalking across my hardwood floor? NO. Please! Negro could have called and said a little something-something. Any excuse is better than a no-show. Any crazy excuse. You know, like:

"Sorry I can't find my white sequin glove."

"The zipper is broke on my Thriller jacket and I feel naked without it."

Or "Sorry I can't watch it 'cause I'll have a J-5 flashback and start roboting across the room and won't be able to stop."

Any excuse. I mean tell me anything! What's up with that?

Isaac

What calls? I didn't get any messages. The "Motown 25 Special"? What? I checked my answering machine, too. There were no messages. I haven't been back to the firehouse, I'm on my off shift. I didn't talk to any of the brahs. What messages?

Bebe said, "I left them. Maybe your machine isn't working right. But I know I talked to Dash once and asked her to tell you to call me. Ask her."

I was angry that Dash didn't give me the message. I know Dash can be shy and aloof around the women I bring around but she usually just stays clear. To deliberately not give me a message was wrong. I was waiting for her when she came home from school. I asked Dash about it as soon as she walked through the door.

She looked all bummed out and said, "Yo D, I forgot! I'm sorry! She did call once. I totally forgot on the mental tip. I was studying for that math test for the advance placement next year in high school. You know I've been studying like a dog for that and I just forgot! Tell Bebe I'm really sorry, please?"

Okay, I was getting angry at first but when she explained I realized it was just a honest mistake. I called Bebe back and explained what happened and told her Dash apologized and Bebe had an attitude. She said, "Isaac. You don't really believe that story, do you?"

Bebe just basically called my daughter a liar. I didn't like that at all.

Bebe

Do I look like Boo-boo the fool? Or as one of my girlfriends says, Suzy Sausage Head wearing wheat bread for a hat? Dash was lying and he was believing her with ease. I didn't call the girl a lie, though I know she was. I simply said, "Isaac, you don't really believe that?" I was just trying to be sure what I was dealing with. I mean, Dash is Isaac's daughter—these were his chromosomes cuttin' up, not mine! Obviously the crazy count is a wee bit high in the Sizemore family.

My homette Sandy? She was like, "Bebe, don't jump to conclusions. You have to work at relationships and any time there is family involved in anything it's going to be a little crazy."

"Yeah, but goddamn, this little Sesame Street hooker—no offense to Miss Piggy—is going to be a trip."

"But, Bebe," Sandy said, "she hasn't got a mother there with her. That's painful for a child. Can you imagine what that is like?"

Sandy sho' can bring it on home for ya. The girl can get a sob story going. "I know. I know. I just think it's hard enough getting to know someone without extraterrestrial drama."

"Bebe, just give it time. She'll cool down, really. But the real question is, how is the romance heating up?"

"Girl, don't take me there. It's okay but it's not hitting it for real."

Sandy said, "You do like Isaac. Yes?"

"I do. I really like this guy. I think this could be something," I said. "But the sex . . ."

Sandy interrupted. "But—don't trip. Because you know how you can get . . ."

"Hey-hey! Watch out now, this ain't no time for the dozens, girl!" I teased.

Sandy spoke easily. "But you know I KNOW YOU. So, just understand that time will work it out. The sex will get better as you get more used to each other. Dash, that's a harder thing to deal with, but she'll come around too. A relationship worth having has to be worked at."

"Al'right-al'right, okay! Oh, girl, I'm sorry. I'm so into my thing, I forgot to ask you about work, is it better?"

"No, Richard is walking around like the Massa ordering everyone around, dipping his nose in everything. I'm just swallowing my anger and trying to wait him out. He's got to tone down at some point, surely."

"Chile, it's a low-down dirty shame, though, that a sistah gotta go through so many unnecessary changes in life!" I said.

"Bebe," Sandy said, "like you say, you ain't never lied."

Dash

Daddy asked Bebe over for lunch. He's all excited and what not. I want to go with Tasha and my crew to the music store where Usher is going to be signing his new CD. Usher is fine and his music is the bomb! All my posse said, "Yeah, Dash, that's messed up!" But didn't none of my suppose-to-be-girls volunteer to suffer with me, huh? What happened to, "All for one and one for all, Tupac lives!"? Forget them shoot!

Daddy is making his spicy chili that I like. Daddy says only the-the—how's he say it?—the-the lionhearted can eat his chili.

Bebe gets there and she looks kinda nice in a lilac pants suit. I told her, "That outfit is on." Bebe and Daddy start chitchatting and I'm hungry. Maybe if we eat fast, I can catch up with my possee! "Yo D! Can we eat? I'm starving!"

"Hold on, girl. Hold on!" Daddy said. "I've got to take Uncle Lucius his mellowed-down version."

Then Daddy took one of the two pots off the stove and headed upstairs. That left me and Bebe downstairs.

She said, "I'm starving too."

I just nodded.

"I like hot food. Your daddy says this chili is one of his secret recipes."

"Daddy's very sensitive about it," I said. "He says that only wimps CAN'T eat it and he gets his feelings hurt and what not if folks don't like it."

"Oh, okay," Bebe said. "I gotcha. Honey, where's the bathroom again?"

"Around the corner, door on the left," and I watched her go. That's when I got the bomb idea. As soon as she left the room, I ran over to the stove and got the pot of chili and put it on the table next to the portable lazy Suzy in the middle that had a pitcher of water, a pitcher of iced tea, and salt and pepper. I dished out everyone's bowl. But Bebe, in her bowl? I added some extra pepper and as much Tabasco sauce as I could shake in it. Then, then like, like I heard my daddy coming. I sat down quick as I could. Miss "I Like Hot Food" was in for a real treat! This was gonna be funny as a mug!

Bebe

Hot-cha-cha-cha!

Isaac knows this chili is too goddamn hot! I'm crossing my legs and rocking in the chair like I gotta go pee! My eyes are crossing! The Frito Bandito hisself couldn't eat chili this hot!

If the boy could get NASA to put this in the shuttle tank, that thing would go in orbit and stay. Never would have to refuel, okay? I took my napkin and got to fanning and rocking. I looked like I was in some storefront church somewheres down South on an August morning.

"Good?" Isaac asked me.

Couldn't answer the boy back. My voice was hidin'. It wasn't about to try and swim up through that lava with rocks that this man called chili with beans! So I just waved my napkin yes, 'cause I wasn't about to hurt Isaac's feelings. But what's killin' me are two thoughts: one, if this chili is burning this fierce going down, it's gonna be burning rubber for real when it comes back out. And two: how is it that the two of them are able to eat it? They've got happy tummies and I got stomach à la blazing!

I reached for the water and Dash rolled the lazy Suzy to her side. "Excuse me."

Then she poured all the water, the last of it, in her glass and sipped and looked at me and smiled. I got so nervous that I dropped my napkin and when I reached down to pick it up I saw it.

Isaac

Bebe is acting funny. Maybe she doesn't feel well? She's rocking and not talkative at all. Dash is quiet as a mouse but has this silly grin on her face. I was just about to try to jump-start the conversation when the doorbell rang.

"I'll get it!" Dash said. "That's probably the sweatshirt I ordered!"

"I'll get you some more water," I told Bebe and took the pitcher over to the sink. "Don't be nervous around Dash, Bebe. You can relax, talk more."

I put the ice cubes in the pitcher, poured Bebe a glass, and she drank it down in one gulp before saying, "Yeah, I got something for her."

What?

Bebe

Aww yeah, aww yeah. I did, too. When Miss Dash came back to the table she had a package ripped open, showing us this sweatshirt with the BET logo on it.

"That's sharp!" I said real easy.

Isaac said, "Okay, put it away and finish your lunch."

"Yes, let's finish our lunch," and I took a bite of chili.

Dash took a big spoonful of hers and swallowed. Her eyes got big as Don Knotts's in that fish movie, okay. She looked at me and I looked at her. She looked at her bowl, then she looked at my bowl. Yeah, little homette, I switched bowls, chile. Then Dash looked at the water pitcher, then she looked at me. Oh no, Baby Godzilla, I thought. Then she went to swing the lazy Suzy her way, I stopped it and rolled it back my way. Back and forth, back and forth.

Isaac said, "Hey, what—"

Dash yanked it hard and the pitcher spun off the table and spilled right on her sweatshirt! "No!" she moaned. "Daddy, she did that on purpose!"

"Isaac, she put Tabasco sauce in my chili!"

"You the one said that you like your food hot! She did, Daddy, and I put just a little—"

"A little! You could be arrested for arson for what's going on inside my stomach right now!"

"Hey!" Isaac shouted.

"What?!" both Dash and I yelled, turning toward him.

What did my man Isaac do? Brother man Isaac just looked at both of us, dropped his head in his hands, and moaned like Rodney King, "Please. Can't we all just get along?"

Isaac

"I say, I say, boy, what's your face all drooped down about?" Uncle Lucius asked me.

My Uncle Lucius is like a father to me. He's an old dude who looks like a black Colonel Sanders but skinny and he doesn't have no chicken millions. And Uncle Lucius has a gravelly voice and a razor-sharp snapping sense of humor. But I wasn't in a joking mood now. No. I had actually gone upstairs to talk to him and had decided to punk out. "Nothing's the matter, Unc. Snapping beans, huh?"

Uncle Lucius stared at me, then shook up a soggy paper bag of fresh vegetables he had at his right side. Slowly he reached down and picked up a big white porcelain pan and situated it between his knees. "Came to watch me work? Or talk? Cards?"

I shook my head and sat down next to Uncle Lucius on the old broke-down love seat by the window. I flicked the curtain back with my hand and looked out.

"I say, I say, boy," Uncle Lucius said. "Holding something in is liable ta bust open yo' belly. That's what old folks used ta say. Wonder if it's true? You let me know, 'cause look like you on the road called 'Bout Ta Find Out.' "

"I was thinking about Alicia. Unc, she-she-she still gets to me . . . sometimes."

"Boy, who do you think you are—Superman made of steel? That gurl hurt you. I seen chickens with their necks wrung that felt less pain than you been feeling over the years."

"I've been doing well—I—"

"Ain't said nothin' 'bout you not handlin' yo' business. Never heard that jump up outta my mouth, but I see you holding back something. But I'm not one to get in a grown man's business. That gets folks' lips and head busted, being in other folks' business. But if you was to talk out loud to yo'self you could figure it out. But I ain't listening, 'cause it ain't none of my business."

"Well, it's just that Bebe . . . I like her and it's that I feel very good around her. She's so emotional. Very inside person. I open up so easily with her, then I catch myself . . . and I try to throw up my dukes and I don't want to. I'm tired of that."

"Alicia has got you scared of closeness."

"But I want to be close to someone, I miss that feeling, but I'm nervous sometimes and I draw up . . ."

"If'n it was me, and it ain't none of my sweet affair, but I'd fight it and keep trying . . . work through it. But course, that would be advice and I ain't one for gettin' in nobody else's business. Naw-suh."

I shifted around in my seat. "I've been tense and I know I shouldn't, and Dash, she's been acting up and I've been letting it slide."

"I say, I say, Miss Dashay can be evil. Got that from her great-grandma, my mama. Sweet as pie when she wanna and nasty as old vinegar when she wanna."

"Dash doesn't like Bebe . . ."

"Them family tree branches stretch long! Dash just a little ole twig but got my mama's ways sho' as you born."

". . . she's been ditching my calls and rolling her eyes at Bebe behind my back and that chili fiasco . . ."

"Being sneaky, now gurl GOT that from her disappearing-acts mama!"

"Uncle Lucius!"

"But I ain't talking to nobody but these beans I'm snapping. I love that child, she good as she can be ninety-nine percent of the time. Maybe you've been letting Dash get away with stuff and that's keeping you from having another real relationship because it's easy to use her as an excuse."

"Humphf!" I said. I was letting his words sink in and it hurt a bit.

"Look like ta me," Uncle Lucius said, "look like Dash run this house, a grown man should run his own house. And a man ain't shame' to find fault in hisself if he'll work to move pass it. Take care of your feelings first, make an effort with this lady. Then, if'n it's good, worry about Miss Grown later."

I sat there for a long time, breathing heavy, watching Uncle Lucius's knotted hands snap and drop beans. I thought about how much I loved him and I said, "You're a cool old dude."

Uncle Lucius smiled at me and I laughed 'cause he didn't have his bottom dentures in. He looked down at the beans in his lap. Then he looked up at me. "Sho' is a good season for fresh beans."

Dash

I busted a move upstairs to Uncle Lucius's house and he said, "I say, I say, I'm gettimg more company tahday then they get when they hands out free food at the church!"

I just shrugged and plopped down on the couch.

"Gurl, what you coming up here with your mouth stuck out like a slide rule for? Huh?"

"On punishment."

"Humpf! Serves yo' narrow tail right."

See? He buggin' too now! I rolled my eyes at Uncle Lucius.

"Don't you roll your eyes at me! I ain't ya daddy! I'll slap the taste outta ya mouth."

I dropped my eyes on down-low 'cause Uncle Lucius don't play that.

"Now, that's right. Get yo'self together. Now look up at your Uncle Lucius."

"All y'all buggin'. I wasn't tryin' to make Bebe sick or nothin'. It was a joke!" I grumped.

"Ain't funny, now is it?"

I shrugged. I was looking for a dose of sympathy up here and all I was getting was more of the same old, same old.

"Po' child," Uncle Lucius said, "you can't help being a thief."

"A thief!" I shouted. Buggin'! "What did I steal?"

"Genes," Uncle Lucius said.

"These my jeans!" I said, grabbing the def creases in my pants. "Tommy Hilfiger. Seventy-five dollars!"

"Naw, gurl!" Uncle Lucius said, getting up to grab our old photo album off the shelf. He sat down again. "Come by here."

I went over and sat down next to him. "You good as gold ninety-nine percent of the time, it's that other one percent that'll make you wanna call the po-lice." He opened the photo album. "See here, you get that from your great-grandmother. My mama, Bessie."

"Straight up?" I said.

"You got her *genes*—and I ain't talking about them Tommy Hill Climber britches you got on."

"Hilfiger!"

"Whatsomever! You stole everythang she got. Looka here at this picture. She took this picture the day she headed to Memphis from the country. You got old Bessie's eyes, pretty brown eyes . . . those are whatcha call 'I'm too pretty to pick cotton' eyes."

"These my daddy's eyes!" I said.

"He's a sneak thief just like you!"

And Uncle Lucius and I both laughed. Then Uncle Lucius said, "She lit out with no money, her good dress on in hopes of hitchin' a ride with some church traveling folks, and walked to Memphis. She wanted to be a blues singer."

"I didn't know that! Daddy said she only sang and played piano in church."

"Humphf, boy always half tellin' a story! That was a ways after Mama bombed in them blues clubs 'cause she'd get evil with the managers when they skimmed off some of her money. I'm supposin' they did everybody like that but mama she got evil 'bout it. She got ornery and wouldn't half sing right though folks was coming ta see her. Heck, they just stopped giving her work. You got her voice and her evil ways too."

I tensed up but kept staring at the old picture, brown around the edges, with this pretty woman in a heavy-looking blue dress staring up at me.

"Got ta where she was 'bout ta starve and she went to a church and asked for food and met a deacon there that was tall and handsome as the day is long!"

"I know! I know! Great-grandpa!" I was up on some of this roots stuff, yeah!

"Right! I takes my handsomeness after him! Yes suh. We all take after somebody somewheres."

"Our family is pretty cool, huh, Uncle Lucius?"

"Yep. Exceptin' when those evil traits start warming up. Like you giving yo' daddy and Miss Bebe a hard time, yep, can't say you didn't get it right on from down the line. But good as you can be when you wanna, and you oughta wanna do better."

I dropped my head on Uncle Lucius's shoulder. I'd lighten up some but I wasn't making no promises. He caught my play on the down-low. Uncle Lucius kinda hip and what not for an old man.

Uncle Lucius, yeah, gave me static
Says I got attitude & he's just about had it
Told me, girl, give Isaac and Be a play
And stop showing out with yo' evil ways

But what about me, what's the deal?
I'm only 13 but what I feel is real

Who knows, huh, I just might get left out
I'm a little confused, I've got some doubt

Stuff is changing and I don't know if it should
'Cause sometimes change ain't always good
I'll cool out some, but you know how it is
I'll try but I ain't making no promises.

Sandy

Richard is giving me the flux. I say left, he says right. I say up, he says down. A job just ought not be this hard and stressful. Is that what work is about? Game playing? Power plays? Stress management?

Bebe said, "You need to chill, and me too, after that chili craziness with Isaac and Dash."

"You're right," I told her. "Meet me after work at Carol's Jazz Box."

Ever drown your sorrows? It was easy at Carol's Jazz Box because she was a client and I'd had several events at her place to help get the club name out there, so drinks were free. Bebe and I were on our second round of drinks when they announced that tonight's quartet had canceled due to a death in the family. When they announced the replacement act, I almost choked on my ice cube.

Bebe slurped, "Awwww shit!"

It was T.J., my ex-boyfriend. T.J. Willet, Jr., jazz pianist. I got a rush of emotions when I saw him: smooth jet-black skin spread over high cheekbones and long firm hands. He stroked those keys and I had thoughts of his touch and the love we made. I . . . was . . . in thought as the music, an original jazz piece, massaged my body and jolted my memory. Late nights. Candles. Touching lips and entangled legs and tongues. I said to Bebe, "He's still a sexy somebody!"

Bebe said, "Fine motherfucker he is . . . but he ain't 'bout jack, remember?"

I began to remember . . . the betrayal . . . that led to the downfall of our relationship. I pressed my thoughts to think of other things and hoped my hormones would do likewise. But when he finished playing his song, T.J. looked over as we applauded and he saw . . . me. Then T.J. began making his way back to our table. I said, "This could be interesting."

Bebe

I said, "This is gonna be some bullshit!" The man played my girl like that piano. I know he look good but he got some low-down ways like his player daddy, Speed. I told Sandy, "Don't go there again. You know how hurt you were."

"I know, I know," Sandy said. "It's over. I just want to see what he's going to say."

"Some shit!" I told her. She was already in a state of emotional flux 'cause of work. I was trying to tell the girl not to revisit the scene of the crime with the crash dummy. But naw, don't nobody wanna listen to the Be!

T.J. came swinging them narrow hips over to the table, in that I-talian suit, and he kissed Sandy on the cheek, then kissed my hand. "What a pleasant surprise," he said.

"How have you been?" Sandy asked.

I thought, Why you wanna know? Say hey and good-bye or you'll get caught! He's too fine!

T.J. said, "I'm doing great. I've got a new CD coming out in the fall."

"Oh, congratulations!" Sandy said and she hugged him.

Bad move! Bad move! I sipped my drink.

"How's your old crazy daddy?" I asked, thinking of Speed and his ripsnorting, fun-loving self.

"Daddy's doing well. He's actually staying home a bit more, or trying at least!"

"That's a change," I said.

And T.J. said, "We've all made some changes. Me, too."

And he looked dead at my girl Sandy and don't you know that troll kicked me under the table with her foot?

Shoot, I got the hint! But I sho'll kicked her right back before I got up and left. Don't matter, 'cause the Be was going to get the scoop later.

Sandy

"What kind of changes?" I asked T.J. Maybe he had changed? Maybe there could be a rebound here? Was there too much water under the bridge?

"I'm engaged."

Now why did that make my head hurt? I knew he wasn't right for me. Yet that news made my head hurt and my heart sank. I thought I was completely over him, yet there was still a little left . . . just enough to hurt.

"I just wanted to stop back here and say hi and give you my good news. How are things going with you?"

"Fine," I said.

"Work?"

"Fine," I said.

"Personal?" he asked.

"Fine," I said.

"Well, you deserve someone special, it just wasn't meant to be with us. But you really do deserve someone special. Just do me a favor when you find him?"

"Yeah?" I said.

"Don't give him the body caress. Keep that especially for me," T.J. said, then kissed me on the cheek.

Bebe

I'm tryin' to stay over here by the washroom but it's killing me!

Uppghf! Kissing her on the cheek a-gain. This boy know he's smooth and there he goes, finally!

I get back to the table and Sandy looks okay, just a little sad.

"What's the deal?" I said, sliding into the booth next to her. "What-he-say, what-he-say?"

"Engaged." Sandy shrugged.

"Whaaaaat! G'on, Mr. T.J.," I said. "I ain't know the boy had it in him! You okay? You all right with that?"

"Yeah," Sandy said very soberly. "He wasn't right for me. He just wasn't and there's no reason to force it or try to make it fit. Relationships are hard, Bebe. Getting them right is hard, huh?"

"Yeah, girl," I said, ordering the next round of drinks. "You telling me, that's why I'm trying to work with my man Isaac. And it ain't no easy deal."

Isaac

"Is-eye, what's up with you and this new woman?" L.A. asked. We were sitting around the firehouse—me, L.A., Cliff, and a couple of the other fellas.

"Get out of my business, L.A.," I said playfully. I really didn't mind his teasing because I was happy that I was working on my relationship with Bebe. We had gone to the movies at the Chatham 14—the first black-owned movie theater chain in Chicago—and a few concerts at the new Regal Theater plus lunch at the too hip Shark Bar, and a reception for a friend of hers that was opening a clothing boutique. We had home-cooked dinners savored by candlelight and desserts eaten with one spoon. We were enjoying each other—I was keeping Dash and her feelings out on the fringe, at least for now.

"Isaac, you haven't been in the mix lately, jack," Cliff said. "Spending serious time with this female. You have to be careful with these women out here! They want you to take care of them—buy them expensive clothes, take them to fancy restaurants, help take care of their kids and you're not even the daddy!"

L.A. said, "Yeah, be careful, Is-eye! Dog, females say they want us but they don't let us take the lead like we should. They want to run everything. We're the men. We know how to show them affection, to protect, but they won't let us, goddamn it."

"I hate to agree with nutty L.A.," Cliff grinned, "but he has got a valid point. They too headstrong and they try to pimp you. I was dating this one woman and I was crazy about her the moment I saw her. I went in with my heart and my wallet open. That was my mistake, know what I'm saying?"

Couple of the brothers grunted and slapped high fives.

"Was that Kim?" I asked.

"Yep." Cliff nodded. "Kim played me and I ain't ashamed to say it either. Had me running around, courting her like crazy jack, and wasn't coming across enough with the pussy! And when I questioned her about it? She blew me off. See ya, wouldn't wanna be ya! I felt like she got all the money and presents that she could get out of me before dumping me!"

"You won't see that in *Waiting to Exhale*," one of the fellas in the back called out.

L.A. kicked in. "Then they get mad if we try to keep a little distance, a little macho to protect our feelings. We got feelings too. We need to be cautious too. I asked this one slim to step at a club and we got our groove in for quite a few songs. I asked for her number—her phone number, not her Social Security number. The honey gave me so much attitude and mumbled something about women having to watch out for men. Shit, we gotta watch out for them too, huh?"

Couple of the fellas said, "Right on!"

"Yeah, but admit it, y'all," I said easily, "most women aren't like that. Just like there are a few skeezers out there giving sisters a bad name, there are some low-down dudes out there giving the brothers a bad name."

Some of the fellas moaned and L.A. groaned, "Naw, dog, don't go there!"

"Isaac," Cliff snorted, and popped a stick of Juicy Fruit gum into his mouth. "You heady, man, bookish. People relationships ain't like those poems, mythology, and all that other shit you read in those books, jack."

L.A. took a jab at me too. "Yeah, dog, we talking about stepping to folks, romance, heat, knocking boots, and making the thang work, Is-eye!"

"I'm not crazy, I know it's hard. I'm just saying we've got to be more patient about getting to know each other and hanging in there to get to know each other."

"Well, Is-eye, tell ya what, dog. You bring your slim around here for the boys to check out then," L.A. offered. "We'll see if she's your caliber, man!"

"L.A., the way you chase panties, it's a wonder anybody lets you around their woman." Cliff laughed.

"Wish you looked good as me is all." Then L.A. started patting his 'fro. "So just shut yo' runt butt up, Cliff. Man, you so short, you sit on the curb and kick your feet!"

Before Cliff could get L.A. back, one of the fellas called out from the back, "L.A., phone! Your bookie!"

Everyone knew that L.A. gambled. We played poker in the house but the games never, ever got ugly or too serious. But L.A.? He gambled on boxing, basketball, baseball, the horses, anything anybody wanted to lay some money on. I glared at him.

"Back in a sec," L.A. said, dropping his eyes and jogging toward the back.

Cliff looked at me. "Better talk to your boy about that shit, man. He's getting out of control."

I walked to the back and heard his conversation. L.A. said, "Yeah. I know I owe you fifteen hundred, G. Listen, I can't talk now. I-I'll get it to you this week, promise. You know a Negro like me? I'm good for it, straight up!"

I watched him hang up and I said, "L.A., I thought you were going to take care of that."

"Aww, dog, that's an old debt. I'm leaving the bookie alone and just playing some poker here and maybe a little lotto every once in a while. That's it. I'm just clearing up that last bit of debt," L.A. said.

Was he lying to me?

But before I could say more, it happened. *Thor slammed down his hammer; the buffalo spirits sprinted across the plains, Prometheus lit his torch.*

FIRE. The alarm sounded.

Dash

Me and my girl Tasha were hanging out in my room getting our groove on. We were listening to TLC, Jodeci, and talking on the phone. Out of my entire posse, I like Tasha the best. Tasha and me go way back, all the way to preschool. Tasha is tall, cute face, and got body already. High school boys try to talk to her all the time. Tasha's got a nice smile and her hair is braided in a def style. She wears bangin' gold chains, too. Her mother is real cool. She lets Tasha listen to gangsta rap, get her hair done all fly, and lets her stay out till eleven o'clock—even on a school night. I try to get Daddy to give me some play by pointing out how much freedom Tasha's mom gives her. Daddy says, "My name is on your birth certificate—not Tasha's." He ain't tryin' to hear it.

"What time you gotta be back?" Tasha said with a nasty little smirk. "Nine?"

She knew I didn't like it, and even though she was my girl, Tasha liked to tease me about my daddy being strict. "Mr. Sizemore wants his little girl in the house, huh?"

I rolled my eyes and gave Tasha the finger. I went over to the mirror and grabbed the new belt I had bought. It was smokin'. It was made out of bottle caps and hung low at the waist when it was buckled but I left it unbuckled, hanging open.

"Booty!" Tasha said, 'cause she knew it was fly. I pulled out the new jacket Daddy had bought me because I'd gotten all A's. It was smokin' too. It was black leather with no collar and had two zippers. I had told L.A. which one I wanted and he hooked me up by going with Daddy when he went to buy me something special. Later, L.A. told me that he had to twist Daddy's arm practically to get him to buy it because Daddy said it was too grown. But L.A. came through for me! Tthw! I just might marry L.A. one day.

"Like my jacket?" I said, showing it off to Tasha.

Tasha nodded. "Yeah, but it don't go with your look, Dash. It's nice, but it fits you too tight. You should have got it loose, big, where it can hang, then it would be really straight!"

"Twwth! Yeah, you right, Tasha. My daddy picked it out."

"Dash, you know it's dangerous to let a parent loose in a store buying clothes for you. They'll have you looking corny-crazy 24–7!"

"Can I wear one of your jackets?"

"Naw! We can't start wearing each other clothes. People'll talk about us like a dog. We'll be looking all cheap and what not! You know it's all about the benjamins!"

True. Then I got an idea. Daddy's fireman's jacket. He and his crew had chipped in and had them made special. It was black with a yellow stripe around the sleeves and a silver emblem on the single-breasted pocket. "Wait!" I said and ran and got it.

Tasha helped me put it on and she said, "It stinks!"

I smelled the sleeve. Yo, Daddy's jacket smelled like smoke. "Smells good to me!" I said.

It did. Like, like it reminds me of when Daddy would get off work late and stand in my doorway, blocking the light. I used to like to sleep with the bathroom light on—but I was just a shorty then and what not. Like Daddy would come over and tuck in my covers tighter and brush his hand across my face. And up jumped the smell. Smoke. And it smelled straight to me 'cause that was him, Daddy.

"Hey now!" Tasha said, checking me out after she pushed up the sleeves. Then we went over to the mirror and eyeballed ourselves. Tasha had on a big running suit, Reebok, and had one leg pushed up over her high-top patent leather Air Jordans. She had her jacket zipped up and a big, loose Fila windbreaker on with the collar up. "We all good now!" Tasha said. "It's on. Let's roll!"

I hesitated. "Maybe I better ask my daddy about his jacket."

Tasha rolled her eyes at me. "Baby."

I shoved her big rock head! "Shut up! I'm not a baby. I don't appreciate you dissin' me all the time and what not."

"Sorry!" Tasha said, leaning up. "But your daddy acts like you a little girl so you need to take your attitude up with him!" she said, all the while wiggling her neck like crazy.

What could I say? Nothing because Daddy was always babying me and what not! I just reached over and got my phone and started dialing the firehouse. I let it ring for a long old time but I didn't get an answer—and I thought, Umph-oh.

Isaac

FIRE.

The piercing drill of the alarm. There is no time and space for that moment. When that fire alarm sounds, your mind goes blank. Your body, however, moves toward trained instincts. Then your mind is filled with urgency, and you're about the business of dealing with fire. Fire is a mother. It's elusive and destructive. And there's nothing more dangerous than an elusive spirit running wild with the power to destroy whatever it comes across.

So, of course, really without thinking, L.A. and I dashed for our gear and began putting it on. There was no talking, just swift movement and a sense of purpose. I headed for the truck first. I'm the driver. The brahs decided that because I've got the most skill and the most speed. They couldn't figure it out, why I could get around traffic jams and could get to the fires faster than anyone else. But the truck isn't just a truck when I drive—it becomes Pegasus, the winged horse of Olympus. Pegasus defied air with magic and speed, carrying thunderbolts for Zeus. I'd crank the engine, and my red Pegasus would just take off!

My crew was aboard now, I cranked the engine, and we peeled out of the stall. Pegasus, away! We were headed to the Dan Ryan Expressway. There was a report of a fiery multi-car accident on the outbound ramp near 55th Street.

I was weaving in and out of traffic, in and out, lights flashing and siren screaming. I started heading down the expressway ramp and I saw that all the cars were backed up. Pegasus, away! I veered right, and started riding the shoulder. I could see the smoke out ahead, a wrenching black twist rolling up into the sky. As we got closer, we could smell gas. I spun the truck around the last group of gapers and I squeezed between a concrete embankment and a state trooper's squad car that had halted traffic about twenty feet back from the wreck.

It was bad. I looked at one car, a compact that had the front passenger headlight smashed up against the windshield wiper. The windshield was shattered, the glass broken into a spider-web pattern. Flames were coming out of the side of the vehicle, the tire was even burning. There was a man slumped against the steering wheel as our crew ran over and started working on dousing the flames. I could see through the back of the car that the steering wheel was bent, pinned against his chest, I saw blood on the side of his face and his head was bobbing up and down as he moaned.

Cliff yelled to me, "Out! Out!"

I had grabbed a crowbar out of the truck as soon as I jumped down. The door handle was smashed and dented in, along with part of the door itself. Could I break the glass? No. The guy could get cut bad by flying glass. I saw a crack in the door and I stuck the crowbar in and fell back with all my weight.

Bobo yelled, "Hurry!"

The fire was still going.

I didn't like the smell one bit.

I gave one more full body thrust and the door popped open!

"Help!" I yelled. Other guys were working on the victims in the other two vehicles. We had no time to secure this guy on a stretcher because the car was really smoking.

"Isaac, hurry!" Cliff yelled.

I spun around, leaned my body against the open door, put my foot on a lever next to his seat, and stood up on it with both feet and pushed. Sweat was pouring down my face. The seat popped back, relieving the pressure against his body. The guy groaned. Two other fire fighters were with me now; one flicked open the seat belt which had saved this guy's life, and the other fire fighter grabbed him out and the two of them carried him running backward toward safety.

I trailed them and Cliff trailed me. As soon as we got back about six feet, the first ambulance pulled up and as soon as they hit their brakes I heard . . . BOOM!

The car blew loud and to pieces. Shit just flew through the air. Life for me became rubber-band motion, from seeing Cliff and some of my other crew covering up, falling backward, hips high with rubber boots bottoms out. Rubber-band motion in and out: I went sailing through the air. I felt the wind and little sharp pieces of debris pricking against my neck.

I thought, Protect your head! I thought about the flames shooting out from the car and felt so hot I could swear they were on my back. I covered my face with my arms, hoped for the best, and thought about my baby . . . my baby Dash. We'd had talks about how to handle bad news, about the possibility of getting hurt or killed on the job. I wondered, how would Dash really cope?

Dash

Umph-oh! I hate it when I don't get an answer at the firehouse. I know he's on a call. I was kinda worried about Daddy but I told myself not to. My daddy is the best fireman in the world. When I was a kid, he used to say that he could blow out a house fire by huffing and puffing and lettin' go just like the big, bad wolf in "The Three Little Pigs"—except he was the good guy. After a fire, he'd come in and say, and say, "Dash, the Big Bad Wolf took out that fire!"

Wherever he was, the Big, Bad wolf was going to take out that fire, too. Cool. I wasn't worried. We had talked about the chance of him getting hurt. Daddy told me not to be afraid, to pray, to mind Uncle Lucius and believe in God's strength and believe in my faith 'cause God only lets things happen that are for the best.

I looked at the jacket I had on again. It wasn't my fault that he wasn't there to say, yeah, that I could wear his jacket, was it? When in doubt, the answer is yes! Straight? Straight. Tasha and I had to go upstairs to tell Uncle Lucius 'bye.

"Uncle Lucius!" Tasha smiled as we ran upstairs.

All my friends love Uncle Lucius because he's so funny. We knocked on his door and he was sitting on the couch eating pinto beans and fried chicken. Uncle Lucius keeps his part of the house cold no matter what time of year it is. It's not even summer and he was sitting on the couch in a white cotton T-shirt, a pair of blue polyester shorts, white silk socks that came all the way up to the knee, and white patent leather shoes. He's almond brown with bushy eyebrows that he stole from my great-granddaddy.

"Chil'rens, come on in! Want some chicken?" he asked.

"No!" we both said. We were ready to break and what not.

Uncle Lucius was eating by the window.

"We're—"

"Wait!" Uncle Lucius said to me as he peeped out the window. He leaned over and raised it up and started yelling at this guy who always hangs out on the corner. "Hey, you—you rock-headed, rock-smoking-need-to-shave-ya-neck-and-cut-your-throat, too, NEGRO, get away from this block with that mess!"

Tasha and I laughed as he slammed the window shut again. "We're going to the mall, Uncle Lucius," I said. Tasha cut her eyes at me and giggled because we knew what was coming next.

"Then raise your right hand and repeat after me," Uncle Lucius said as he sucked the last meat off a chicken wing.

We giggled and followed his order.

"I promise to go straight to the mall . . ."

We repeated, ". . . straight to the mall . . ."

"Not stopping for any boys we know, thought we knew, or think we wanna know . . ."

We laughed and repeated.

"Not stopping for any strangers or rappers—not even Hoolio or Kung Fu . . ."

"Coolio and Wu Tang!" we corrected.

"What-SOME-ever . . . Promise!" Uncle Lucius said.

"Promise!" we said, and Tasha was nudging me and I was nudging her back.

We both hugged Uncle Lucius and ran for the door, but froze

when he yelled, "Hey! Don't forget. Keep the top on your cookie jar, hear? A fast tail will getcha a big belly. Y'all got home training, X-AH-SIZE it!!!"

We ran. We stopped back downstairs to my room and Tasha called Kendra and Melody and told them to meet us by the earring place on the second floor.

"Dash!" Uncle Lucius called, and I heard him coming downstairs.

What now? I rolled my eyes. It was easier to get out of jail than to get out of this house!

"Dash, your daddy's hurt . . ."

My heart grabbed the inside of my chest and wrapped itself up in a knot.

"He's all right, for the most part. Got a cut on the hand that required a few stitches. They're bringing him home now," Uncle Lucius said.

I felt my heart start back to beating again. I told Tasha to go without me, I was going to wait for my daddy. I went in his bedroom and picked up the family Bible, read the Twenty-third Psalm, and thanked God that he wasn't hurt bad. Then I stripped down Daddy's bed and put fresh sheets and stuff on it so he could rest good. Daddy likes tea. I put some water on for him. When he came home, guess who brought him? Bebe. Why was she bringing him home? Why didn't L.A. bring him home? Was L.A. hurt too?!

"Where's L.A., is he okay?" I asked.

"He's fine, still at work. I just needed someone to drive me because my hand is sore," Daddy said, holding up a bandaged thumb. "Six stitches! Bebe came to the hospital to—"

"You needed help and you didn't call us? Uncle Lucius and me could have come and got you."

I was mad and I was hurt. She was moving in. Bebe was bum-rushin' our stuff and what not! I know they'd been dating but I didn't expect it to get too serious. If he needed something, Daddy should have called family first. Is Bebe family? No!

"Dash," Bebe said, "I live close to the hospital and so it was easy to just call me and I could get over there quickest."

"I'm not talking to you! This is an A and B conversation so C your way out!"

"Dash!!!" Daddy yelled.

"Isaac, never mind, she's upset . . ." Bebe said.

Who needed her to take up for me? See? See? Pushin' in! Crowding in! "I don't need you to take up for me or take care of my father! You need to ride out!" And I felt tears coming on. I wasn't about to let this chick see me cry. I ran to my room and slammed the door.

Isaac

What was that big blowup about? I could have killed Dash! Why'd she have to show out in front of Bebe like that? Dash slammed the door on us.

I told Bebe, "I'm sorry about Dash. I don't know what her problem is. But I'm going to get her butt right now and make her apologize to you."

Bebe stepped back and gave a half smile. "Don't do that, Isaac. She's upset about you getting hurt. I don't want you to embarrass her. That'll embarrass her. Really, I'm okay with it."

"No, it's not okay," I said. And it wasn't. "She embarrassed me! She's a child and we're adults. She's got a bad habit of wanting to be grown before her time!"

I shouted this last part, hoping that Dash could hear me.

Dash

I heard that. I want to be grown? I am growing up and Daddy just doesn't want to let me. That's his problem. Plus, plus, okay, Daddy just brings Bebe in here like she's Flo Jo Nightingale and what not out of the history books. I saw the way she was hugging him around the waist, acting like she was helping him to walk. Psych! It's his hand that's hurt. What's that got to do with her huggin' his waist and helping him up the stairs? What's up with the dumb stuff? Ain't nothing wrong with his legs! He can walk. Why couldn't she just drive him home and leave? I could have taken it from there. No, Daddy wanted her to help him when he was in trouble. Bebe-smeebe. And did you see her? She ain't fine or nothing, and she got all those hips and that butt! It's a miracle she got balance! And she's old! At least he could have gotten somebody a decent age and what not! Later for them. Later for them both!

I leaned over across the bed and—Daddy can't stand Tupac's music—I blasted it as loud as it could go. I don't give a care if he don't like it neither! I don't care if Daddy puts me on lock down! And I certainly don't give a care about Miss Bebe!

Bebe

Run for your life. Cover your head and your butt, World War III had started and shit was flying ev-er-y-where, people! Obviously little Miss Dash had a problem with her daddy having women around him. I didn't have to plug into the psychic network to pick up on that, okay?

That's why Dash and I kept clashing. This kid was hurting. She gave us both the nastiest look when we came up the stairs! Who?! If she could have snapped her fingers and stomped her feet and made me disappear, she would have been doing a Mexican hat dance, okay? Anyway, she threw her fit on me and Isaac and he was embarrassed, yeah, but that was okay.

"I'm going in there and throw that Tupac tape out the window and drag her little butt down here and make her apologize," Isaac said.

I stopped him. I said, "Isaac, don't. She wasn't ready for me. She saw me invading her space and she wasn't ready. Really, Dash was probably scared about you being hurt and she wanted, naturally, to take care of her daddy. She wanted to . . . not some woman her daddy has just started dating. She's hurt. Don't bless her out or punish her, talk to her."

And then I exited stage left 'cause, as mad as little Miss Thang was, she was liable to throw another award-winning fit. But from the look on Isaac's face, he was about to get a Best Blowup nomination his own self.

Isaac

"Dash, open the door!" I ordered like a drill sergeant.

Nothing.

I kicked the door with my foot. "Turn that junk off and open this door or I'm gonna break it down and keep working my way until I reach you and it AIN'T GONNA BE PRETTY!"

That door came flying open!

Dash looked at me with watery red eyes and then just fell back on the bed, face buried in her crossed arms.

The first thing I did was knock Tupac out the box. Then I started bawling out Dash. "You know you showed your tail today for nothing," I said angrily.

She sat up. "Nothing! You-you . . ." And she fell back on the bed. "I hate you!"

"And right now I can't stand your rotten butt either! Dash, just for your information I'm going to tell you what happened. Just for your information, because I don't answer to you, you answer to me.

"After the explosion, I didn't want to drive because my hand felt like it was about to fall off. The other guys were still working, so why pull one of them? Bebe lived close, so I called her. Yes, I was glad to see her. Yes, I was glad I had her to call. No, I didn't forget about you.

You and Tasha had the phone tied up. Y'all talk on it like it's going out of style!"

Dash still didn't say anything.

I sat down in a chair next to her stereo that was on top of the dresser. I found out the hard way with a thunk upside my head that Dash had hung one of her speakers just above the chair on the wall. I looked up at it and leaned forward.

"Dash, you had no reason to go off like you did today. It was wrong and you know it. You acted a butt and for what? For nothing, that's what. You're smart. You're clean cut. You mind most of the time. I'm proud of you and I should be able to bring a lady friend home without you throwing a fit. She's not stealing any affection I have for you and she's not more important than you. I don't know how to explain it any better than that. I like Bebe a lot. She's fun. We enjoy each other. I don't get mad when you sneak and call Noah."

Dash leaned up with a guilty, surprised look. "You know about Noah?"

"Yeah. Parents aren't dummies like you kids think. We were kids first, remember? Every sneak you wanna sneak I done snuck first. I know Noah likes you and it's okay to call, talk on the phone—but still no dating. Period. You're too young and, besides, you're still my best girl."

Dash sniffed. "I'm sorry, Daddy. Sorry for all that." Then Dash wiped her nose with the back of her hand.

"Don't get snot on my jacket, Dash," I said playfully.

She reached out and hugged my neck. I decided to wait a bit and let the dust settle before I got her and Bebe together again. I had two feisty females on my hands.

Bebe

Mama said knock you out! Isaac and I are going to watch the Holyfield fight on pay per view. I digs me some Evander 'cause the *Real Deal's* body is ripped and his mind is righteous. He's a Christian brother who knows how to give back to the community. *My man!*

I drove my old struggle buggy over to 35th Street. There was a bar on the southwest end, near the park where the White Sox play. I was going to pick up Isaac. It was a couple of weeks after his injury and he was getting back to his old self.

We were going out to the Park West, which is a club-slash-theater on the North Side, to watch the fight.

Now quiet as it AIN'T kept, I'm a sports fan of the highest order. I love basketball—y'all know Mike is all right, Zo' got the flow, and Grant is just *sexy.* I like boxing too . . . timing, skills, the fierceness of it, but I ain't gonna lie, don't got the nerve to watch it ringside and that's the truth. Isaac digs sports too, so he said that we should watch the fight together. Isaac decided that he was going to hang with his boys for a while before we went to watch the fight.

I ran into some construction on the expressway on my way and I just started daydreaming about me and Isaac. We were spending a lot of time together, just cooling out and talking.

Like last Wednesday.

Me and Isaac were at my flat, just kicking back, cooling it. The bank closes at one and Isaac was off that day. I made us some lip-smacking, finger-licking, tummy-pattin' lunch: fried chicken, potato salad, corn bread, and lemonade. Isaac likes to eat just like me and so, quite naturally, the chicken legs had no prayer. We greased. After we finished, Isaac went into the front room to stretch out after eating all that good, hearty food.

Now I know Julia Child and them is down on fried foods, saying they're bad for your blood pressure and increase stress. But I'll be doggone if my mama's top-secret recipe for fried chicken could be bad for anybody. C'mon-c'mon-now! Black folks been eating fried foods, cobblers, cakes, macaroni and cheese all they lives and getting fat and sassy and old. My great-grandmother put the o's in old and soul food and lived to talk smack until she was a hundred and three—old girl was bah-bah-bad!

The only problem with this particular type of food is, dang if it don't make you sleepy. You wanna knock someone out? I mean, put them damn near in a coma? Whip up some good old-fashioned soul food and see if they don't get full and pass out on the nearest chair, couch, or floor.

Isaac headed for the floor and tucked one of the pillows from the couch up under his head. I fell out on the couch; swung one leg up high, one arm down low, one arm up high—I was too comfy, chile.

"I'm hugging you like this pillow," Isaac said.

"Ain't nothing like the real thing! C'mon over here and get a snuggle!"

"I'm too full to move." He groaned with pleasure.

I cocked my head and looked at him and we both smiled. Chile, I was too full to move too. The only reason I could get to the remote was because I was *laying* on it. I flicked on the stereo and it was on WVON-AM, talk radio. They had a white guy on who had given a controversial speech at the University of Chicago about black folks and why they aren't successful in America. Guy said that there was no patriotism in the black community.

Bah-duh?

We looked at each other, then at the speaker and frowned.

I mean really, how much more patriotism can we show? We helped build up this country from scratch for free. Got our culture snatched and the country reneged on our forty acres and a mule. We get our butts kicked by racism on the social and economic fronts, yet we're the first to fight for our country and out front, if you please. Check it out: from Crispus Attucks and the Revolutionary War . . . to the brothers manning the front lines in Doubeya-Doubeya I and II . . . to 'Nam . . . to Colin Powell in the Gulf War.

Isaac said, "Turn that fool off, please."

I did and I thought a minute, then I told Isaac, "You know what the problem is?"

He said, "What?"

I said, "White folks and black folks see patriotism differently EXCEPT for the 'ism' part. See, 'ism' at the end of any word means full of, loaded. Like racism. Now when white folks see the word 'patriotism'? White folks, they concentrate on 'pat' as in, a pat on the back like 'that a boy' and 'good job'; 'pat' as in pat on the head, like "there-there, everything is okay, nothing's wrong.' See, they think patriotism is fighting for your country and then keeping quiet, pretending everything is Howdy Doody for all Americans."

"Oh-kay," Isaac said, leaning up on one elbow. "But black people . . ."

"Black people," I said, "see patriotism and they pull out the word 'riot.' We will fight like crazy for our country, but we gonna talk shit too, and let you know that we don't like being treated badly and misused. We gonna do what we have to do but we're gonna let you know that we ain't happy about some of the unfair stuff that's going down. That's right. We may dis America sometimes but we die for her too."

I could tell by the half-smile on Isaac's face that he liked my theory. Jump back, Sally, jump back! My brother wasn't the only thinker in the room. Naw, sir, so I blew him a kiss.

Remembering that conversation with Isaac made the trip to the bar seem faster. I finally got there around 8.30 P.M. Isaac was supposed to be waiting outside but he wasn't. Where was this boy? Here was that time thing happening again but I wasn't going to trip. I waited fifteen minutes before going inside.

The bar was packed and it was sho' nuff cute. There were wooden tables with little miniature toy fire trucks in the middle of them. Lighted shaved, scented candles were pressed into the back cabins of the trucks. There were pictures of different fire companies on the walls, each separated by a memento. A fire hat. An ax. A jacket. A blunted hose.

There was a stout, bucktoothed bartender mixing drinks in a silver shaker with a mean motion. I asked him where Isaac was and he said that crew was in room C. I looked to the back and there were apparently three private rooms, so I went for room C. It was noisy in there and no one heard me open the door.

There was a big color TV set on a high shelf in the right corner of the room. About twelve guys were sitting around drinking beer looking at the prefight shows. They were all attractive guys, just laughing and joking. I could feel the kinship that they had, feel it in how they sat next to each other, leaning in and grunting at each other. Isaac was off to the left and in a couple of seconds he noticed me and instantly he smiled, then he got a little blank look as if he realized that I had stepped in what was clearly a masculine domain. Isaac hesitated, then waved me over and said, "This is Bebe."

I got a torpedo for a mind. I'm dead on! Can't nothing stop the Be
. . . not the girl. From talking to Isaac about his friends and looking
at them now, I knew exactly who they were even before Isaac introduced them. There was stout and solemn Cliff. Then there was L.A.
with his sleepy eyes and quick smile jumping up to give me a mack-
daddy going over with his eyes. "You doing mighty fine, Is-eye," he
said.

I guess that was supposed to be a compliment to me. Check that
out. "I ain't mad at cha, L.A. You doing mighty fine yourself," I said
and just smiled.

Isaac said, "Let's go. I'm ready." Then he started to throw back his
last beer.

L.A. said, "Why go? We got the fight rigged up in here and why pay
twenty dollars apiece and drive way over to the north side and pay to
park too, huh?"

I looked at Isaac and Isaac looked at me. Then my eye caught Mr.
Clifford, who was giving me the once-over. Uh-unh! Can't fool me no
time, not even on April 1! Cliff ain't want me in here.

Isaac

Cliff did not want Bebe there. No. So far, we had not brought our ladies to any of the sports stuff that we had in the private rooms. After work, meeting each other for drinking, yes, the other guys had invited their ladies. But this back section had just been open for about two months and we had watched basketball games, wrestling, and boxing and there had been no women. There was no verbal agreement, it was just working out that way for some reason.

Now Cliff had just been dogged out by a woman, so he was a bit down on the whole female species, and he was sizing up Bebe. Cliff was not going to be rude or uncouth about it, but he was sizing up my lady. Cliff is a good guy but it was clear in his mind that this was the brah man's section of the bar. He was serious about his sports. But like the cool brah that he was, and after L.A. offered, he didn't object, so we stayed.

Bebe sat next to me and after a few minutes and a cocktail she and everyone else relaxed. Excitement was building as we waited for the main event. Bebe was talking with the guys and she was getting along with everyone—Cliff, though, was quiet.

L.A. said, "Man, I can't wait for Holyfield to step out there, dog, he'll go down in history as the greatest boxer of all time!"

Now both Bebe and Cliff said at the same time, "Please!"

WOW!

They looked at each other. Bebe knows her sports and so does Cliff. He eyed her and said, "Know a little about boxing, huh?"

Bebe said, "Yeah." Now I didn't know she knew about boxing. I know she knows basketball but boxing? Cliff looked at me and I shrugged. "She says she knows, she knows."

Bebe

See, Cliff was tryin' to play me because I'm a woman and he figures, and figures wrong, that I don't know my sports!

Aw, yeah, I know! My father loved boxing and he used to tell me about listening to Joe Louis on the radio when he was a kid and he talked about seeing Sugar Ray number one fight in the Garden and Sugar Ray number two on TV in the Olympics.

Awww, yeah, there were some Doubting Thomases and Cliffords up in the room, so I started to *sport* my sport knowledge. I said, "Holyfield could have beaten Joe Frazier and George Foreman. Their techniques were sloppy and they didn't know how to block and counter well enough."

"What about against Ali or Louis?" Clifford asked real quick.

"Holyfield is my man, but ah, I ain't going to weave no fable to-night. Holyfield never would have beaten Muhammad Ali or Joe Louis, that's another skill level altogether."

All the guys in there agreed, I could feel it. Cliff tried not to look impressed but I think he was. Then he said, "If Joe Louis and Ali fought each other, who'd beat who?"

I thought a minute. That was hard. I stuttered a bit.

Then Cliff said, "Ali. He had the ultimate power, technique, speed, and a razor-sharp mind. He was a thinking boxer all the time."

And he was right. "Yeah, I said you can't beat brains no day of the week."

A couple of the guys laughed. Cliff didn't laugh or smile but by now the main event was coming on.

The introduction at ringside ended up being longer than the fight.

"Man-somebody-oughta-kick-Don-King's-ass-for-putting-these-pooh-butt-matches-on," Bobo said.

Cliff slapped his thighs with both hands. "Fine with me! L.A., give me my ten, man! Told you it wasn't going to last three rounds!"

L.A. reached for his wallet and pulled out the ten and as soon as he laid it on Cliff's palm, he said, "Wouhda if your mama was in the ring!"

I'd heard about Cliff and L.A. and their famous Yo Mama matches and here I was 'bout to witness one.

Isaac

Like the boxing announcer says: *"Let's get ready to rumble!"*

Cliff said, "Yo mama so fat, she was the body double in *Free Willy.*"

L.A. said, "Yo mama so fat, you got to grease the tub to get her out."

Cliff said, "Yo mama so fat, she got hit by a bus and asked, 'Who threw that rock?' "

L.A. said, "Yo mama so fat, she went to a dance and the band skipped!"

Cliff said, "Yo mama so stupid, she uses shoestring for dental floss!"

They were rolling and we all were laughing and going whoo-eee and ahhing. It was fun watching these two brahs going at it. Cliff said, "Yo mama so stupid, she thinks a quarterback is a refund."

And then L.A. went dry, brah went dry and couldn't think for a second. He said, "Ah . . . yo . . . yo . . ."

Then Bebe just had to help him. I wanted to tell her NO as soon as she put her drink down. But she blurted out, "Yo mama so stupid, she sit on the TV and watch the couch!"

Too late.

Bebe

Got-dog-it! My mama always said, "Bebe, ya talk too much!" I know it. I know it. Sometimes it seems like my lips got a separate set of mind and motor skills of their own; and even though a mind is a terrible thing to waste, lip service ain't! What can a sister say? I goofed.

Cliff looked at Isaac and Isaac gave him a pitiful look like he was askin' for mercy for me. *Please!*

Cliff said, "Yo mama . . ."

Isaac said, "Ah, naw, brah."

And I said, "I'm here." I knew if Isaac took up for me now they'd ride him about it forever and Cliff never would give me a break. Ever. So I was about to get whupped but not without a fight.

Cliff said, "Yo mama so fat and old, she knew Burger King when he was a prince."

He was good and I was an amateur. I could remember one more and that was all I knew, "Yo mama so fat, she cut her finger and gravy poured out."

Then Cliff fired off about four and I couldn't get a word in at all and I didn't know any more anyway. Cliff ended up with, "Yo mama's hair is so short, her French braids look like stitches."

By now we all were laughing and I just waved a surrender to the boy because he was tops, for sure. And Cliff appreciated it. And the guys were telling me, "Nice try" and "Go, girl!" just for taking it like I did and I knew it was in fun and so did Isaac and he looked pleased and we stayed there the rest of the evening and had the best time.

Isaac

Bebe surprised me with a gift. A chain necklace with the letter *P*. She said, "The *P* is for that Greek homeboy you told me about."

"Prometheus."

"Yeah, the necklace will bring you luck," Bebe said.

I had told Bebe the whole story of Prometheus. He and his brother Epimetheus were Titans and the god Zeus gave them the job of creating animals and man, using clay and mud. The "E" man gave all the good stuff to the animals he made—courage, strength, speed—and when it came to man, the bag was basically empty. That left Prometheus hanging, he didn't have anything to finish his job. His brother "E" messed him up. You know how family can be. Anyway, Prometheus decided to sneak up to the realm of the gods and steal a little fire by lighting a torch by the sun. He wanted man to be superior to all animals and with fire he was.

But this pissed off Zeus and the other gods so they got together for the big payback, so to speak. They each gave a virtue to a woman who they created and then sent to earth to punish Prometheus for giving fire . . . and man for taking the fire. That woman was *Pandora*. And you know she let all hell break loose by opening that box, Pandora's box, with all the evil in it.

"Yeah, yeah," Bebe had smirked. "Blame it on the sister. You just hang on to that necklace for luck."

I had a surprise for her, too, that she'd get the next day.

Bebe

"Delivery for Bebe Thomas," the young man said, smiling. I looked up from my work and he handed me a beautifully wrapped package. The paper was gold with red, blue, orange, and white thin streamers tied together in one bow. It was huge! Everyone in the bank was looking. I mean everyone. All my co-workers, nosy like me, the security guard who usually nods off sitting in the chair by the door, and all the customers in the line.

"Somebody's got a secret lover," said one of my tellers stationed closest to my desk.

Since I was the show, I batted my eyes, "Ain't no secret to me!"

Then I opened my package. A dozen long-stemmed red roses were inside. They were arranged inside a vase that was tinted red and clear for a pinstripe look. And around the mouth of the vase was a braid with little peppermint candies dangling from it. The entire bank let out a collective, "Awwww!"

I blushed.

One customer asked, "Is it your birthday?"

I shook my head no.

Another customer said, "It's not Valentine's Day."

I looked at the card from Isaac and read it out loud, "Just be-cause . . ." And I smiled. I felt a ray of happiness burst inside me and I just grinned and couldn't help it.

A third customer said, "Oh, it's a lover's holiday."

Isaac

I sent Bebe roses, just because, like James Ingram sings in "Find One Hundred Ways." I sent her roses just because she and those roses have a lot in common. Bebe is colorful, desirable, fragrant. I feel good around her. She's very easy to be with and that's new to me.

So I did like James Ingram said. I sent her roses just because I like the way her arms fit around my waist. I like the way she tells me about herself and the way she always asks about me.

"Isaac," she asked, "what makes you love being a fireman?"

"Bebe, I love it because fire is a wild spirit that needs to be tamed. And when you're a fireman you're the master of the spirit. I respect fire. I love shaping, molding, changing, knocking that spirit out. You get a rush of power because you know that you've saved something— a house, building, factory, or somebody. Oh, and yeah, I love being with the brahs too."

"Now, you didn't know that you would love it so much until after you started doing it," Bebe said, snuggling up close. "What made you want to be a fireman?"

"Okay, let me see," I said, wrapping her arms around my neck. "Bebe, do you remember right before King got shot and killed? It was a stone-to-the-bone ugly time. You know, Uncle Lucius had lived in Alabama all his life up until then but had to come to Chicago because things were so bad down there! I remember Mama said they busted his head open with a brick after he tried on a shirt he wanted to buy at a white store. A mob outside damn near kicked him to death for it, too.

"We picked him up at the bus station one evening a couple of weeks later. His head was bandaged with a piece of cloth. I recognized the cloth. Grandma, he and Mama's mother, kept it rolled up behind the bread box in the kitchen along with sweet oil, rubbing alcohol, and some herbs. She would cut off a strip and use it and her medicines to doctor your hurt. Grandma had cut off the cloth for me a couple of times when I fell or tripped playing in the woods near the creek down there in 'Bama. I spent a week with her every other summer when I was little. I was a teenager now looking at my Uncle Lucius and it was the first time I ever saw him and he wasn't laughing or trying to tell a joke.

"My daddy had taken off work at the meat-packing house so we could all go pick him up. Daddy muttered something about dirty white folks and helped Uncle Lucius into the car. He sat next to me and didn't crack a smile or a joke. He was real down. A few weeks later it happened."

"What?" Bebe asked.

"King got shot and killed. Everybody was crying, mad, or both. I was sitting outside on the stoop of the building where we lived, talking with some of my hanging buddies. We were talking about racism and this and that and Uncle Lucius was standing behind us and we didn't know it. Bebe, none of us really knew about hard-core racism. We stayed pretty much in our houses, on our blocks, and all our families had fathers and/or mothers both working. We had nice clothes, plenty of food, and went to good schools. The only real ugly racism we saw was when we went down South in the summer, visiting relatives who walked like they were beat and kept their eyes down and their voices low. We weren't stupid. We knew there was racism in Chicago for sure, but the city being so segregated, it was harder for us to feel first hand because we were so sheltered.

"Uncle Lucius let us know that, too. That day he told us stories that I cannot, will not repeat. He told us story after story of bad things that had happened to relatives and to people he knew. By the time Uncle Lucius finished, we were mad as hell and rioting had already broke out. Mama wouldn't let me out past the gate, watched me like a hawk.

"Finally that night Mama was asleep and I was laying on the cot in the living room mad because I was missing out on the protests! And I saw Uncle Lucius sneaking out of the house. I put my clothes on as fast as I could and followed him, ducking behind bushes and stuff. He stopped and said, 'Isaac, get your ass ov'r hur!' I was busted but he said, 'C'mon, but you got to be careful and be a man. We need to show 'em we ain't playing no mo'.' And he grabbed me by the shoulder, but now I wasn't sure I wanted to go anymore. I was scared but I didn't want him to know it. So I got my courage together and we met a group of men who lived just outside of our neighborhood but I had seen them a couple of times. They were rough. They knew Uncle Lucius. He told them I was his blood and was cool. Now we were moving in a pack. One of the guys had a radio and I remember hearing Stevie Wonder's "I Was Made to Love Her" . . . and Aretha's "Chain of Fools" . . . as we were walking. The pack was just moving. There is something about numbers that give you strength and make you feel unbeatable.

"We got down to the hot spot, with all the action. People were rioting like crazy, smashing windows and looting and screaming and crying. Without a word, we started hitting stores—throwing bricks and shouting—and there were police cars that we outran and it was a mess. Somebody yelled from a back porch to be careful because

Mayor Daley had given the order to shoot to kill. Shoot to kill anyone with a brick in his hand!

"The crowd broke the window to a TV shop. We ran inside screaming; most folks took things. Uncle Lucius said not to take anything because we weren't thieves but he sure started busting up TVs left and right. I joined him. After a few minutes I heard a poof! And I saw that a fire had started in the back. But fire is funny. Something, some kind of accelerant, was on that floor because that fire cut a wide path across the wood. I ended up on one side, and Uncle Lucius and the other brahs ended up on the other side. Flames separated us."

"Did you get burned?" Bebe asked.

"Wait, wait, I'm going to tell you. You see, some guys ran, but Uncle Lucius and another fella tried to beat the flames down with their jackets and that only fanned the flames. Then, from like out of the sky, came this arch of water. It slapped those flames down like pow! I was drenched, then I looked and there was this white fireman standing there. He was hosing down the other corner where the fire was still burning. I was stunned. Couldn't move."

"Where was Uncle Lucius, Isaac?"

"He was standing there yelling for me to c'mon but I couldn't move. I don't know why. I kept looking at that white guy. Then, out of the corner of my eye, I saw a gun being raised to the back of Uncle Lucius's head. It was a cop in riot gear. But the fireman? He yelled, 'No!' He told that cop that we had helped him put out the fire. Whether that cop believed it or he really didn't want to shoot to kill, I'll never know, but whatsomever, as Uncle Lucius says, he didn't shoot. He lowered that gun and backed off. And we ran.

"After that, the entire West Side has never been the same. And for years after that Daddy would cuss about, quote, the dumb niggers that burned down their own shit. Uncle Lucius and I never said a word. He started working with Daddy at the packing house, and retired from there. You met him and can see for yourself that he went back to his old, crazy, joke-telling self. And me, I'm a fireman, not an engineer like my daddy wanted, but I'm happy."

"And I'm sure they were proud, just the same," Bebe said.

I nodded. "Uncle Lucius always says Mama was crazy for moving back to Alabama to retire after Daddy passed away. I keep telling him that things are different down there now, but he says a visit is okay but never again to stay. Tell me a story about you growing up, Bebe. Fair is fair, huh?"

Bebe

Well, well, well . . . Mistah Isaac. He wanted to hear a story about the Be. He wanted to share old memories with me. Memories are stone-ta-the-bone somethang. A pitiful memory never jumps in your mind or throat. Never. What jumps in your mind and throat is a memory with bang. No wimp or pooh-butt memories can dig their way out of the steel cocoon that protects our insides. Shaft-Sheba Baby memories are the ones that come bustin' a move out of you, for real.

I remembered driving in the car, oh, I must have been ten, driving down South to visit my great-great-aunt who was low sick. We'd gotten the call. Two hours later with a wicker picnic basket full of fried chicken, oranges, potato chips, and candy necklaces . . . my mama, daddy, me, and an older cousin were on I-57 headed out of Chicago.

Ridin' made me LAZ-AY! I'd play dead on the back seat, holding real still. Ya see, my senses would tell the story. In the city, looking up and out of that back window was like looking into my dirty fish bowl; it was cloudy and little things were floating around and only every now and then would there be a flicker of light struggling through. And the air? The city air smelled like car exhaust. And the road? The city road sounded like a hard and fast turn at double Dutch.

In the country, it was different. The sun would sit its fat butt on the window, legs spread, and I'd have to turn away 'cause, ooh, chile, the view would be hurting my eyes! And the country air? The country air smelled like boiling water; clean but heavy. And the road? The country road sounded like somebody playing jacks but steadily throwing and picking up ten all the time.

It was a long-long drive and Daddy was so mannish he didn't ever want to stop to stretch—just to pee. And he peed like Speed Racer. Shoot, we had to unfasten, squat, pee, and drip dry too! Speed Racer would be behind the wheel gunnin' the engine. He had no sympathy for women whatsoever. And I was always littlest and last, running to the car soggy-legged 'cause they had rushed me so. But hey, I didn't want to be in those trees too long no way. One time a bee mistook my butt for a hive. I had to run like crazy!

By the time we made it to the country, my head ached, back ached, and tail ached. So fourteen hours later, getting out of the car you were a livin', breathin' Raggedy Ann doll with your hair standing on top of your head, your legs wobbly, and your toes pointed crooked.

Mama always made Daddy stop about ten miles out. Then she would pour water on a face towel and wipe me and my cousin down. Then she would comb my hair. Whooooo!! It was a half an hour ordeal; ten minutes to catch me, five more minutes to threaten to REALLY give me something to cry about, and fifteen for the actual process. Mama would sit on the hood. I'd sit on the bumper and wrap my arms around her knees and lock them tight underneath. Mama would get that comb and start to pull as hard as she could to try and get the naps out. One time, she pulled so hard she threw the car out of park! Chile, we almost rolled into the river—car, bags, naps, and all!

This day we were cleaned up and pulling up into the dirt driveway. It was paved by the constant licking it got from my uncle's big-wheeled tractor that was straight out of the "Green Acres" TV show. I wondered how he talked them into letting him borrow it? But my Uncle Caleb could talk the devil outta his pitchfork! Folks said I was just like him. My Auntie Corey always said she saved my uncle from himself. She said when she met him he was a slick-mouthed gambler down on his luck. Auntie Corey said Uncle Caleb was poor as a snake, didn't have a coffee can to sip out of, and had enough dirt under his fingernails to fill a shallow grave. But the love of a good woman, she often said, made him prosperous in planting and life planning.

Uncle Caleb looked sad that day we arrived because my auntie was so sick. He whispered in Mama's ear and she started to cry on his shoulder and Daddy had to grab her waist and hold her up. Uncle Caleb came over to me and said my Auntie Corey had waited to see me and wouldn't eat or sleep till she did.

I went to her. Aunt Corey liked to sit up on the back porch. But wasn't sitting up this time. Nope. She was laying down and the doctor was closing his bag, talking about "pencil shots" and "miracles" in medicine. Aunt Corey didn't even have her eyes open and didn't look like she was breathing. She ain't wear her sickness light at all. And I thought, Miracles. That's what she needed, a miracle. And I thought about the word. I kinda knew, but didn't know, how you went about getting a miracle.

Aunt Corey's face was puffy but her body was poor boned. There was a blue and white bandanna sucked solid against her forehead by pomade, sweat, and fever. I went straight for Aunt Corey and took the bottom of my T-shirt and dabbed at two drops of sweat bubbling on top of her eyelids. She opened her eyes slightly and smiled. And I told her, "You need a miracle and how can I give you one?" She just closed her eyes.

I thought about miracles and all the ones I had ever heard about were in the Bible—though I had heard Mama say that it was a miracle that she didn't kill Daddy, the way he acted sometimes. I ain't wanna fool with that kind of miracle. I thought Bible miracles. Miracles that put rainbows in skies, that fed multitudes with two fishes and a loaf of bread, that made sick folks well.

I climbed in the bed with Aunt Corey and she was hot! Sick feels like you're getting burned, I remember thinking. It was so hot! But I didn't care. I laid down next to her and I prayed for a miracle and I prayed until I started seeing red, wobbly circles even with my eyes open.

Later, somebody said they tried to move me, but me and Aunt Corey had locked arms like we were cemented together. Later, somebody told me that we stayed like that through the night and every time someone tried to touch either one of us—they fingers got shocked, like we had static cling, not on our clothes but in our bodies. I don't remember none of that, a-tall. Period.

But I'll tell you what I do remember. I remember waking the next day because somebody was patting on my face. I can't stand nobody playing in my face. I remember thinking, I'm gonna knock them into next Wednesday if they don't stop playin' in my face!

But it was Aunt Corey, eyes open and patting. She had color in her skin. She had a shine in her eyes. And Aunt Corey had that mouth back, saying, "What they feeding you up North? You sho'll is gettin' to be a big, pretty, fat old somethin'!"

I was a miracle worker! I didn't care what my cousin said about me being too little to do things, my hair being nappy like BB shots, or none of that. I was a miracle worker. And that snoop-footed doctor with a rotten smile had the nerve to try and jump up and snatch all the credit! Can you feature it? He said it was the pencil shot that saved Aunt Corey. I knew then and still believe now that it was prayer. I told Isaac, "I'll never forget the power of prayer."

Isaac

I had one more question and I hesitated to ask it. Now I am not a shy man, literally speaking, but I do try to stay clear of uncomfortable moments if I can. And right now Bebe and I were very comfortable and I thought, Why shake it up? But I'm a bit nosy, not in an annoying way but in an inquisitive manner. I mean, inquiring minds want to know, so some big mouths should ask!

So I did.

I asked Bebe, "So tell me . . . why hasn't a woman like you ever been married?"

Bebe

Hold up, hold up, stop the bus, baby, I need a ride!

Didn't Isaac know that you weren't suppose' to ask a woman a question like that? I started to hem and haw and say something funny, or witty, or smart-alecky, but I actually leaned back on the couch and put my feet up, and thought long and hard.

My mama used to say your soul is a big pot and throughout life sometimes it's empty and sometimes it's full but most of the time it's 'tween and you're trying to stir up something good. I felt Isaac's question down in the bottom of my pot. So dig it, dig it, I started answering his question by questioning myself.

"Well, I have been in like, in stupid, and in comfort, which all can make a woman go ahead on and jump tha broom!"

I looked down at Isaac and his eyes were right up on me, too, just invading my space but drawing my thoughts out of me. Isaacman had me dipping into my pot and I wanted to satisfy him and myself.

"Let's see, the time that I was in comfort? I was dating a Missouri man who opened a branch of his construction company here in the Chicago area. He built that big fabulous complex in suburban South Holland. Homes with three thousand square feet, three bathrooms, a fireplace, and so on and so on. He gave me a pair of diamond earrings and the brother even owned a skybox at the United Center, okay? I was in *Southern comfort,* y'all! I could have married him because it was headed thataway but I had to break away instead. I found myself caring more about what he gave me than the man himself. I was a black Madonna—a material girl on the real tip, and that really wasn't me. It wasn't. I really wanted caring. But I was in comfort, which just ain't enough to satisfy.

"Then I was in stupid one time. I was right out of high school then and I was crazy about my boyfriend Al. Al was the first man that, well, tellin' you true, made me feel every inch of being a woman. I felt that I had picked the lock on a magic box with his name on it and all the glitters and charms that made me happy were inside. But that wasn't for real—it was some cubic zirconium stuff! Like the record says, I had to let it go 'cause it was another love TKO!

"And, yeah, Isaac, I have been in like before. I liked one gentleman so much that we almost got married because my clock was tickin'. I was turning thirty-nine and getting afraid that I would be an old maid, no family and no children. I thought, I'm in deep like? It may not get any better than this.

"But 'wake up, Little Suzy,' and, Bebe, don't you sleep neither—I woke up to the fact that deep like wasn't going to be enough. I couldn't just grab something out of fear and make believe it was something it wasn't. Ain't that much imagination in the world. So, I guess I just haven't found the right man, the right feelings, and been in the right situation yet. That's why."

Isaac looked at me and said, "As far as relationships are concerned, you've been in like, in stupid, and in comfort. What are you in now?"

"Suspense," I said.

Isaac

Suspense.

I thought about what Bebe said for a couple of days. That was a hell of an answer. I noticed that she didn't say that she had ever been in love. Bebe is a cautious lady. Very cautious. I think that it's sad, her not having been in love.

I've been in love.

I waited for a day when Dash was going over to Tasha's house and Uncle Lucius was going to a bid whist party and I put on the Spinners, "The Love I Lost."

I played that when I thought about Alicia, wondered where she was and what she was doing. Alicia and I met at a rent party for Jump's cousin, who lived over on 57th in Englewood. I had my 'fro picked out and my comb with the handle made into a black power fist sticking out of the top of my head. Bell bottoms flaring, I was jamming in that tiny little basement with my friends and I spotted Alicia across the room. She took up space in a room not with size but with attitude. Alicia acted like she was a star, like she was someone you had to know. She was cute, petite but shapely, and she had lovely hands that she rested by the thumbs in the belt loops of her hip huggers. I asked some of the guys about her and they said she was stuck up. I had pride and I liked someone who had pride too, who was selective like me, too.

She blew me off, that night. The next week. The week after that. It took two months for Alicia to even dance with me. I remember the way her hair brushed against my ear and the musky, sensual smell her body gave off as we locked into each other and tried to tear our clothes off as we moved to each note of a Temptations song and I thought that she was the sexiest thing I'd ever seen. Alicia was love at first sight for me because I never could get her out of my mind after that first time I saw her. And why would I want to? Thoughts of her made my thing big and I wanted to explode each time I touched her. I loved her and wanted to take care of her. We got married and I thought we'd stay together forever.

What went wrong?

That's the kind of question a chemist asks when he can't fix a formula, or a cook asks when a cake doesn't rise, or a mechanic asks when the tuned-up car engine comes back smoking. It's those daily things, the simple irritations that you want to put that kind of question to, NOT about a love you lost, the wife and mother in your family that you lost.

What happened?

Yes, that's better. That's a safer way to put it. Wrong points to guilt. Wrong points to fault. Someone is wrong and someone is right. What happened means that more than one circumstance was at work. More than one thing didn't kick in and go the proper way and that's what I think happened. Alicia never really seemed into the marriage. It was obvious that I loved her more than she loved me. She was into the world more than she was into me. She kept a globe on our bedroom dresser. She would spin it with her hand and stare at it for what seemed like hours. I thought that was so silly! I never said it but I thought it and maybe one day when I wasn't careful, when I wasn't really careful, maybe she saw it in my eyes in the reflection of the mirror. I hated that she had that globe. Her mother said Alicia always wanted to see the world. Ever since she was a little girl, Alicia knew that one day she'd travel around the world and meet exciting people.

Dammit, wasn't I exciting? I felt excitement when I brushed up behind her, my thighs against her rump, and wasn't that excitement to touch our tongues together? Wasn't it exciting to take a carriage ride and Alicia could have pretended that we were gliding down the streets of Paris rather than Chicago? And years and years would pass and she would become more and more restless and I felt that I was losing her but I tried to keep her and I felt that she would fly away and I . . . I-I cheated.

Alicia never wanted children. Even after all those years together, she never wanted children. I cheated. I wanted children but was willing to not have any for her. But I cheated because I felt like she was going to fly away and I wanted to weigh her down with a part of me, with a part of what I wanted out of life, so I pricked a hole in my condoms to get her pregnant.

Dash. Dash. Dash.

That's how she got here. Can that be considered planned parenthood? Guess so, huh? I just knew that Alicia would settle down when she saw that tiny face, heard that needy cry, and was touched by those shriveled-up fingers. I thought she would drop-kick that globe into the back alley when she first felt Dash's lips sucking life from her breasts.

Alicia loved us, I do believe, there is no doubt there, but just not enough to settle her. Where she got that desire to roam I do not know. Where she got the courage to leave first me, then Dash I do not know. If you can call that courage. I wish I knew where she was so I could ask her. I would not try to bring her back because I see now, I know now, that you can't hogtie someone's heart but I would like to know if she's happy. That would be something to know, huh? Wouldn't it?

Bebe

I'm trying to get to know Dash. But Dash doesn't want to know me. When I call and she answers the phone? Dash talks real dry like she's got a mouthful of sunflower seeds and needs to spit out the shells. She says, "Tthw! Huh? Uh-huh." Then she breathes heavy into the phone, sighs, like it's oh, so much trouble to get her daddy.

I tried to make conversation with her last week. "Dash, how's school?"

"How was it when you were a kid?" she asked.

"Fine," I said, kind of surprised.

"Well, it's still the same," Dash said.

Super smart mouth?! Okay? I never would have talked to an adult like that when I was a kid. Never. I'd be afraid they'd go upside my head and rightly so, then tell my mama and then I'd really get it— twice! Not these kids today. They've got a smart answer for every-thing. And Dash is right on in there with them. She's heady though— don't do it in front of her daddy. Dash gets me on the solo. Sample: I talked to her one day and I said, "Oh, you going to the sale at the mall? I went yesterday." You know, just making conversation.

Dash said, "Yeah, but we ain't going to the BIG woman shops!"

That little Sesame Street hooker! She was trying to crack. Yes, I got meat on my bones, but I'm solid and shapely, but she tried to make it sound like I needed to go to a tent sale. The little troll!

I wanted to tell Isaac, but why? What was he going to do? He can't make her like me, and if he gets on her about her mouth, she'll really hate my guts then. Everybody wants to be liked but I truly don't want to kiss no little kid's ass, okay? But I know it must be tough growing up without a mother. That has to work on her mind. But Dash is dancing the twist on my nerves. Whenever I go over there? Dash will go over to her girlfriend Tasha's house or go to her room and get on the phone.

That phone! The child has a phone growing out of her head! Dash just tucks that receiver under her ear and struts around, no shoes, just white athletic socks on. Dash has more phone cord than the telephone man. She walks and unravels cord—got it tacked onto the wall and just walks and unravels cord, reels it in, rolls it out. She looks like she's laying pipe or something.

Dash will be on the phone for two hours and won't say two words. I asked her one time, just playing, mind you, I said, "Are you alive or on life support?" She just rolled her eyes. I'll try to ask her something and Dash'll look bug-eyed, as if to say, I'M ON THE PHONE! So what? What business she got at her age? None! I'm just getting tired of all this attitude she's giving me. I know Isaac sees that she doesn't seem to care for me too much and I can tell how he tells me to say "Hi" to Dash, or for Dash to say "Hi" to Bebe. He just wants us to get along. I'm trying, God. I'm trying.

Dash

Bebe this. Bebe that. Forget Bebe?! She ain't all that, but Daddy seems to think so. She's too frantic and eager. She's trying too hard! You know, I answer the phone and she sounds too cheery-fake. "Hi, Dash! How's it going?"

Chill already. She wants to ask about school and shopping like she's my mother or something and she's not. Daddy wants me to like her, I know, and I'm trying to be fair. I'm not trying to be mean and what not. But it's like we ain't clickin' right now and you can't make folks hit it off. I've got my own mind and what not.

Daddy came to my room the other day and said, "Dash. I'm going to invite Bebe to go skating with us on Saturday, okay."

He said it just like that. Daddy wasn't asking me because he said what he was going to do and what not. And Daddy didn't say it in an up tone like, "Okay?" Naw, he said, "Okay." Like done. Like she in there.

Bebe

Roller skating?! Awww, naw! My big butt does not need to be on skates. I couldn't hardly roller-skate as a kid. Now I'm going to wait until I'm in my forties and get out there and roll around, falling all over the place, killing myself in the name of bonding? The only thing that will be bonding is my butt and the rink floor! Humpf! And the way Dash looks at me sometimes, she's liable to roll me right out into traffic! Skating?! Why couldn't Isaac say, the movies? Why not the Du Sable Museum? No, he wants me to go out with him and the roller derby queen, Miss Dash. I wanted to say no. I wanted to say, hell, no. But I couldn't! Look like it was so important to Isaac. I said okay. And as soon as I said okay, he gave me a big kiss and grinned from ear to ear. I felt a sick feeling in my stomach about it though. Dash wasn't going to give me any play on those skates. Maybe if I appealed to her, asked her to show me how to skate when we got to the rink, she'd kind of teach me and that would put her on a higher level than me. Dash could help me, show me something. I started to feel better. It might not be so bad, huh?

Sandy

"It'll be fun," I assured Bebe.

Bebe and I were strolling through an African arts fair at Daley Plaza. I was so glad to catch up with her. The anxiety I'd been feeling at work and the way I'd been hustling to impress Richard had put us out of touch for a little while. You know how it gets sometimes? You think about your girlfriend but don't get the opportunity to share a meal or swap eye contact or a call.

This arts festival was on. The toasty rays of the sun melted through the thick, angled glass windows. The unusual warmth was part of nature's way of clawing through a Chicago spring. All the colorful paintings, jewelry, fabrics, pots, and crafts caught the light and burst energy through the entire building. The Picasso statue, always in my mind African, loomed gracefully, tossing a warm and protective shadow across the arts fair. In the comfort of that setting I tried to ease Bebe's fears. "Girl, don't be nervous about Dash."

"Sister girl, this child got a fierce dislike of me, I'm here to tell you."

"You're not scared of a little kid?" I said, squaring her shoulders and giving her a sarcastic smile. "Not the Be!"

Bebe grudgingly flipped a smile back at me. "I just don't want a whole lot of mess and be all stressed out and stuff."

"You'll be fine if you just keep being yourself," I told her.

I wanted so much for things to work between Bebe and Isaac. I'll tell you why. Bebe, Isaac, and I had gone to a concert at the Park West to see George Benson. George Benson was outstanding, but J-108 was cosponsoring the event and I'd seen the show the night before. So my eyeballs and instincts were trained on evaluating Isaac and Bebe. Isaac is classy, cool, and into Bebe. Bebe is into Isaac. She likes his style, which doesn't cramp hers. I was very pleased at how comfortable they were with each other. And Bebe was on; upbeat and funny, just being Bebe. I liked them together.

"Bebe, this is what you should do. You need to stop trying to make Dash like you and be yourself, and she'll like you naturally in her own time. Period."

"*Stop*. I am not trying to make Dash like me," Bebe said.

"You are too."

Bebe's response: "*Oh, but no.*"

"I'm going to throw a fit on you if you don't shut up and take my advice," I scolded. "Try, Bebe. Promise before I have to go to this meeting with Richard and Harvey."

"Is Richard still sweating you?"

"Yeah! He walks around the station as if he owns it. That's why I want to go to this meeting and get out of there early. Richard claims that we can trim the budget. How? I do not know. But Harvey wanted to have a meeting to see what Richard has to say."

"The two of them got thick awful fast, huh?"

"Yeah, Be. It's like when they get together it's just the two of them there and I'm not taken seriously at all. I've had meetings with them and they talk all over me. I make a suggestion and it vanishes into the universe, they never seem to hear it. It's irritating. It's like they have this man thing going. I'm surprised at Harvey but maybe he's just trying to schmooze Richard because of his powerful connections with S.E."

"Sandy, that's some B.S. You know good and well Richard must be some kind of a fuckup if his brother is that high up in the company and they dumped him—a white man in America—off as a consultant at a small jazz radio station."

I agreed wholeheartedly.

"Ditch the diplomat role you're playing, Sandy, and put old boy Richard in check," Bebe advised.

"I'm trying to be cool and professional, wait him out," I reasoned to Bebe and myself.

"Just like you're telling me about Dash? Then I'm telling you about Richard—he's gonna do what he's gonna do anyway so, just to feel better, let him know you've got some dap. You've got to go off on him some kind of way," Bebe said. "Fair is fair, now. Promise me like I promised you."

"Well," I said, drawing the word out to several syllables. Then I exhaled. "Okay."

"Give me some love," Bebe said, and we hugged before I rushed off.

I was in a hurry for my meeting. It was Saturday morning and I was dressed casual, wearing a pair of slacks and my college sweatshirt. Harvey and I had had meetings like this before and we always came very casual.

I got to Harvey's office and Richard was inside sitting down, wearing a polo shirt and jeans. He smiled warmly and I smiled back. "Where's Harvey?"

"Running late," Richard said. "Say, great school!" He pointed at my sweatshirt.

I smiled. "Yes, I know. I'm a graduate."

"Really? So am I!" Richard said and just grinned. "I was there a few years before you, of course. Aaah, I loved it!"

"Me too! We have something in common," I said. Maybe we would start getting along better. I hoped. I hoped.

"You know my father met my mother at the homecoming game their sophomore year," Richard said.

"Aww, that's nice. College sweethearts," I said, taking a seat at the circular conference table with Richard.

"Yeah, it's a great school," he went on to say. "You're lucky you got in while affirmative action was still big."

"Excuse me?"

"Affirmative action. The way they hold spots for minorities. I never will forget how my best friend Jerry was turned down. He was a real bookworm, Jerry, smart, but he didn't get in. I remember how he cried about it. But we realized the problem, affirmative action. If we had been in the same class, you very well could have gotten his spot," Richard said and leaned back in the chair.

Richard didn't say it nastily. He didn't say it in a mean way. Richard said it like he was reading it out of a book, a book like the Bible. I started to let it go but the very idea of it made me angry and I was about to digest that anger, but my promise? Remember, I promised Bebe.

"I think I was awarded the spot I was supposed to have," I said very evenly. "I was an excellent student."

"Yeah," Richard said assuredly, "but everybody knows that affirmative action cuts slack for you people. They save spots for minorities, ESPECIALLY women, too. You're a double quota. That leaves a lot of white guys like my buddy out in the cold."

I couldn't believe what I was hearing. Richard said it all just as nice as pie, as if he didn't mean any harm. But I was insulted. I said,

"Richard. My SAT score was high. I graduated fifth and was secretary of my high school class."

"I didn't say you weren't bright. I'm just saying that my buddy didn't get in because of affirmative action. There were two black guys at my school that did get in and their grades weren't as good as Jerry's. Hell, Jerry had better grades and scores than I did even," Richard said.

"Maybe their test scores weren't as high, but they could have had more activities, or they could have written better essays, or submitted better letters of recommendation. But your friend Jerry, you say, Jerry had better grades and test scores than you?" I asked. I'd caught something here.

"Yeah, bright guy! Sharp!"

"And you say you were a legacy—a double legacy?" I asked.

Richard nodded.

"Well, I used to recruit. I know that there are only six percent minorities on the campus. But forty percent of the campus is made up of legacies. That's some coincidence, huh? Seems they're setting aside nearly half the spots for legacies. Now the college didn't even admit minorities or women in any real numbers until the mid-seventies, we know this. So nearly all these legacies are white men. So there you have it. If they saved a spot for me, then surely they saved your spot for you. That's the biggest affirmative action program going. Maybe we both got in on affirmative action and you got Jerry's spot."

Richard looked like he wanted to die! He nearly went to glory right there before my very eyes. I was so pleased with myself that I crossed my legs. That left only my right foot and Richard face's flat on the floor. I couldn't wait to tell Bebe. I wondered how her skating adventure was shaping up?

Bebe

Skate time! I was psyched. I got to Isaac's house and we gave each other a big hug. "Let's go," I said.

"We're waiting on Dash," Isaac said. "I needed her to run to the store for me."

We went upstairs to sit awhile with Uncle Lucius. Now I'd met Uncle Lucius the day I brought Isaac home from the hospital and we had also sat with him in Isaac's kitchen a couple of times and played Tonk—laughing and lying, the three of us—but I hadn't been upstairs to his part of the house. Uncle Lucius is real. He's got a Southern, gravelly voice and sounds just like the big red and white cartoon rooster, ("I say, I say, boy!"), Foghorn Leghorn.

"Miss Bebe," he rumbled, smacking his gums. "Say, gurl, I wondered when you was gonna get up here to my place for a visit!"

Chile, the place was the most organized clutter I'd ever seen. He had glass juice jugs lined up against one wall—all filled with pennies. He had stacks of tools on the floor—hammers, screwdrivers, paper cups with nails in them in another corner. He had five fishing poles in another corner and a big plastic bowl in the center of the cocktail table full of beat-up decks of cards. On the floor next to the television set there was a stack of crumpled, ancient girlie magazines—not *Playboy,* but *Bronze Thrills.* And you know what? He was saving pages in them, turning the corners down. It was stuff like that everywhere, clutter stuff, but neat in spots and places.

"Sit down!" Uncle Lucius said and I went over to the couch up against the wall and sat down—plop! The corner went smack down against the floor.

Uncle Lucius and Isaac both laughed as they helped me up. They wasn't foolin' the Be. It was clearly a setup.

"I say, why you do tha gurl like that, son?" Uncle Lucius asked, grinning. "Don't do hur like that!"

"I forgot!" Isaac lied, winking at me.

"See," Uncle Lucius said, raising the end of the couch with one hand and sliding a small block of wood under the leg to prop up that side of the couch. "Now, that's how to work it."

I sat down very carefully; I like my hips and want to keep them intact, big and bad as they are, thank you.

Uncle Lucius said, "Isaac, go get us some of that lemonade I made in the icebox there! Go on now!"

He headed toward the kitchen and Uncle Lucius said, "Turn the radio on."

Isaac stopped by the old upright radio and turned the round knob. It clicked but no sound came out.

"You forgot how to work it?" Uncle Lucius said. "Go on to the icebox, son!" He went over and plugged the cord in. "It's always on!" Then he picked up a smashed-up coat hanger and stuck it in a little hole in the back and bent it to the east. B. B. King's "Let the Good Times Roll" from 1976 came blaring into the room.

I spied a clock on the wall that didn't work. Every time you looked at it, you thought you should either be asleep or eating lunch because it was stuck on twelve straight up. I said, "Uncle Lucius, why don't you get rid of that clock?"

"Huh," he grunted, "oh, say, it looks good, and even though it's broke—it's still right twice a day!"

Chile, the whole house was broke. Uncle Lucius lived in a broke house!

"Say, Bebe, look a here, open that drawer in the cocktail table right there by your foot."

I tried but couldn't.

"Let me tell you how to work it," Uncle Lucius said. "See that ruler there on the side. Yep. Take that, stick it in the corner, slide it down till it's tight, and now yank the handle! That's it!"

I opened the drawer and pulled out two pictures on top. Woo-wee, they were too cute! The first one was Isaac as a baby, nude, flat on his back, his right hand palming his head and his left hand playing with his navel.

"I like this Kodak moment!" I said.

Then the other picture was of Isaac at about maybe three and he had on short pants, suspenders, and a white shirt with a rounded collar and sleeves that stopped at the elbow. "He looks like a black Spanky in this one!"

Uncle Lucius and I hollered. Isaac came in with the drinks on the tray and he just sighed, "C'mon, Uncle Lucius!"

"Baby, you getting rerun checks from Our Gang Comedies or what?" I asked. Uncle Lucius slapped his knees and pointed at his nephew.

I took a glass, a shiny old jelly glass, off the tray and so did Uncle Lucius. Isaac sat down with the tray and the last glass. "Stop showing those old pictures!"

We started sipping our drinks.

"Uncle Lucius!" Isaac scolded. "Where are your teeth?"

I started laughing.

WOW!

Uncle Lucius smirked at me. "They used ta be in that jar she drinking out of."

I like to choked, but then I looked up and Uncle Lucius was winking at me. Then he pulled out another baby picture of Isaac and waved it! Isaac tried to grab the picture out of Uncle Lucius's hands. He flipped the picture over to me and I doubled over and clutched it to my chest. Isaac started tickling me in hopes of making me turn the picture loose. Nope! Uncle Lucius got as much fun out of our playing as we did and we all laughed ourselves silly.

Dash

"Dash, I haven't heard your daddy laugh like that in a long time!" Tasha said as we came up the steps with the groceries.

She was right. I didn't say anything 'cause what Tash had said stuck in my head. We put the stuff away and then she went home. I went upstairs and Daddy was laughing with Uncle Lucius and Bebe. And yeah, he was giving her that look. Daddy looked happy. Not that he was really unhappy before. But happy is all I can think of, and yeah, he looked like happy.

"Ready to go, pretty?" Daddy asked me and I nodded okay.

"Hi, Dash," Bebe said. "Now you know I can't skate. I'm depending on you to help me."

I just nodded.

In the car, Bebe tried to ask me about the music groups and stuff I liked and I answered her but I wasn't really interested in having a conversation. Daddy had been throwing no's in my face all morning and what not. I asked him about getting braids. No, that looks too grown. I had asked Daddy could Tasha come so I could have some company too, but he said no, and I was still kind of mad about that.

Bebe said, "Your daddy says that you can sing?"

"Yeah, but I want to rap," I told her. Tasha and I had been practicing over at her house because Dad can't stand rap music. I love it!

"It's fun. Rappers make bank and they wear fly clothes and everything! Me and Tasha can jam, too. I've been trying to get Daddy to let me get some braids so that the look for our group will be more better," I said.

Daddy said, "Dash, I keep telling you, no. Those braids make kids look too grown. I don't like them and they cost too much money, too!"

"I can't do nothing. Can't even have a pager," I mumbled.

Daddy sighed. "I used to think only doctors and drug dealers had pagers. Now all these kids have them. That's too much technology for me. And you're a child, what would be that urgent?"

"Well, if I can't have the pager, why not the braids? I can't do nothing the other kids do!" See? Daddy acts like I'm some little kindergartner or somethin'.

Bebe said, "Well, if she doesn't get extensions and just braids a little hair in with her own it could be cute."

Daddy shook his head. "I don't know. I just think they look too grown on the girls I see."

I said, "Just think about it, Daddy, huh?"

He looked at me in the rearview mirror, then at Bebe, and shrugged like yeah. A little hope was better than no hope at all.

"Cool, if I can get my look together and stuff, I know our rap group would take off! Plus me and Tasha are going to be in the firemen's talent show, too. And, Daddy, don't forget, rappers make a lot of money!"

Daddy said, "Yeah, but money can't buy a beautiful singing voice. And folks my age started rap anyway!"

Bebe said, "Yeah, it's nothing new! Think about Gil Scott-Heron! He was rapping back in 1975!"

Daddy played Gil Scott-Heron's records every now and then. That was cool but it wasn't really rap. It was more talkin' than anything else. It didn't have no driving beat or nothing like that. "Now stuff is better," I said and folded my arms across my chest because I was sure.

"It's different and that's good," Bebe said. "But don't forget the start."

My daddy nodded his head and said, "Tell her, Bebe."

Please?! This was going to be a long afternoon. I just hoped that we would have more fun once we got started skating.

Once we got inside the rink, me and Daddy put on our own skates but Bebe needed to rent a pair.

"Dash, would you help me pick out a pair?" she asked me.

I already had my skates on and I said, "Fine. Just stay here with Dad and I'll bring you back a pair. What size?" She told me and I skated away. I wanted to yell at Lance anyway; his father owns the rink and Lance works at the counter where the skates are. He's fine!

"Hey, Dash," he said and smiled at me.

Lance is old enough to vote and I wasn't trying to flirt with him because I'm not fast like that for real but he's fun to look at and fun to pretend we're the same age and maybe can hang out with each other.

"Hey, Lance," I said and grabbed a pair of skates off the counter.

"No, cutie," Lance said with a smile. "Take the next pair. That pair has a slightly warped wheel. You skate a few feet and it hangs up and makes you fall."

Then he winked and turned to wait on someone else. I glanced back and saw that Daddy had his arm around Bebe. He was just as comfortable as could be. And she was just sinking him too. Bebe was reeling my daddy in! I don't know why. I'm not sure if I'm ready for that or not. I wanted him to have fun but I just felt funny about all of this. Lance gave me a big smile and touched my chin with an open hand (wait till I tell Tasha!) and said, "Smile." I did. I grabbed Bebe's pair of skates and rolled back over.

Bebe

Little Miss Tabasco Tail!

Uh-huh! I spotted Dash just flirting away with this kid handing out the skates. Isaac wasn't paying much attention, he was watching ESPN on a television they had rigged up in the waiting area. But I saw little Miss Tabasco Tail doing her thing. Yeah, Isaac was going to have to eyeball her 'cause that boy was about twenty or so, I know. When we came in, his name tag said, "Lance." Good-looking young man, *Sir-Lance-I-got-a-lot,* but he needed to be flirting with girls his own age.

Finally Dash tore herself away from him and brought me my skates and we were off to the rink! I was ready to hit it. But I never dreamed I'd literally be hitting it for real! I mean—bam! Get up. Roll a bit. Bam! Down again. Up and down, up and down! Everythang was twisted: my legs, my clothes, and my face. But I was trying, trying to creep along.

Isaac was going, "C'mon, you can do it!"

The man was holding his hands out to me like I was a toddler learning how to walk.

Bam! Hit the rink again.

Dash was skating around backward, on her toes, bopping and

169

weaving, the show-off! I wish I could skate close enough to trip her little tail!

"I can skate backward when I want," Dash said with a smile.

"I can go shopping when I want," I shot back before, bam! I hit that floor again. God, my butt was hurtin'!

"You're not listening!" Isaac said in a gruff voice.

Ain't that a bitch?! I wasn't listening! He wasn't listening! Didn't he hear my butt smacking against the ground?! Huh?! I was killing myself and he was barking orders, hollering about "turn this way and that way" and "move your feet like this." "Man," I said, "you crazy!"

I got up and bam! Went down again. I stayed there this time and whispered, "Lord, help me or take me right here!"

That's when Dash skated over with a pitiful look on her face. "I'll help you."

I prayed for an angel and got sent a little devil.

She said, "Bebe, try relaxing your legs. Take smooth, even steps!"

Dash took me under the arm and we moved slowly. I started going pretty well with her holding me up. Isaac came skating over, "Now just—"

"You shut up and g'on!" I said, giving him an evil look.

Isaac just laughed and started rolling around us in a circle. He started dancing, bending his knees and stuff, and bobbing his head. That's where Dash got her show-off ways from, okay? I could see that trait was swimming the back stroke in their gene pool.

"If I could get my hands on you!" I said, half mad and half joking.

Isaac stuck his tongue out and kept dancing around. "I'm sooooooo goood!"

I whispered to Dash, "You gonna let him play me like that? Girlfriend to girlfriend, you gonna let me go out like this?"

It was the first time Dash smiled at me. "Naw, let's get him!"

She grabbed me by the waist, lunged forward, skating fast, and we rolled forward and I hip-checked Isaac and knocked him flat on his butt! But I kept going! My arms were windmilling because I mean I was determined not to fall. Dash grabbed for me. "Let me be," I said, and don't you know I didn't fall? I had my balance, brought my knock-kneed stance together, and stood straight as could be. I leaned on the rail, thank you, Jesus, I was by the rail, and crossed my legs. Dash skated next to me and smiled. I smiled at her, then I looked at Isaac on the ground. "How ya like me now?"

Isaac

They got me. Bebe and Dash had got me. They got me good and I loved it because Dash had helped Bebe. I was pleased that they were getting along even just for those few minutes. I decided, Okay, this is as good as it's going to get today. Don't push it. End the skating right now. I said, "Y'all win! How about some deep dish pizza?"

Dash said, "Antonio's!"

Bebe groaned. "Only if they've got padded seats."

We helped her off the rink and went over to return her skates. Bebe sat down and took them off. I handed them to Lance at the counter.

"No wonder you kept doing so bad," Lance said, looking at the skates. "These are the broke pair. Dash, I told you that."

We all turned and looked at her.

Dash had a stunned look on her face.

I was so angry! How could she be so mean? A child of mine could not be that mean! I grabbed Dash by the arm and jerked her up, "You mean to tell me that you deliberately gave her these broken skates? What is the matter with you, Dash? She could have hurt herself! Well, say something, huh?"

Dash

"I didn't do it on purpose! For real, Daddy," I said. He was mad! But I didn't! I looked at the skates and at Lance and at Bebe and everybody was staring me down. How'd it happen? I don't know.

"Dash!" Daddy said real loud. Too loud. A couple of other kids turned around and were starting to stare. I was so embarrassed. They weren't going to believe me, I know. I know they weren't! I felt a hot something run up my face on the inside and my eyes started burning on the inside, too. I didn't want to cry and I was trying to hold it in bad. I didn't look at anybody, I just kept looking down at the floor and I said, "It happened by accident, y'all. I turned around and saw you and Bebe hugging and I reached back and I wasn't looking and I grabbed the wrong ones. You see they all the same color at the top, blue. I just grabbed without looking. It was an accident, for real."

Then I just looked up, 'cause I knew nobody was gonna believe me and I was going to get it—get yelled at right in front of everybody.

Bebe

Look, up in the sky it's a bird. It's a plane. *Naw-naw, baby!* It's the BE coming to that poor grown-ass child's rescue. Don't ask me why, but I plucked her out of a pool of trouble. I threw little homette a lifeline. I said, "Wait, Isaac, I believe her."

Dash looked up at me and I could see a tear just hanging on the edge of her eye. She ain't wanna go there, I know. I gave her a stern look like, Little girlfriend, you'd better wipe your weepin' eyes and let your backbone slip into place and get ahold of yo' self! Dash caught my meanin', good old-fashioned. She sucked back those tears and stood up straight.

I told Isaac, "I believe it was an accident like she says. I don't believe Dash is ornery like that."

Isaac looked at me and his face softened, even *Sir Lance-I-got-a-lot* dropped the surly look he had on his face. I believed Dash. That was too hateful of a thing to do, even for Dash. Baby Godzilla gave attitude, not bruises. It was still a little tense so I said, "Isaac, why don't you let me and Dash hang out together ALONE sometime soon?"

Thought the man was gonna faint! Then he nodded his head up and down hard as he grinned. Isaac looked like one of Bay-bay's kids OD-ing on ice cream.

"That's if Dash wants to," I cooed.

174

Honey chile, Baby-go-for-bad was so glad I saved her little narrow butt that she would have agreed to try and sell shade, two for a dollar, in the summertime. Dash was truly grateful!

The next subject was tricky. "Isaac, if you say okay, I'd like to braid her hair for her. I can give her a style that isn't grown at all and it could be real cute. I can braid my butt off—what's left of it." I'd gotten a pain and had to shift around on the folding chair.

"Well," Isaac said, dragging every letter out to the fullest. "Not too grown, okay?"

And Dash leaped over and gave her daddy a big hug. I just eased back in the chair and relaxed 'cause I was very pleased with me.

Isaac

"Is-eye!" L.A. said. "Enter, my brother!"

I stepped into his apartment with a bagful of chips and beer. L.A. and I were going to watch the Bulls play the Knicks.

"You got the popcorn popped, man?" I asked him.

"I just poured some of the corn in the bowl, man. Hit the tube and get the game on TNT!" he said, taking the bag.

I looked over at the spot where L.A.'s Toshiba thirty-two-inch, picture-in-a-picture stereo surround sound television set was. Excuse my slang, but where it was—was where it ain't. He had one of those huge wooden entertainment centers with the glass door and cabinet that you slide the panel out. Yes, inside there he had a twelve-inch set. Where the Toshiba deluxe CD stereo system was supposed to be in the entertainment center he had a component set made by Lennox. I went straight to the kitchen and L.A. was grabbing some tall beer glasses and had a six-pack under his arm. I said, "L.A., where is your set?"

"Awww, dog," he said, "that thing was using electricity like a mo'fo! My electric bill was high! So, hey, outta here!"

"And bought that little thing? Why not at least a nineteen-inch set? Brah, on that set the players are going to look like little ants running around," I said.

L.A. said that he got it from his cousin for a few bucks so he saved some dollars. I asked about the stereo. Same story. L.A. must think I'm a fool. I said, "Did you sell them to somebody for money or did you just give them outright to your bookie?"

L.A. bumped and rolled me, saying, "You don't like what I have to offer, then you ain't got to be up in this motherfucker, man. Don't make me feel small about my shit, Is-eye."

I had made a few calls and had found the number of a gambling hot line. The hot line had the addresses and phone numbers of where meetings are held in the city for folks with problems. I wanted to tell him about the hot line but L.A. had sworn that he was okay. I had to ask him again. I went into the living room and I sat down next to him on the couch. I scooped some popcorn up in my hand and tossed a few kernels in the air. "What's the deal, L.A.? I just don't want to see you mess up. Are you still gambling? Because if you are, you are on the wrong track."

L.A. looked at me and said very seriously, "I still owed that money that you heard me talking about on the phone. I've been making weekly payments but I had to give up some merchandise as collateral. Hence the tube and the sounds. When I pay off the debt, I get my 'dise back. That's it. I ain't making any new debt, Is-eye. I'm trying to wipe away the old to start clean. Period. I'm a little embarrassed, but hey, I'm a man and a man pays his debts. So how about this? How about some peace, my brother?"

I popped open a beer and took a sip. I believed him. He didn't blink or hesitate. I sipped and said, "Peace."

Bebe

Isaac called me and said that he had a family emergency with Dash and could I help? At first, a jolt of nerves sliced through me because I didn't know what he was talking about but I felt kind of uneasy that he was pulling me into it. I was hesitant about getting involved and I didn't even know what the problem was . . . but I care for Isaac, so I told myself, Bebe, push that stuff outcha mind, girlfriend, and see what's going on.

Isaac said that Dash got her you know what.

Her what? I repeated and I didn't get it. Really I didn't.

Isaac copped an attitude. "You know, Bebe. What y'all get."

Oh! Now I knew! But was I going to be a good girl and let on? Was I going to let Isaac off the hook? Course not! "Y'all get what?" I asked him and covered the receiver so he couldn't hear me laughing.

He just started breathing hard.

"C'mon, baby, what's it called?" I prodded, still laughing and trying to hide it. Can you say period?

"Menstrual cycle," Isaac finally huffed out.

Boy, was it killing him or what?! "High 'fluting, ain't we? Period will do just fine."

"Bebe, cut me some slack. This is important. I don't know how to talk to her about it," Isaac moaned.

I started feeling sorry for the boy and I broke on down and decided to help him out. "All right! You want me to come over later tonight?"

"Come now!" Isaac pleaded. "And bring some, some supplies with you."

"Supplies! Boy, tampons!" I corrected.

"No! I don't want nothing going up there yet."

"Isaac," I said, "you're talking crazy!"

"No, I'm not. I don't want her getting used to nothing going up there—not yet! Get the big napkins," he said.

"Pads, knothead!" And I laughed. "Isaac, they don't make them all bulky like that anymore."

"Oh, I remember them being thick. One time when I was eight me and my friends were outside playing doctor. I was the doctor and they were the patients. I didn't have any bandages. So I went and got a box of my mother's Kotex out of her bedroom closet. I bandaged the kids' legs with them, their heads and elbows too."

I cracked up imaging a neighborhood full of kids running around bandaged up with those big huge pads on them. "That was a sight, I'll bet!"

"Yeah, my mother thought so too. She whupped me good, made me get money out of my little bank, and made me go to the store and buy her some more. I was so embarrassed! She made me carry them and wouldn't let the man put them in a bag. Boy, did I get talked about like a dog. So, you get them, okay?" he said.

"Sure, baby," I said. "I'm on my way."

Dash

My back is hurting right in the middle and my stomach is twisting up in knots and it hurts. I told Daddy I knew what it was, I told him, "Daddy, I'm starting my period."

You'd think I told him I'd gotten shot or something. He made me lay down, which I was going to do anyway, but he was so frantic! Man! I knew what it was because Tash got her period last year and what not.

I went to the bathroom because I felt like I needed to pee-pee, but when I sat down to go, I pushed but nothing happened. I felt this little pulling down there but I didn't feel like I had pee-peed but I knew something happened so I wiped myself and there was this little smear of pink. I knew what it was but still I lost some of my breath. I didn't think anything right then. My mind was blank, know what I'm saying? I didn't think anything and that's hard to do for real. There have been times like when I've tried to make my mind blank and what not like, like, say, when I'm thinking about a boy I don't want to think about, okay? But like then, when I wanna, I can't get my mind to go blank for nothing. But this time my mind was empty. Then I finally snapped out of it, and thought, Duh, dummy, you need some help. So I went to my room and called Tasha. Tasha's an expert, for sure. She's been on her period for a year! But Tasha wasn't home.

I remember Tasha telling me that she woke up in the middle of the night screaming because the front of her gown was sticky, wet with blood. She was only eleven and a little kid, that's why she tripped, Tash said. She said her mother gave her a tampon to stop it. Tasha and my other girlfriend Rhonda both got their periods before me. They acted like I was not part of a secret club or something, whispering and talking about it and what not, and when I ask, "What?" They say, "Oh, you wouldn't understand!" Ain't that stank! And I told them too, "Y'all stank!" I was jealous! And now that it's here and I'm in, I'm not sure I want to be in—'cause when you in, you're in for a long time, Tasha says. It's messed up to be this uncomfortable for days and have to go on about your business like nothin' is up.

I heard a knock at my door and I just knew it was Daddy back from the store, so I said come in and it wasn't Daddy, it was Bebe. She had a bag in her hand and she gave me a little smile. "Heard you might need a little help?"

"Dawg! Just broadcast all my business!" I yelled and squashed my pillow over my head. I hope I smother myself!

I heard Bebe move across the room, take a seat next to my night-stand, and put the bag on the table. "He's a man, baby, and he didn't know what to do, or what to say, or if you were nervous or scared or what. Isaac told me to bring some supplies!"

"He's tripping," I said.

"I know. He don't know we ladies can handle this—our bodies change so drastically and show us our changes in such dramatic ways that it scares them because they don't understand it—and certainly couldn't take it!"

"Think so?" I asked and sat up a little bit.

"Girl, if men had to deal with periods, having babies, and meno-pause they'd be jumping off the Sears Tower left and right," Bebe said.

Then she made a diving motion with her index and middle finger and smacked her palms together going splat!

"My stomach is hurting, not real bad, but will it hurt like this all the time?" I asked her.

"It depends. Everyone's body is different. If you're getting cramps now it's likely that that will be one of your symptoms. Some people get cramps, or backaches, or muscle spasms. Some women are easily irritated or get bloated, or a combination of any of the above," Bebe explained.

"Aaagh!" I said and buried my head back under the pillow.

Bebe took it away and I laid there like a log. She rubbed my shoulders. "It won't kill you, little homette. Here, let me give you a massage on your lower back—and I've got some herbal tea on downstairs to ease those stomach cramps for you."

And Bebe massaged my back real good and it wasn't hurting so bad. Bebe said, "You were surprised this time, but not anymore. You'll start to feel signs that your period is coming. An early backache is one sign or you'll feel bloated or you'll start craving salt or sweets or just junk food, period."

"It's on the same day every month. Tasha told me." I knew a little some-something.

"It's about the same time every month but it can skip around if you're sick, like with the flu or something's got you stressed out or if you're on birth control—"

My eyes got big when she said that because I didn't think she would mention anything at all about sex because Dad was so uptight with me about that kind of stuff.

"We don't need to have that conversation, do we?" Bebe said very carefully.

"No!" I yelled. I wasn't crazy!

That made Bebe smile. "My girl. Cool. Cool." She left my back and opened the brown paper bag with the supplies in it.

"I bought tampons and pads both. Now your daddy told me he didn't want you to use the tampons because he didn't want nothing going up there . . ."

"Oh, pah-lease!" I groaned.

". . . but I know we're sophisticated enough to talk about them— and I don't think he's going to want to know the details of this conversation anyway."

I giggled.

Then Bebe told me all about what to do. . . .

"I heard one of the deacons at church say once that it was a curse for women because we made Adam sin," I told Bebe.

"Ththw!" she said, sucking in air. Then Bebe slipped off her shoes and put her feet up to relax. "Drown that nut-nut in the baptizing pool! It is not a curse, it's part of nature. You know God don't curse nobody! Please! Your period is your body letting you know that you're a woman who can give life. And it's time that you crossed over into a new arena of your life."

"I can't wait to tell Tasha and Rhonda, they got theirs before me! Now I've got mine too!" I said, real excited like.

"Cool, tell your girls but let me tell you it ain't no cause for celebration. I heard of birthday parties, rent parties, anniversary parties, but never a period party! It's a trip! It's a mess and it ain't no fun at all! You'll get cranky some days, ornery some days because your hormones are inside doing the-the . . . what's that dance you and Tasha do?"

"The tootsie roll?" I asked, hugging my pillow.

"Yeah, your hormones are in there doing the tootsie roll!" Bebe said.

And don't you know she jumped up and did it? She did the dance and I didn't know she could! I laughed at her old butt 'cause she looked funny doing my dance and Bebe even laughed at herself. But she was doing it though.

"If you have any more questions ask away," she said. "You go take care of business and I'll bring you back some tea."

And I felt better already.

Isaac

I came into the house with a bag of groceries full of all the things I needed to make my famous meat loaf. Bebe was coming over tomorrow to braid Dash's hair and I wanted them to have something good to eat. When I came in the door, I heard Dash singing. Usually she was rapping along with one of the records and I'd ask her to tone it down. Today, she was singing a cappella. I just stood at the edge of the stairs and peeked up. I could see her standing in front of the mirror with a brush as her mike and she was singing, sounding great. When Dash finished I applauded.

Dash looked embarrassed but that sheepish little smile said that she liked the compliment. "You should sing more, Dash, I keep telling you that. I'm not going to get on you like I have before, but really, you ought to work on that side of music instead . . ."

". . . of that rap stuff," she said, finishing my sentence for me.

I shrugged and just said, "All right, echo—be my shadow, too, and keep me company while I fix us dinner."

Dash eagerly agreed, grabbing a book off her dresser. It was my dog-eared copy of *Their Eyes Were Watching God* by Zora Neale Hurston.

Dash took a seat at the opposite end of the counter near where I would be working. I started getting everything ready for the meat loaf.

This is what's in it: I put peppers, green onions, celery salt, finely diced tomatoes, a dash of barbecue sauce, cooking wine, corn bread crumbs, and a tablespoon of honey. I put the "me" in meat loaf because no one else has ever touched my recipe. It's distinct and it's mine and it satisfies every time.

Dash was reading and I could hear the faint, pleasurable release of her breath. Dash is a straight-A student and her leaning is toward math, but I have always liked to read and I know that if I don't push her to read she won't read as much as she should. *Their Eyes* is the first book that I have given Dash that she hasn't complained that it was too long or too boring.

"Daddy," she said, looking up at me with puzzled eyes, "will Janie ever find somebody who loves her?"

"You have to finish the book!" I said, happy that it was holding her interest and she was asking questions.

"She's awfully unhappy with this Joe Starks guy," Dash said. "I don't know if I like him or not. I think he's kind of doggish, huh?"

"No," I said because that's not how I saw it.

"Yeah," Dash said, flipping through the pages that she had already read. "Uh-huh!"

"Dash, Joe is not a bad man. He loves Janie and only wants the best for her. Sometimes you can love someone and you can make a mistake by loving them so much that you don't see them for who they are, for what they want, for what they need," I said.

"But if you love someone, won't you automatically know what's right or wrong to do?" she asked.

"Baby girl, love is good and it's wonderful but it's not the end-all, be-all—make everything right. There are people who love each other but just can't live together, can't get along. They love one another but one has a problem, maybe drinking or drugs, and it breaks the love down. You see that Joe Starks loves Janie so much that he wants to put her on a pedestal. But she's not that kind of woman, she loves people and having fun and you can't smother someone like that. You can't change somebody."

Then I started thinking about Alicia; maybe I smothered her. Maybe she needed that air and had to fly away to get it. Maybe I had been her Joe and loved her too much and couldn't see what she needed. That's the thought that was running through my mind. And you know what? Kids are something. Kids are really something because Dash had to feel it by looking at me. She knew I was thinking about her mother.

"Or maybe they don't love you enough to let you know what's up," Dash said. "I think if they love you enough they'll let you know and try to fix it. That's what I think. Janie just didn't pull up and leave. She tried to stay but Joe just didn't get it. So I think Joe Starks has some fault, but Janie was tripping too. And sometimes stuff just turns out just whacked like that. And really, you know, Dad, it's really like nobody's fault it's just whacked like that."

I looked up at her and our eyes met for a minute. My baby girl was right, she was growing up. I was pleased and a bit scared at the same time. But I knew not to tell Dash that.

Bebe

Boop! We kicked my man Isaac to the curb this morning. It was ladies' day! Hair braiding is not for the faint of heart. It's like the Olympics. The participants need to have a slew of S's like stamina, strength, style, and speed.

Now, a couple of days ago, Dash and Tasha took the El and got off at Cermak to go to a wholesale hair place in Chinatown. I gotta give the little divas some dap—they did a good job of picking! They got a nice grade of light brown hair with a hint of red. But then they nutted up! Dash also bought some beads—big white beads. Who'd she think she was, Venus Williams or somebody, with her hair flipflopping up and down the tennis court? I ain't going there.

"Ditch the beads, homette," I said.

"Ththww!" she said.

I was ready for attitude. But I wasn't havin' no attitude. "Dash, those beads look too out-there and, besides, your head is going to be hurting enough the first few nights without you having to try to sleep with a bunch of rocks in your hair. Besides, every time you turn your head, it'll sound like somebody playing with click-clacks."

"Click who?" she said.

"Oh, right!" I laughed, she didn't know anything about that crazy toy. "It was a fad toy I had when I was a kid. Two metal balls on heavy string and you'd jerk your hand up and down and they swung back and forth, making a loud click-clack sound."

"Huh, sounds like you all were deprived in the toy area if that's the best y'all had to play with—two balls on a string!" Dash laughed.

I wasn't going to let her crack that tough. "Well, we didn't have all the stuff you guys have now but we still had fun. Y'all video babies don't know how much fun it is to play with simple things or to just play with each other. Double Dutch rope. Dodge ball. Tag. Red light. All that was some cool, pure fun."

"Give me Nintendo any time," she said and gave me a look like she felt sorry for me. "Y'all had it rough way back then."

Was it time for a rocking chair? Did I need Geritol with a straw stuck in it? Was I about to get a Social Security check and didn't know it? What? I'm not ancient! The girl had me scratching my head. "I still say ditch the beads. If you think about it, you only see real little kids with beads now. All the teenagers and adults just have straight braided hair—no beads. Plus we promised your daddy that you would look good and I don't want him mad at me or you, see my point?"

"Okay," she finally said.

She gave up without us going a whole bunch of rounds and I was truly glad.

"But I want the tiny, tiny braids and I want them to hit me here," Dash said, turning around and showing me with her index finger.

Lord! If the girl was light-skinned she'd look like she was Chinese or something with her hair way down there. "Dash, that's a little much, don't you think? One minute your hair is at just below your ear and the next minute it's dustin' your butt?"

"Tththw! I saved my benjamins for months to pay for it, didn't I?" Dash said. "So it's my hair."

"Yeah, it's yours now. But just because you paid for it doesn't mean you have to use all the hair in the bag, huh? Remember, we want you to look cute and chic, and that's a shorter style, I think. Besides, you know how much longer it would take to braid that much more hair?"

"Tthwth!" Dash said again.

Cool! Chile, I was fightin' for this little child's fashion sanity! I was not gonna let her look crazy no matter how hard she tried. We were just about to get started; this braiding thing takes forever and a day, chile. I figured that even with the short style it would take about eight hours. We settled into the living room. I put Dash on a short stool and I stood to get leverage. I put a metal dinner tray on my right side for the hair, the oil, extra combs, and a pitcher of ice water and two glasses.

Dash decided that she wanted to listen to some music. She'd fetched down a little leather case with her tapes in it. She popped one in and it seemed like I'd heard that song before. I just hadn't heard it like that. Call the po-lice—it was criminal! I could hardly recognize the song but Dash was just bopping to it. Then I realized that it was one of my old cuts! And it sounded like s-h-double dot that i-t! They had hip-hopped it to death! You could hardly recognize the original recording 'cause it was getting whupped to death by some vicious generic downbeat. You know how shot car speakers sound with the bass on high? That headache sound? That's what they had done to this song. It was pitiful! It was a violation!

"What's the matter? Bebe, you look like something hurts?"

"Yeah, my ears!" I said and just turned down the stereo. "A good song ruined."

"What? That's new," Dash said, looking confused.

"New? Hello! BET news flash, baby, that song came out twenty years ago. That's some counterfeit version! Dash, nowadays y'all are sampling so many of our grooves and remaking so much of our music that you won't even have any dust records of your own! When it comes to music, you guys ain't Generation X, you're Generation Re-run! It's all our music, chewed up and spit back out!"

"Oh, don't go there! It's not that bad, and what's wrong with put-ting a new sound to an old record? It's all good!" Dash said, settling down on the floor.

I decided to show Miss Thang something. I said, "You got all the latest stuff there, huh!"

"Yeah!" She smiled.

"Okay, wait a minute," and I went over to Isaac's record collection. The man had his stuff alphabetized and he had records from way back in the day in mint condition. I called out the names of a few songs that I knew had been remade. She found some of the tapes in her case and a few more she had to run to her room to get and bring back. I got the records from Isaac's collection.

"What?" Dash said, looking confused.

I took the first tape from her, "Love Don't Love Nobody!" I played as much of the counterfeit as I could stand. Then I said, "The cut: Spinners 1974." Then I played the record.

I went on, " 'Killing Me Softly With His Song.' The counterfeit. The cut: Roberta Flack 1973. 'Sweet Thang.' The counterfeit. The cut: Chaka Khan & Rufus 1975. 'You are Everything.' The counter-feit. The cut: Stylistics 1971. 'Rock With You,' the counterfeit. The cut: 1979, Michael Jackson when he still looked black and before Latoya turned snitch!"

Dash just sat there with her mouth open.

"Close your mouth. I know it's hard to take but I just wanted you to know, originality is not your generation's strong suit," then I put on the Isleys' "Harvest for the World" . . . and patted the stool. "Hop up, girl, and let's get started."

Dash

When Bebe offered to braid my hair, I thought that I was going to be whacked sitting there for so many hours with her alone. I did. But it wasn't bad at all. She scratched my scalp and it felt so good to have my scalp scratched and massaged like that. Bebe said that the warm sensation going from the fingers to the scalp helped soothe the brain and relax the mind. I asked her how she knew and she said that her mother told her. Bebe said that her mother used to oil her hair in the kitchen, by the stove with a pressing comb. Bebe said she would duck her head and hold her ears. Bebe said every now and then her mother would get to talking and not watching as careful, and sizz! She'd accidentally burn the tip of Bebe's ear. Bebe said she'd have little chocolate kisses from a straightening comb on the top edge of her ears.

I asked Bebe about her mother and what not. Ya know, I was on the nosy tip. In Bebe's business. Bebe said that her mother was tall, strong, and had good hair, better than hers. Bebe said that her mother cooked the best blackberry cobbler and always told her to use her mind, keep some money hidden, and know that most men think the way to a black woman's heart is through her legs but that ain't so, know it ain't so.

When Bebe asked me if I missed my mother, I was surprised. I was like, like why she go there? But we were just talking and she was braiding and we were relaxed and I think it just tripped out of her mouth. I had felt before that she made sure she ain't ask me about my mama but this time, here I think the question just tripped out on accident. I held my breath because I didn't want to seem mean, because I wanted to say, "None of your business," like I told other people because it kinda hurt to think about it, not to mention going into a conversation about it. That was my way of throwing up my guard. I wanted to say, "Ride out—leave me alone!" But I didn't say that this time and I'm not sure why, except maybe I wanted to say something different for a change. I said, "Miss her."

Bebe said, "That's good. If you still miss her that means that you still love her. And you should always love your mother no matter what. A mother needs a child's love just like a child needs a mother's love."

I blurted out before I knew it, I said, "I get postcards every now and then from exotic places. My mother is a world traveler."

"Uh-huh," Bebe said and kept braiding.

I'd look back at Bebe every now and then with a hand mirror I had sitting in my lap. I said, "I know my mother loves me wherever she is. . . . I don't need a new mother."

I felt Bebe's rhythm catch for a second, then keep on. She said, "I'm not trying to be a replacement or anything like that. I'm enjoying your father and he enjoys me. I'm trying to help us be happy. I'm not a replacement model, I'm original. I'm just Bebe. Nothing more or less. I'm not trying to change your life, Dash. I'm just floating around in it some, just think we ought to let each other live."

She kept braiding and braiding and I didn't say nothing, just thought. Bebe wasn't so bad, huh? Tasha came over around lunchtime. Tasha is so antic-frantic sometimes!

"It's going on, Dash! Miss Bebe is hooking you up!" Tasha said.

I had to admit my hair was looking good and it was looking even better since I knew I was getting it done for free. Bebe accepted Tasha's compliment and then said she needed a break. We all sat down and got a plateful of Daddy's meat loaf. It was slap-yo'-mama good. Tasha and I talked about our latest rap song we were writing. We were trying to figure out what music to sample under it and I know Bebe had just cracked on that so I didn't expect her to be interested but she was interested and what not.

Bebe said, "Hey, baby girls, I know y'all don't have the music together yet but show me your stuff? Why don't y'all turn this into the Sizemore Supper Club," she said and crunched on a mouthful of salad.

Then me and Tasha busted out a rap for her. We did our best to smoke it, too. We finished, smiling at each other 'cause we know we did good. But what did Bebe think?

Bebe

Aww, *sucky-sucky* now! They were good and I told them so. Dash and Tasha had presence and their words weren't just mumbo jumbo. I'm sure it would sound even better with music behind it, but they needed to work on their look and mannerisms. I'm sorry, but a sister gotta speak her mind. That gangsta hip-hop look? It is not going on for them. It's not. But they had talent. Their voices were strong, clear, distinct, and together they had chemistry. I just thought that they should change their look and make it more *say-say*—feminine! So I laid that notion on my little homettes, too. You'd-a thought I told them to jump in Lake Michigan naked.

"Aww, we ain't going up on no stage looking corny," Tasha said.

"For real," Dash said, shaking her half a head of braids. "We straight like it is!"

They couldn't see it. The two of them had 'bout as much vision as Ray Charles and Stevie Wonder. I commenced to breaking it down for them. "Hear me out," I said. "Suppose you ditch the concrete look. The running suits. The dark colors. I'm not saying be corny, just chic. Like En Vogue but rapping. That'd be different, huh?"

"Yeah, but who would take our rap seriously?" Dash questioned.

"Everyone will!" I told them. "See, you'll be the only ones with a different look and style. So that'll make everyone notice and remember you."

"I don't know," Tasha said but they were looking at each other with doubt.

I kept pulling at my girls. "Look, get something kinda sophisticated for your rap. Then get your moves in synch, like the old clips you used to see of the Temptations or the Supremes, and I'm telling you . . . you'll stand out and everybody will be going crazy. I promise you. When is the talent show? Your dad told me but I forgot."

"End of next month," Dash said.

"Okay, practice my way for a couple of weeks, and if you don't like it go back to the old way. Period. I'll come by and check y'all out, okay?"

They still looked like I was expecting them to take that leap into Lake Michigan. I sweetened the pot. "And for trying it my way for a couple of weeks, I'll spring for the outfits. . . ."

"Whoa!" Tasha and Dash shouted together and started doing the dance, the tootsie roll. "We're gonna look good and get our groove on!"

I had to shout over them, "Within reason! Within reason!"

Sandy

Who on earth wanted layoffs?

That weeble-headed Richard. Weebles wobble but they sure can screw up! It was Richard who drafted a proposal for Harvey that would lay off about ten people. We only have a staff of about thirty-five as it is. So he wants to lay off about twenty percent? To use one of Bebe's phrases, is he on the crack pipe or what?

Richard showed me the proposal in a meeting with Harvey. He whipped it out and put it on the table like it was some brilliant proclamation. Crap was what it was, but Richard was just as happy and proud as he could be. And Harvey bought the idea once Richard told him how much money the station would save and how the stock would go up in value. It didn't matter how much I protested about people having families, and bills, and leaving the rest of us at J-108 to be overworked.

Thinking about the layoffs sent me home in a foul mood. I was glad Bebe was coming over. She is a pick-me-upper. I was sewing a dress for her. I saw the pattern in the store and it looked just like Bebe. She had picked up the material for it and we were just about done. I really like to sew. It's fun and creative and lets me blow off a little steam.

"I don't know if I want to let you near me with needles and scissors with that sour look on your face," Bebe said as she slipped into the shell of the dress.

There was no lining and no sleeves in yet. Bebe and I both thought that it might be cool to use the sleeves off another pattern—they were three quarter and fitted as opposed to the short, cuffed ones that went with the pattern.

"I had another horrible day at the office," I said, trying to smile. "Richard just comes up with these elaborate plans and then throws them off on everyone else. When they don't get done or don't turn out well, he trys to pit one person against the other to keep up a lot of tension."

"Humphf," Bebe said. "Richard is a gatekeeper. Don't do nothing but *delegate* and *instigate*. That means we need to investigate!"

"Investigate what?" I asked Bebe.

"Investigate into finding someone to whup Richard's behind!"

"Bebe!"

"Girl, you know my friends on the West Side don't like anybody messin' with me or my friends. Hey, for twenty dollars they whup his butt!"

"Twenty dollars?" I said in disbelief.

"Hey, it ain't gotta be a new twenty-dollar bill. It can be one of those laundry twenties, the ones that got forgot and were washed in cold and dried on hot . . ."

"Bebe . . ." I scolded.

". . . or hey, they like kicking butt so much, may could hand them some Monopoly money, chile."

"Bebe!"

She laughed. "I'm just kiddin' . . . but I'm just sick of him, ain't you?" Bebe said, turning around on the footstool, checking her hem.

"Absolutely, it's as if Richard is my personal burden. The fool wants to lay off twenty percent of the staff to save money," I said, lowering her hem about an inch.

Bebe raised the hem two inches and said, "Girl, you kiddin'! Wheez, that many folks! For what?"

"Just 'cause," I said, watching Bebe raise the hem. "We turned a solid profit last year. But Richard has sold Harvey on the idea."

"What are they doing—smoking crack? Don't they know times are hard? People gotta eat. Folks have to pay bills."

"Richard cares about Richard, period. Maybe S.E. Heck, he doesn't care about Harvey or the radio station but Harvey is too dumb to see it. How he can stand all that kiss-ass stuff is beyond me. Girl, it's sickening to watch it," I said, lowering Bebe's hem three inches before sticking a pin in it. "There!"

"Shorter!" Bebe hollered. "You know me and Tina Turner were separated at birth!"

"Who's the seamstress?" I asked, looking up at her.

"Who's wearing it?"

I raised the hem two inches and said, "There now."

Bebe looked satisfied and said, "Cool. I've got to show a little leg now. Isaac likes my legs, don'tcha know!"

"Speaking of Isaac and a little leg, what's up with y'all?"

Bebe

Sandy was dipping in my biz and I mean with a long ole straw! Now you ain't gotta have Johnnie Cochran cross-examine me, I confess I'm nosy. But usually Sandy isn't. This chile has been hanging out with me for too long! I told Sandy, "Yah getting a little nosy, huh?"

"Hanging with you, yeah," she smart-mouthed.

"So you wanna know the downlow?" I asked her.

"Oh, picking up slang from the Sizemore house, eh?" Sandy said. "Well, give. I'm waiting! What's up with the sex? You said . . ."

"I know, I know," I admitted.

It was just that I hated to sound selfish or demanding because Sandy is always in my shit about being too critical and too hard on men. Well, if I am, then she's too soft. Simple as that. Break it on down, break it on down. Isaac is a good man, a good father, funny, well read, a gentleman, but he was just not ringing my bell 'tween the sheets! It's just as plain Jane as that.

"It's still weak," I told Sandy.

"Hmmm," she said. Sandy let me step down off the stool and she went over to the counter and looked at the pattern she had out.

"Hmmm what? I've got to say something. A zipped lip ain't doing me no justice," I said, starting to sit down.

"Stop!" Sandy said, her hands clenched in two soft fists. "You'll get creases and stuff in the dress and throw off the hem that I just pinned."

Boy, was I uncomfortable! I stood there looking like the tired mannequin that I was. "I've got to say something 'cause it's driving me crazy! I don't see how he doesn't know. It's not that it's bad or anything, it's just that I'm left hanging, I'm not satisfied. I'm going to say something."

"Be," Sandy said in one of her maternal tones. She can dig one up every now and then. "Let me give you some advice."

"Aww, please let's not get on that advice tip. Know what I say about too much advice?" I cooed.

Sandy looked up and raised her brow, "What?"

"It's just what it says it is. Ad . . . i.e., piling on. Vice . . . i.e., flaws, trouble. Too much advice can be more trouble than it's worth, chile!"

Sandy chuckled. "Thought of that yourself, huh?"

I nodded, all proud.

Sandy ignored me and went ahead anyway. "My advice is don't be pushy with it. Don't be tacky."

Who was she calling tacky? There isn't a tacky bone in my big-boned, superfine body! "Excuse me, Miss Thang. You are dippin' and dappin' and don't know what's happening. Tacky? I'm not tacky! When have I been tacky?"

Sandy put her left hand on her hip and started swinging the tape measure she had looped around her shoulders. "Don't make me clown."

"You can join Ringling Brothers Circus if you wanna. I am not tacky! I'm frank, and frank is a cool brother to be every now and then when necessary," I told her. Tacky? She had nerve! "You got nerve!"

"Don't get mad but you can be pushy and blunt and Isaac is a nice guy. You don't want to mess up a good relationship over a sex thing. You don't want to scare him," Sandy said.

"Scare him? The man runs into burning buildings, for Christ sake, how am I gonna scare him? Please! You don't know what you're talking about."

"Bebe," she said, "I'm just saying, think it out before you say something. Men are sensitive about sex."

"I know that! I pulled your coat to that, remember?" I went to sit down again. Sandy started yelling and couldn't stop me. Shoot, I was tired of standing up. Tired of not saying what I needed to say to Isaac! Tired of not having my bell rung! I was tired!

"I'm going to talk to him later tonight," I told Sandy. "I'm going to be frank but gentle. I've got to, Sandy, because I really, really feel something for Isaac and I'm hurting us by not saying it and he deserves truth in this relationship just like I do and I don't want anything being less than it has to be. Ah-huh now, leave it alone. My mind is made up!"

Isaac

I can't believe it. I can't believe Bebe. I came to her house with a bottle of champagne, cologne splashed generously on my neck, and my tapes of the Chi-lites' greatest hits. Bebe had asked me to bring the tapes because she wanted a dub of some of the songs and I said fine. We heard: "Have You Seen Her," "Stoned Out of My Mind," and "Oh Girl."

That's when music was music and lyrics meant something and were written from the heart. Then "I Like Your Lovin' Do You Like Mine?" came on. Bebe said in a clench, in a soft, warm snuggle, she said to me, "Isaac, do you like my loving?"

"Oh, yeah," I said, feeling warmer, softer, and wonderfully comfortable. "Do you like mine?" I asked back, playing along with the record, you know? I waited but she didn't answer. I raised my head from the snuggle position I had made against her breast. We looked each other in the eye and I didn't like what I saw.

"Well, baby, I think it could be ahhhh lit'le better," Bebe said.

I was stunned and totally embarrassed. There was no one else in the room but I felt embarrassed. "You're not happy?" I asked her. Wasn't she? I thought that she was. We felt so good together and had so much fun together and she wasn't happy? Why hadn't she said anything?

"It's not that I'm not happy," she tried to explain. "I'm happy with you, Isaac, and that's the truth. It's just that when we make love, I-I'm not all the way there and you leave me, baby. See what I'm saying? I want us to be on the same page, see?"

"No, what I see is that you've been lying to me," I told her. I didn't want to hear it. I was mad and I was hurt, my pride was hurt and I was mad and even I didn't know that I could get that mad and hurt that quickly. I'd prided myself on remaining cool in a heated situation. This was a major blaze smoking inside of me. I didn't want to talk. I didn't want to debate. I didn't want to screw. I wanted to cut out.

I said, "Bebe, okay, just let me get out of here."

"Isaac, stop. Hold up. Let's talk—don't leave like—"

And that's the last of her words I heard before walking out and slamming the door.

Bebe

Slam-bam-good-bye-and-goddamn! Isaac was too through! He left carrying a big old sack of mad on his back. But I-I-I'm lost. I can be sharp as a switchblade most of the time but, like that blade, I do have my dull moments—and that's dangerous. I was crazy-confused, chile. Was I stank about it? Was I tacky like Sandy said?

I call myself trying a smooth way to sneak up on the subject. The Chi-lites helped me out. I didn't break on Isaac, play the dozens on him, or anything low class like that. I care deeply about him and I would never, ever hurt him like that or try to embarrass him or shame the boy. But I needed to, had to, talk about it, huh? It was becoming a block, and every block I ever saw needed to be removed or climbed over. And that's the God's honest truth.

What am I going to do? Should I call him? Go over to his house and talk to him? Will he talk to me? How am I wrong? I needed to get the message across and I wanted to be frank and frank fucked me up. Okay, apologize? Why? Not for what I said but for how I said it maybe? I had to say it wrong, put it wrong, for him to get that mad. But what was all that happy stuff? That's some leftovers from somebody else. I think leftovers from Alicia the ex-wife-ee-pooh with the magic carpet that went poof! I better call him—but I'll wait till tomorrow or so to let it blow over.

Isaac

I'm stuck on a mad and I can't help it. I feel insulted and ornery. Who does she think she is criticizing me like that? I've been doing my thing for years and never had any complaints before. And who does all the work? I do. I'm the one with all the pressure and the physical exertion. Me. It's all on me and it shouldn't be, but that's the way it is. I know Bebe just isn't there not participating, not enjoying and helping. But the lion's share is on me. I'm supposed to be all knowing and all doing and all that. I was doing my best and I get criticized?

I thought she was happy but she's not. Maybe it's not me and maybe it's her? Women don't think that men have feelings like they do. They aren't the only ones who are sensitive. What, God only gave them emotions, feelings of tenderness? What, God only gave us egos, feelings of selfishness? People are mixed inside. Mixed! Bebe stepped on my feelings. She made me feel poorly and it hurts me to think that I'm not making her happy.

Can I stand that? Can I stand not being able to make her happy? I don't think so. I-I can't help but think about Alicia. Alicia and I had great sex and we loved each other and yet and still I didn't make her completely happy and she left me. I'm not holding on to her like some kind of a token or a memento of something lost. I know I have to move on. When your heart is hurt it's always best to throw it out of your mind and move on to the next thing. You have to keep going. Put your head down and keep going. Love yourself and keep going. I'm a lucky brah 'cause I've had Dash with me to help fill some of the void and now Bebe has come into my life and she makes me happy and we have fun but can I trust her to tell me always what she is feeling right away, no waiting? She didn't this time and I know that it's not fair to hold her to a standard that I didn't tell her about, but it's hard to think about fair when it comes to the heart. Your heart doesn't know anything about fair. All your heart knows about is hurt and feeling good and anyone that has felt good sure doesn't want to go back to hurting bad.

I've been feeling good and I don't know if I can deal with another woman putting me back in the bad. I don't know. I know I need to talk to Bebe but I don't know if I can, at least not right now.

Bebe

I'm too old to play hide-and-seek, jacks, or love games, okay? But the way it's going, it looks like I might be playing old maid for a while. But all jokes aside, I'm too old for bullshit. I know I hurt Isaac's feelings and I'm truly sorry from the bottom of my heart. I sho' can mess up sometimes. I was trying to wait for him to call but he hasn't so I've called him. Hey, there is no shame in my game. But he won't call me back. Dash swears she's given him the messages.

"No joke, I told him," Dash said.

I believe her.

Right now we're about as together as Sonny and Cher. How could this mess us up so? We've talked about some of everything. We've disagreed on about a third and never once did we leave each other mad. The boy is just being ornery. Or is he that sensitive? Obviously. What did he want me to do, just leave it go? That wasn't going to fly. It wasn't. I must be satisfied sexually. It's a must. Sandy may say that it's tacky or ghetto to say it but I don't give a fuck, literally. That is one of life's necessities. And it's not like I'm some immature child, I'm not expecting to go on the roller coaster every time but I need that ride or thrill every now and then.

I'm not trying to push my Isaac away. I don't want to mess this up, 'cause I'm feeling good about us. I need to fix this and I'm not sure how to fix it . . . not just for him but for me too.

I've been putting a World Wrestling Federation headlock on my pillow for the last few nights. I just can't sleep! The sandman won't come visit. Isaac won't come visit. Can't get a man in my bedroom to save my life, chile! Pit-i-ful!

I've just been turning over and over looking out my bedroom window, and not a single star is adding style to the sky. I stare out, unfocused, just staring for so long that I start looking cross-eyed and thinking crazy! It's like I'm going gaga!

Tonight I got up and started playing some old records. Now you know I'm sad, putting them albums on with the hiss, pop, and skip to 'em. I listened to Average White Band's old school cut, "Person to Person"; and like the band sings, our communication is weak . . . we need to do something person to person. That funky downbeat is right in synch with my heart bebopping against the inside of my chest 'cause it's lonely and missin' Isaac. The slow thunk-thunk-ha! of that characteristic sleigh-bell sound is driving tears down my face 'cause I'm lost, y'all, and I ain't got no answers.

I can only do what Bible-reading sister-girl knows how to do. I'm going to just stop and sit still. If I sit still, what I should do will come to me. When you don't know what to do, don't do nothing, my mother used to say. Rushing in, you'll make a mistake. Running away, you'll trip and fall. Wait. Just wait until the answer becomes clear to you, my mama used to say. I'm waiting.

Dash

Ththw! Ththw! What is up with the two of 'em? They trippin'!

Bebe called again the other day and asked me had I given Daddy her message. I was like, yeah. I wasn't playing around anymore and what not. Then when Daddy came in later, I told him again. I said, "Bebe called you twice and I gave you the message, right?"

He just nodded, all nonchalant and what not.

I said, "Daddy, you heard me, huh? Bebe called and . . ."

He went all off and stuff. "I heard you, Dash, okay?!"

Dawg! What'd I do? I mean, c'mon now—what's up?! He went to his bedroom and shut the door. Yep, they fightin' about something and I don't know what. Unhhhhh-huhhhhhh! I been checking him out and what not, bumming around the house and stuff. He's all whacked. Yep, he's got something on his mind all right. It's Bebe. Now when me and Tasha went over to her house to practice our rap, she was encouraging and nice and fun but when I mentioned Daddy she just gave me a fake smile and what not and said everything was fine. And Bebe ain't good at them fake smiles neither.

Grownups think we're so stupid. But we be on it. I took my book and went into Daddy's room. "Hey, Daddy," I said, "I finished *Their Eyes Were Watching God.*"

"Good," he smiled. "What'd you think of it?"

"Well, let's see," I said and flopped down on the bed next to him. Daddy was laying there with his night light on, reading. "I really loved Tea Cake! I'll bet he was fine!"

Daddy started tickling me. "Fine, huh? Fine? Whatcha know about fine? Huh? Huh?"

And we just laughed. Then I said, "I think that Janie loved him because he accepted her for her. That Joe Starks guy was looking to make her somebody, trying to make her do like he said, like he wanted? That wasn't gonna work, not with a woman like Janie. But Tea Cake let her be what she wanted to be and let her come go with him, hang out with him, and be what they could together. They could talk to each other, you know? They could tell each other what's what and that's cool."

"Yeah, Dash," Daddy said, picking up the conversation, "they could feel what each other wanted and needed and they were able to give it. It'd be nice if life was like some novels, huh?"

I said, "You can learn from books and apply it to real life, that's what you told me, huh? That's what reading is about, you said, huh, Daddy?"

"Yeah, Dash, yeah," he said and Daddy just got quiet and thoughtful. He patted my shoulder. "Well, don't you worry about me and Bebe."

"I'm not thinking about her, I'm worried about you," I said. That was as much as I could tell him 'cause that was all I knew and I hoped that that little something helped.

Sandy

Harvey says he's going through with the layoffs. That's it. Richard is happy and I'm miserable. They want me to tell the people in my department. Hit woman. We each take a third and do the firing. Isn't that something? I wasn't in on the planning. I wasn't in on the selection of the people. Now I'm an important part of the management team and I'm needed. Yeah, I'm needed for the dirty work. I tried to get out of it but Harvey got this blank look on his face, then he smiled again. "Sandy, I know that you will rise to the occasion because you are a professional."

And that's how it ended—with me feeling like a *professional fool.* What made me think that Harvey would take my side? His secretary Diana can't stand Richard either—he acts like she's his secretary too. We had lunch the other day and she said that S.E. had taken their managers and top business associates—including Harvey and Richard—on a weekend trip to Las Vegas. Diana said that S.E. paid for the whole thing. Di said that Richard had Harvey eating out of his hand. What choice did that leave me? Just one. Do my job; stop worrying about what I couldn't change and had no control over.

Bebe came over for the final fitting of her dress. It looked good! It needed to be taken in just a hair at the shoulders, then I could put in the sleeves and be all done. I was waiting for Bebe to say make it shorter and I even joked, "Want to show more leg for Isaac?"

Bebe shrugged and said, "Naw, it's fine."

"What are you going to do, Be?"

"I'm just ah waitin'," she said.

"On what? A telegram? A message from God? What?" I asked her and laughed nervously. I knew. She didn't think I knew, but I knew. Bebe loves Isaac.

"Homette, I'm waiting on a feeling, a sign or something, on what to do. On how to handle it. Until then sister*girl* myself ain't budging," she said, turning around in the dress.

"Bebe, don't wait too long," I said. "Isaac is a good man and a good man can get gone in a hurry with all these sisters out here looking, huh? Don't stand on the tracks looking and get caught watching someone else catch your train."

"You ain't never lied," Bebe said with a heavy touch of worry. "Fix me a drink, huh?"

And I went and opened a bottle of wine, got two goblets, and poured us each some. We took long sips and I said, "Be . . ."

"I gotcha-gotcha. Don't worry me now, Sandy, 'cause my nerves are already shot to hell and back with me worrying by my lonesome. Don't you worry me too. You my girl and I know you're right and I don't want to mess this up any more than I already have. We both know that but I can't take a chance on making another wrong move. See what I'm sayin'? The next move I make has gotta be like writing on the wall, clear like the lines in my palms. See what I'm sayin'? If it's clear to me, then it'll be right. For real, for real. I feel it in my gut."

I took a sip of the wine and I savored the taste and the passion in Bebe's voice and I backed her up. "Okay, that's the plan then. You don't make a move until it's clear what you should do. But don't do it until you run it by me first, okay?"

Bebe nodded okay.

I drank down the rest of my wine, then Bebe said, "All right, cool. Now, flip the record over. How you gonna play what's going on with you?"

"Me, what?"

Bebe reached over and playfully smacked my leg. "Girl, I hate it when you play the nut roll. Later for all that. Are you going to fire all those people?"

That made me mad. Now I'm not clear on why it made me so angry but it did. I said, "I'm not firing them. J-108 is firing them. I'm just telling them the news and telling them what their severance will be."

"Uh-huh," Bebe grunted.

"I'm just the messenger, that's all. It's not my fault and there's nothing I can do about it," I said.

"Uh-huh."

"I can't save them, so why should I jeopardize my job for a lost cause?" I said.

"Uh-huh," Bebe moaned.

"Will you please stop arguing with me about this!" I shouted.

"Uh-huh," Bebe quipped.

I drank down the rest of my wine and went over to the kitchen counter where the dress pattern was laid out. I was checking the sleeves. Bebe came over behind me and rested her chin on my shoulder and sighed. I said, without moving, "I know there is more room in this big old apartment."

Bebe didn't move; she just sighed and let her body rest heavier on me. I said, "If you don't get off me, I'm gonna knock you out."

"You and which branch of the armed service, Army or Navy?" Bebe laughed. Then she said, "Just do what you think is right and don't stress yourself out."

"Okay," I said, relaxing a minute.

Then Bebe's eyes dropped down to the pattern in front of us. There was the one that came from the store, then there was another very different one hand-drawn by me.

I explained to her, "That's what I use to help me decide which part to change and what to sew first. I make my own little pattern and use letters. It helps me know where to go."

That's when something hit her! Bebe said, "Ooh!" and picked up my pattern and started shouting for joy! Then Bebe hugged me and did a shake dance in her partially finished new dress. I was totally confused. Then Bebe explained, "I've got a plan!" It was a plan that would hopefully solve all her problems.

Isaac

Me, Bobo, and Cliff were in the TV room of the firehouse shooting the breeze, waiting on L.A. He was late, about an hour late. We were rehearsing our lip-synch act for the talent show at the community center. It was L.A.'s idea that we get in it. We were going to lip-synch to a medley of songs—the Temps, the Jackson Five, Tavares, the Time, and the Ohio Players.

We had been practicing for a couple of weeks. We're going to be bad! The medley starts out slow with Tavares's "Remember What I Told You to Forget," then pumps up with the Temps' "Get Ready," then the J-Five's "I Want You Back," then the Time's "The Bird," and closes on out with "Fire" by the Ohio Players.

We're going to have a partition setup where we can run behind it during the segue downbeats that L.A. had his D.J. friend mix in between sections of the songs. Behind the partition we're going to change—put on a different jacket or big-brimmed hats or big 'fro wigs or like for the last number we're going to put on our fire hats for the Ohio Players' cut. We're just busy now working on our steps and getting our timing down.

"Hey-hey-we're-going-to-be-a-hit!" Bobo said, running his hand over his slicked-down hair. Bobo loves to eat. He'd brought in some salsa and corn chips he'd gotten during his trip to Mexico. Bobo did a shuffle two-step that was part of our act, "We're-going-to-be-bad-Esee!"

"Not if we don't get these last moves down," Cliff said. He was always the worrying one. "Where is L.A.?"

I shrugged. "I don't know, brah. L.A. would be late for his own funeral. Probably with some young lady and forgot about the time. I've paged him twice and he hasn't called. He must be on his way."

As soon as I said that, L.A. came busting through the door. "What's up!!" he shouted. He was bopping and parading and doing part of our dance steps.

"What—you had the best twang of your life?" Cliff joked. "Man, you flying!"

"Awww, yeah, y'all know a Negro like me is always in a good mood!" L.A. laughed.

The rest of us looked at each other, and someone said, "Yeah, right!"

"I just won the pick three—313—for six hundred!" L.A. said and started strutting his skinny behind all around the place. "Wooo-weee!"

Bobo, Cliff, and me started yelling and cheering and slapping each other on the back.

L.A. said, "Straight! It's good to see y'all this happy for a brother!"

Cliff reached over and high-fived L.A. Cliff said, "Yeah, dog, 'cause now you can pay us back!"

Then the three of us did a Temps spin to a stop with our hands out—yah! L.A.'s face flopped but he couldn't say a word. He paid me the three-fifty he owed me. Then he gave Cliff and Bobo the hundred apiece he owed them. Like Dash says, I was waiting for him to get stank but he didn't. If you could get your money from L.A., you'd better get it and fast.

"Y'all satisfied? Am I broke enough for y'all?" L.A. said sarcastically. Like we cared!

Bobo spoke in an upbeat tempo. "Esee-we-glad-to-see-green-in-your-pocket-and-green-in-ours-'cause-it's-been-long-time!"

We laughed and L.A. fell in line. I cupped his shoulders and whispered, "Bank the rest, boy."

L.A. whispered back, "You know a Negro like me!"

"Hey," Cliff said, looking around. "Where's the box with the props and stuff in it?"

"Aww, my bad! My bad!" L.A. said. "I left them at the crib. I'll jet over and be right back!"

All hands grabbed L.A. No, we told him. I decided that I would go because I needed the least practice. I slipped on L.A.'s hooded jacket so I wouldn't have to go upstairs and get mine. L.A. tossed me his keys, since his car was parked right out front. I jogged out the back door and came on around the side. I was putting the key in the car door when I felt someone grab me from behind. It was like a headlock and I choked on my word and that word was going to be "Damn!" But the pressure on my throat and arms was too much and my voice got beat down. In the reflection in the glass of the car window, I saw nothing but arm and chest. I felt nothing but hair from that arm cutting into my chin and the pressure that arm was putting on my Adam's apple. I tried to spin around my body but whoever it was hit me in the lower part of my back. Awwww, God, it hurt! I felt the pain all down in my tailbone just before my knees gave out on me and I felt saliva drip out of the side of my mouth.

Whoever it was said, "I'm gonna fuck you up!"

And my mind screamed, Why? That's what my mind screamed but unless he was a mind reader, he wouldn't know it. I couldn't talk. I couldn't do anything. Not even when I saw the knife come out and move straight for my throat.

Bebe

You know how the Staples Singers croon, "I'll take you there?" Well, sometimes I just go there all by myself!

I've just had a nice hot bath and I'm spread out across my bed, hugged up good ole fashion in a thick and thirsty passion purple towel, y'all. My body is *tingling* but my mind is *tripping*. I've got thoughts of many things, about life and what it's about. Tripped-out stuff, y'all.

Sometimes *I just go there,* you know? Chile, everyone does, I think, or at least I hope so, so I'm not by my lonely-only or on the crazy tip. But yeah, I'm sure other women get ta where they start dealing with their place in the world and their wants.

I can remember when I was a *hormonal* eighteen and my entire menu consisted of wanting a sexy man who would be Kool & the Gang and do just like their hit song says, "Get down on it!" A man who would make my heart and chest dance the bump together in serious "Soul Train" line fashion.

It's tripped out, y'all, when you think about yo' attitude and how it changes. That's what I wanted back then, period, end of record. I had no thoughts of that sexy man having to take care of me because I was always so independent and knew that I could take care of myself. It's crazy, I mean, what you think you want and what life gives you and what you keep.

Now we're still on the Daylight Saving Time tip and falling back, like when sister-girl me was twenty-five. I wanted a good man who could help me get a nice house and a nice car and who would be able to do the *boogie nights* every weekend with me.

When I turned thirty-five, it was like "The Waltons" era. I wanted a man who looked all right but who had a sense of family, who wanted children and a nice home and who would encourage me in my work.

When I hit forty, I wanted a man who knew how to love me inside and out and who made me feel like I was first in the world in beauty and in cause. When the M.C. said, "Here she is, Miss America," the man's thirty-two-inch picture-in-a-picture wouldn't show nobody but the Be. I wanted a man who put me in that kind of spotlight and who could love me inside and out.

Isaac tells me that I'm funny and I'm good-looking. When we're together, makin' like one and one is two, seem like this world is ours. That's what our presence is like together. I feel that Isaac loves me on the inside. It's the outside loving that has hit the snag. And I know it's important to me and I know that it's important to him. He doesn't want to fall short, in my eyes anyway. And I can understand that. If we're both satisfied in every way, look like nothing could bust us up. Look like nothing could hurt our good thing. We can make it together if we've got it going on like that. We're so close, we're so very close.

Chile, I ain't ashamed to testify. No. Being without him has been miserable. I'm feeling sad and I'm hanging by a thread but not a Velvet Rope like Janet Jackson. Girlfriend gets so sad she shoots coffee up her butt. Hey, if it works, "mo' java to her." But seem like to me that when that caffeine jolts those sad cells they wouldn't *die,* they'd *multiply!*

My man Isaac. Wonder what he's thinking about now? Wonder if he's gonna call? I'm opening a CD for someone at the bank and I'm daydreaming about Isaac and the time I gave him a bubble bath. He's on my mind, y'all. Shoot, my brain cells can't move around for thinkin' on Isaac all the time.

But here's how it played out. Isaac had stopped by my apartment one evening. My man came in walking like Fred Sanford or somebody, walking funny and holding his shoulder.

Isaac said that he had played some ball at the gym the other day with some of his boys from the old neighborhood. Isaac said that he had come down with a rebound and got stripped from behind. He said he called a foul and he felt something pull in the shoulder when he went to take the ball out. Isaac was sure it wasn't anything serious because it just tingled. It just tingled, he said, and then Isaac smiled. Boy got a money smile; *he could pay off lottery tickets with that smile.*

An-y-way, I started to rub that shoulder and work that arm on round and round. My touch is Charmin soft too. I was sure to be tender and not hurt him and he rested himself real easy-like on my "come hither" couch. I patted Isaac on the back and told him to c'mon with me. Isaac looked kind of sheepish, like What you gonna do, girl?, but he followed. Oh yeah, Isaac knew to follow.

I ran the hot water into the tub and I poured in my best perfumed bubble bath and Isaac joked about smelling like a sissy at the firehouse and I kissed the laughter from his lips and quieted him. I started taking his shirt off again and I told him, "You getting stripped from behind again and this time ain't no foul!"

I took each item of clothing off one at a time. I peeled them down and away and the motion that my hands took was like, well, the sensuality I felt was like the wind beneath my wings. Yeah, I'm buggin, movin' on. Isaac was still. I barely heard him breathe and his eyes? Boyfriend's eyes were closed, shut tight. I took him by the hand, it was "the fine leadin' the blind," and led him to the tub.

The sponge, of all things, got ta actin' up on me. The sponge was brittle at first and roughed up my palms and resisted the water . . . at first. Then I felt that old sponge get with the program, give in. When it gave in, the sponge sopped up all the water and gave it back just as free as a waterfall. I sponged Isaac down from head to toe and I felt his body tense and then relax, tense and then relax.

Say, say, say, y'all . . . then a sigh left his lips. I knew that it had traveled up from the cellar of his insides 'cause when it hit air it was merely a wisp of voice and breath twisted together. I felt such joy giving him this pleasure and when I finished he, Isaac, boyfriend, said simply, "You."

Turn about is the best kinda fair play, hear me?

And Isaac stripped me down and I stepped into the tub. Chile, I caught a honest-to-God chill and I felt goose bumps "run for the border" all across my love jugs and my nipples got hard. Isaac cupped, held, scooped up my left jug with one hand and sponged, soaked it down with his other hand, and Isaac ain't let the water gush, naw-naw, he let it trickle . . . trick-elllll!

The water trickled down my breast, made a stream down my stomach, and commenced turning my belly button into a hot spring. My butt got tight and Isaac stroked it and I relaxed and he continued to sponge me down. I felt like screaming, Yeah, this is what I like and how I like it too! But I was . . . silent. I was silent in my joy and he was diligent, that's one of my college words now, diligent, he was diligent in his task.

And now I'm laying here and I know that I don't want to lose him and I've written a letter to Isaac and tomorrow I'm mailing it with a stamp, a kiss, and a hope. My mind and my heart wondered, will it work?

Isaac

I felt the tip of the blade next to my throat. I jerked backward and the tip left my skin with a lurch and, when it moved back, I shifted hard to the left and the blade got tangled up in my necklace. I heard the guy grunt and my necklace snap and that knife hit the ground. Then we started to wrestle. He was on top. I was on top. Him. Me. Me. Him. Then I heard Cliff from way behind me say, "Turn him a-loose!"

I got up, spun around, my hood flopped off, and I finally got a good look at the man trying so desperately to hurt me and I didn't know this brah from Adam.

"What the hell is your problem!" I yelled. Do you know he looked as surprised to see me as I was him? He looked at me like it was the first time he'd ever seen me in his life and that was the case too. The guy was big, about six four and two ten with a shaved head and graying goatee. He had on a navy-blue windbreaker with the sleeves folded back neatly around his ashy elbows. There was a tattoo on his right forearm that said, Get Money.

"I thought you was L.A.," brah said.

"I'm over here," L.A. called out. He and Cliff and Bobo and the rest of the guys were standing in the doorway. Cliff and Bobo had axes in their hands. L.A. had a baseball bat in his hand. "I'm here, G-money, and what you had for me, I got for you."

All three of them came out of the doorway and I just took a step in the middle and started yelling, "Wait! Wait! Wait! What is this? Is everybody crazy? Does somebody have to get busted up and bleeding out here?"

That stopped everybody cold and G-money said, "Bitch over there owes me money!"

"I got your bitch," L.A. said, lunging forward. Bobo grabbed him before he could reach G-money, who did not move and only smiled and nodded like he was saying, Yeah, bring your skinny butt on.

"How much?" I asked.

"An ass kicking's worth," G-money said, "now or later."

That made everybody mad! Cliff said, hefting the ax, "If you touch him or anybody else here we gonna go chop-chop on your ass so bad you'll think you're the lunch special in Chinatown."

G-money got that ugly smile wiped right off his face. "L.A. owes me a grand and owes it to me since two months back. He lost three big bets on b-ball and he knows it. Ask him."

We all looked at L.A. He dropped his head, and we all groaned.

"All right," I said. "Give it up, y'all!" And I started taking out the three-fifty that L.A. had paid me back.

"Shit!" Cliff yelled and hit the wall with the ax handle.

"Shit," Bobo repeated, then he started cursing more in Spanish but everybody gave up their money. I got the fifty L.A. had left on him and that was the whole six hundred. I gave it to G-money, "Here's six hundred. Come by Friday and we'll have the rest for you."

"You got a down posse around you, L.A.," G-money said, lifting the left leg of his sweat pants and stuffing the wad down in his sock. "Saved your neck, man!"

"The rest comes with a condition, though," I said, speaking up quickly. "You take no more bets from L.A. no matter what he says, dig it?"

"Straight!" G-money said. "I was tired of chasin' his punk ass anyway. Friday, motherfuckers." And he walked away.

L.A. started going off. "Aww, you should of let us whup his ass, Is-eye! He's been hounding me and riding me and I only owed him four hundred and the rest was bullcrap interest he tacked on and we could have whupped his—"

I ran up on L.A. and grabbed him by his collar and tossed him up against the wall. I was yelling, crazed out of my head. "He wanted to cut you up, man! He could have killed me by mistake! And suppose I had-a been with somebody I love like Dash or Bebe? That guy would have gone after them too! Are you nuts? Man, what's wrong with you?"

Nobody tried to pull me off L.A. either. I went upside his head and got one good lick in before L.A. covered up. "I ain't fightin' you, Is-eye! Is-eye, I ain't!"

That stopped me. Breath was pumping out of my mouth and nose and I was damn near bent over from stress more than anything else. I looked into L.A.'s eyes and I saw some fear there. And that made me glad because what common sense won't make you do, fear will. "You have to get help, L.A., and that's the God's honest truth. Period."

"I am! I am!" And L.A. started straightening up. He shook it off a bit, serving up a bunch of *regular* and *leaded* bullshit. "I know. My bad. My bad. I'm going to look into it soon."

"Tonight," I said and I looked from Cliff to Bobo. "Tonight, you're going to call. There's a twenty-four hour hot-line number you can call now."

L.A. frowned a bit and then he turned and saw that Bobo and Cliff were going to back me. I said, "You're running yourself in the ground and you're running us away. We can't chance you messing up on the job, brah. Besides, your mind is not on what you're doing—"

"Naw, I—"

"Shut up and listen, L.A.!" I said, cutting him off. "We can't go into a burning building with you! Your head is messed up! Who can trust you to take care of business? You're late all the time! You're lying to us! You've got to make a change."

"That's right, that's right!" Cliff said, sounding like a loyal deacon amen-ing my every word.

Bobo jumped in. *"No se si puedo confiar en tí."*

"Speak English, man!" L.A. said angrily.

"I don't know if I can trust you anymore," Bobo translated.

"Y'all full of it, man!" L.A. screamed at us, using the bat like a baton. "Y'all play poker with me! You don't want me gambling but it's okay when I lose up in this mothafucker! It's ah-right if my dough-skee gets lost up in the firehouse! Huh? Yeah-yeah! And tonight, Is-eye . . . Cliff . . . Bobo . . . all y'all was happy as sissies in county jail when I hit that pick three and could pay y'all back! Nah! Wasn't no lecture going on then! Nah-unh! Fake ass motherfuckers!"

"Hey, I'm not gonna be all them motherfuckers, jack!" Cliff said, reaching for L.A.

I jumped in front of Cliff. "L.A.'s right, y'all."

We told him not to gamble but we gambled in front of him. He was right. We took the money and were glad to get it and we didn't care that he won it gambling, and lottery is still gambling and a problem is still a problem.

"All right! The Negro is in the right for once, damn," Cliff growled. "We just gotta make a change."

"Yeah," Bobo said, nodding. "We'll cool all that out."

I told L.A., "We'll even take you to the meetings."

"What meetings?" L.A. said, looking confused.

"The Gamblers Anonymous meetings. Each of us will take turns the first few months going with you—whatever it takes, but this is it.

We're tired, brah, it's not working anymore. You leave us hanging on this one, and we'll all ask that you be transferred."

"Y'all wouldn't!" L.A. said, looking shocked.

"Don't count on it," I warned him.

"What you gonna do, Esee?" Bobo asked, leaning on the ax handle.

L.A. slid down and sat on the ground and he patted the bat against the blacktop. He said nothing for a long time and we stood waiting. We had thrown a lifeline out to the brother and we were ready to pull him in if only he'd grab hold. He had to grab hold. I was cheering him on in my head, C'mon, L.A.! It wouldn't do any good to make him do anything because, if he didn't want to, it wasn't going to work, so he needed to show strength and we were there to help if only he'd try. I heard him sigh and he worked his neck, popping a couple of bones, then L.A. hummed a little bit and finally he said, "Well, what y'all chumps waiting on? Dial the damn number."

Sandy

I wasn't expecting it. No, I wasn't. I went into work early even though I had had problems sleeping. I did. I mean I tossed and I turned and I kept seeing people standing in front of me at work, in front of my desk, and I'm talking to them but I can't hear what I'm saying and all of a sudden they just drop through the floor. One by one. They drop through the floor. And finally, after all my work friends dropped through the floor, then my desk dropped, then my chair, then me! I felt myself falling and falling and I heard my scream echoing and I woke up awash in sweat. My subconscious helped me to make a conscious decision, okay? But still, I wasn't expecting Harvey to react like he did.

Harvey went off. He went off on me.

"What do you mean," he said, "you're not going to participate in the layoffs? This isn't a game! This is business! I'm your boss! You work for me and you do what I tell you to do!"

He was yelling. Yes, he was. He thought because he was my boss he could say what he wanted to me. Is that crap or what? I was stunned! I forgot to close the office door when I walked in, and Diana came in and gave both of us a long, disapproving look as she closed the door.

I told Harvey he didn't have to yell at me like that. My parents didn't yell at me like that. Harvey said that he was tired of my attitude. He said that he was tired of me trying to play the race and sex cards. Excuse me? Harvey was going off the deep end. That sounded like some crap Richard had told him. Why was he listening to this guy? He knew me. Yet he was listening to Richard!

I told Harvey that he obviously had his facts wrong. I had no race or sex card to play. I did my job and I was an African-American woman and proud of it and that did nothing but enhance what I could bring to the worktable. I told Harvey that I had done a hell of a job for him in sales and that he did me no favor by giving me this position. I earned it and I made him money.

Harvey said, "If you want to be part of this team, then you need to act like it."

I said, "I want to be a part of a team that knows that business is best when it's run by people who like what they do and like who they're doing it for. Unfortunately, I'm no longer in that category."

Harvey's face turned the color of a Red Delicious apple, "You ingrate. I gave you a chance to run the sales department at a radio station in Chicago, the number three market. Who else would give that job to someone your age? Huh? I put you on the map! And you pay me back with a piss-poor attitude."

I said, "You gave me a chance, true, but I've paid you back in gold. Your sales department was weak until I got here. I've gotten your major accounts, I helped you put together the S.E. proposal. I've paid you back. I'm still the same old Sandy. You've changed. You let Richard come in and dictate everything and because I don't like it—now I'm a problem. I'm a person. I've got pride. I don't owe you anything, Harvey, but two weeks' notice."

He blew up. "Fine, quit! Go ahead!"

And I did it. I quit right there and gave Harvey my two weeks' notice. I wasn't worried about finding a job. I've got skills. I've got a degree. I've got money saved. And I've got confidence in myself.

I went back to my desk and someone from the mailroom had put a delivery on my desk. I tore the paper off and there was a beautiful plant with a note: "Whatever, it'll be okay. . . . Bebe."

That broke daylight across my face. I sat down in my chair and laughed away the tension that was left in my body. There's something about knowing that you are able to be responsible for yourself, for your ideas, and for your actions in the workplace. There's something pleasing that you feel, I felt an extra shot of self-love, because I was able to know that I can depend on what I've been taught by my parents, by friends like Bebe, and by my own values to keep me up. I don't need to feel stressed out all the time over a jerk like Richard or angry over someone two-faced like Harvey. I'm Sandy wherever Sandy goes, wherever she works, and I bring skills to the table and if those skills aren't recognized, then I need to be excused from the table and look for satisfaction elsewhere.

I felt so good. I called Bebe, told her what happened, thanked her for the plant, and then finally I said, "I'm free!"

Dash

I went to get the mail and there was a letter for Daddy and Mama had sent me a new postcard. I tossed the letter on Daddy's bed with his junk mail and I just stared at the postcard. It was from Hong Kong. It was a pretty card, with letters that you can feel on the front and what not. It had some pretty blues, greens, purples, and reds in it. I just kept rubbing my fingers over and over it and like ta rubbed the color right off, I was so frantic. I flipped it over in my hands and I got a jumping feeling in my chest from nerves when I saw her handwriting. I was, like, thrilled but scared too. I read my own name, "Dear Dash" . . . and I was like stuck on that.

"Dear Dash" . . . I was stuck on it because I knew that that was the only connection thang we had going in the last few years—when my eyes hit these cards that's like the only connection we have and that made me . . . sad.

And I was stuck on "Dear Dash" . . . and after that I read on about how she loved seeing the world and what not and how great life was and how she wanted me to be a good girl and do like Daddy said . . . and Mama wrote that, even though she wasn't with me, she loved me.

And after reading that I looked up in the mirror and I saw myself. I just saw . . . myself. See what I'm saying and what not? I had to

really focus to see the cards, too, you know, the other cards I had
stuck in the side of the dresser mirror. And I felt then, like I knew,
but I knew before . . . I can't explain it. Naw, wait-wait, yes, I can. I
can if I stop and wait a minute and think and try.

I think, naw, I know that in the back of my mind and what not, it's
like, I knew all this time that she's not coming back. I like knew that
but I didn't want to think about that. And I felt something today,
something different this time, looking at this card. I don't know why,
maybe I'm tired or growing up or both or neither or I'm just tired of
hoping because hoping is too tiresome to do too long. It'll make you
sag on the inside and what not. I think that I know that I'm ready to
let go of that hope and accept things like they are and what not. Just
because she's not here does not mean she doesn't love me or I don't
love her and I just want to let go of the hoping because it's too hard
and this card from Hong Kong lets me know she's getting farther and
farther away and I'm getting farther and farther away in my mind
from her and I've got to let it go and I just felt it leave me. Ride . . .
out.

Whatever it was left me and I think what was leaving was the part
that hasn't wanted to really accept her not coming back. But that just
left me. I know she's not coming back and I can accept it and I don't
know why now, maybe it's just time, and I know that the tears coming
right now are okay to have 'cause . . . 'cause they are and I don't
even need to wipe them away. I'll just let them all out and then I'll
keep my cards on my dresser but when I look in that mirror I'm going
to see me and it's cool like that.

Been kinda hoping, waiting for the day
When Mama would be back, back home to stay
Postcards in the mail, stamped from overseas
Are the only connection, between Mama and me

WOW!

This last card, the same as all the rest
Made something snap, snap deep down in my chest
Like I felt for the first time, I really knew
Mama won't come back, no matter what I do

And yeah I'm sad, but not *really* down
'Cause I've got my Daddy and Uncle Lucius around
But most of all, I can finally see
That I've got myself to be there for me.

Isaac

I came home and Dash's door was closed. I opened it and peeked in. Baby girl was asleep. I went to my bedroom, popped in a tape by R&B man Tyrone Davis, and fell out on the bed. I felt some letters jamming against my back. Light bill. Phone bill. Credit card application. And a letter . . . from Bebe.

Seeing her name started me to thinking about two important things: one, the broken necklace that was now on my dresser that had brought me luck just like she said. And, two, something that happened. Something important. I said something, blurted out something after that run-in with G-money. Brah didn't even realize it until Cliff pointed it out to me later. You know what I said? Without thinking, from deep inside, in a fit of anger so there's no doubt it was real, I had said, "Suppose I had-a been with somebody I love like Dash or Bebe?"

Wow! To me, it's absolutely scary. I included Bebe in my circle of love. I'm not mad at her anymore but there's a chunk of hurt pride still in me.

I do love Bebe. It's funny how that fact must have been hiding inside of me. But the signs were there. How much I look forward to seeing her. How I think about her when I'm not with her. How I feel joy when she laughs and when she smiles. I can let this love grow or I can let it go.

Check that out. That's something funny to think about, letting a love go. It's rare to have one and here I am thinking about possibly letting it go. And what for? Because I want to make sure that I can make her happy. It's a bad feeling that grows in your gut when you're afraid of not being able to make someone happy. Most people are selfish. It's a "me first" world but I'm the kind of brah who's not really like that.

This is my thing. I want Bebe to be happy in all ways and if I can make her happy in some ways that could be enough for her, maybe, but not for me, no. That's not good enough for this brother. See, I've been there. I've been there with Alicia.

Right now, my mind is trying to kick this around, and I want to open this letter. My man Tyrone's jamming in the background, he's singing, "Turning Point!" That was a cut back around Christmastime in 1975 and all the way up and through the summer of '76. The turning point in your life. Well, on no better song could I get the guts to open this letter.

I ripped it open with my thumb, put my mark on it, and it surprises me because I don't know what the fuck it is. I have to turn around the first page to get the straight of it. Then I read page two. And I laughed! Bebe, that lady is something else! She is stone' outta her mind. She can't do anything regular—that would be too much like Mars to her. I plan on spending a few minutes on this letter and then I'll call her and make my move.

Bebe

Are you ready for Midnight Madness?

Midnight.

That's when the phone rang.

My new caller ID read, "Isaac Sizemore."

Then came the madness!

Look like the phone's sound turned from a ring into that funky downbeat from Marvin Gaye's version of "Heard It Through the Grapevine." You know that sexy-love-life-on-edge riff. "Dum-dum-dum-dum . . . Da-Da-dum-dum-dum-da-dum-dum . . . !"

That's tripped out enough in itself.

Then look like the Kleenex box next to the phone turned into a puppet version of Isaac, à la Little Penny from the Nike commercial. But only it was Little Isaac in a fireman's hat sitting by the phone, doing an eyeroll from me to the receiver, hunchin' his shoulders, doing a point-point and all the while the riff is going.

"Dum - dum - dum - dum . . . Da - Da - dum - dum - dum - da - dum - dum . . ."

Then back to big-headed *Little Isaac* . . . eyeroll, shoulder hunch-hunch, point-point. Grapevine riff.

"Dum - dum - dum - dum . . . Da - Da - dum - dum - dum - da - dum - dum . . ."

I had to rub my eyes two or three times to shake off that silly dream. Finally I was able to answer the phone. My hello was timid and the breath I took afterward was violent, a gasp of air that seemed as imposing as a twister. And I held it, expecting God knows what, but I held it, waiting for him to say whatever.

Isaac said he'd gotten my letter. Isaac is Kool & the Gang and Coy Floy Joy when he wanna be. My man did not give no kinda freebie hint away in his voice or his words. Isaac just said that he was coming over in about an hour and was it okay?

Awww, yeah! I want to talk! I want us to work this out! And I told him yes and I hung up the phone and instantly my knees drew up toward my chest and I circled my arms around them. Then I started to think . . . about my letter.

Chile, it was a sho' nuff brainstorm I got from the pattern that Sandy had. See-see, this is the deal. The pattern is in the outline of the shape of the dress and has instructions on it on what you should do and where you should go. Now dig it: if you can't sew at all, it's not going to be much help. But if you got some Singer-sewing-skill, and some knowledge, the pattern is what helps you to go all the way and come out like how you want to, see what I'm saying?

Okay, okay. So I figured that why not do a little dip-dap-adaptation, make that system work with my situation? Apply it to my needs?

So I drew an outline of my body and I put letters by key areas. For example, I put an "A" by my mouth. I put a "B" by my ears. I put a "C" by my breast, and so on and so forth. I stopped at the letter "G" because that was good enough.

In my letter I wrote:

Dear Isaac,
I'm so sorry that I hurt you and I know that you know that I wasn't trying to do that. I was just trying to be real and to communicate.

Sometimes what we say comes out too harsh and not helpful like we want it to. I guess that's why God gave us hearts as well as mouths because He wants us to feel and not just say. I feel so close to you and I have missed you and I want to see you again, and talk if we can.

I have enclosed what I think is a little helper for us. It's not just for you, but for us. Sometimes people need help to get in synch. It's not that I'm saying that you are bad, or insensitive, or that I don't care about you very much. I want us both to be satisfied with each other in every way so that we can grow together.

The diagram is of my body and the letters are in special places. Learn it and maybe we can get together and work out the block that has come between us. Can't nothing hurt us but us ourselves, let's give it a go, huh?

Isaac

I packed me a triumph kit. Forget survival. I wanted to triumph. I put in it several packs of ribbed condoms, a bottle of wine with one glass, two cassette tapes of love songs, and scented body oil. I took it with me in a little leather bag that I could sling over my shoulder. Dash gave it to me for Christmas.

I drove over to Bebe's house and she was waiting for me, in the living room with the fireplace roaring. The flickering flames were our light. Bebe had on a lilac silk robe that cinched at the waist. Her legs were tucked beneath her body but I could see the rose polish on her baby toe and she sat in the corner of the couch. Bebe's face was, well, guarded; her eyes were slightly downcast and her lids were low. I saw in her anticipation, a new docile presence, and Bebe seemed—vulnerable.

I slipped off my jacket and put down my bag. I had already made a conscious decision not to tell Bebe I loved her tonight. I didn't want that to add any more pressure than there already was. So I made slow and deliberate gestures, hiking up my slacks by the creases with my thumbs and index fingers as I sat down next to Bebe on the couch and I said, "How ya been?"

Bebe inhaled. "Ah, making it . . ." then she exhaled, ". . . barely."

239

"I missed you," I told her and I let my left arm fall freely behind the couch.

And I watched her blink back a smile and then whisper a solemn, "I missed you too."

There were about three clock ticks or two inhale-and-exhales or five rapid-fire heartbeats that passed between us. I leaned forward and erased half the space between us. "We need to talk. I wanted to talk to you before now but I haven't because, well, maybe I've got too much pride. Bebe, I didn't . . ."

"Isaac, I didn't mean—" she started.

"Let me finish? Just wait and let me finish. My pride has kept me from calling. I'm not ashamed of my pride. I need it. I need it to survive. Pride is my best weapon in this world. It keeps me working toward having good things for myself and for Dash. You hurt my pride and I think you thought you were being honest and straightforward. Well, everybody can't take a full body hit, particularly from a heavyweight like you."

"What?" Bebe said, uncurling her body.

I laughed just a bit. "Not heavyweight like on the scale, lady." And I touched her leg and rubbed it soothingly. "Heavyweight like in being a force. You've got a forceful personality. When you're in a room, Bebe, everyone knows it from the folks to the ceiling lights."

Bebe whispered, "Sandy says that I'm pushy, sometimes." And she raised her eyebrows and looked for me to dispute that.

I kept my mouth shut and said not a word on that. My mind went to the next page. I was moving forward. I had goals to achieve. "We talked about Alicia before. I'm big enough to say that her leaving me had a big impact on my life. It hurt me. It stressed me out, turning me into a mother and father both for Dash. But it put some insecurity into how I deal with relationships."

"I know . . ."

"Would you shut up and let me finish?" I said. Wasn't this hard enough for me?

Bebe gave a hard blink, then nodded.

"By insecure, I mean that once I started dating other people, and it hasn't gone as far or as deep as it has with you, but when I started dealing with these women after Alicia I always worried a bit about making them completely happy. I felt that I had to make them happy in every way. That's because I felt that maybe one reason Alicia left was because I couldn't make her happy in every way and that thought hurt me, and hurts me still. You telling me that you aren't sexually satisfied made me mad because I thought everything was fine because you took so long to say, and I was hurt because it went back to that thing, that sore spot with Alicia. I want to make you happy in every way. I don't want a shortfall. I don't want surprises. I want the best for us. That's what I want, Bebe. Period. Nothing in excess, nothing below grade. The best. What I need from you, Bebe, is a promise of being honest but don't be so in your face with it. Don't be a backdraft. I'm an easygoing man. Subtle works better with me than anything else. Now, what do you want from me?"

Bebe

"I want you to love me the best way that you can," I told Isaac. I didn't want to put a whole bunch of pressure on the boy. I was trying to get us the best just like he was thinking. I obviously went the wrong way with it, or too hard with it, but my intentions were as good and as old-fashioned as Mama's pound cake and I told him so, I told Isaac true: "I didn't want to hurt you and I just addressed it the best way I knew how. I'm not Alicia, though, and that's a straight-up fact. Ain't but one Bebe in this world. Can't no other woman compare with the Be, that's just how I feel about me when it comes to trying to do my best. I want the best for us and the best means that we've got to communicate and never stop. That's what I want from you, a big old free-flowing pipeline with your face at one end and my gorgeous mug at the other. If we got to whisper, that's fine. If we got to shout, that's fine. If we got to read each other's face, that's fine. If we got to read each other's . . . letters . . . well, I hope that's fine too. Let's go for the best, babe. Time is a-wasting, how I see it. Let's just go for the best, huh?"

Isaac

That's what I wanted to hear. I reached over and hugged her tight. I felt more relaxed, more loose than I ever had before. I smelled dusting powder behind Bebe's ear and I kissed the place that was giving off the lovely scent, yet I didn't let her go, not for a long time, and her arms felt strong and good around me.

Finally I opened the wine, poured, and I used two hands around one glass to give Bebe a sip. She used one hand to give me a sip and the other hand stroked the back of my neck. I felt in control and confident and I began to tickle the inside of her ear with my tongue. My hands were roaming, squeezing and detailing, testing the grade of the land that I had visited before and I was enjoying and I listened carefully to her breath . . . yes, Bebe's breathing became deeper, more luscious, her lungs seemed to wrap around the air and blow it back out, welcoming me back with a kiss, and I loved it. Bebe whispered in my ear, "C," and I went there and staked out that area as my own, claiming every inch, hoping for it to give back to me a flourish of emotion. I tended to "C." And to "G." And to "A." However she called it, that's where I went . . . eager to please and pleasing myself all the while too.

Bebe

Baby, I was calling letters left and right, up and down, all around the world! I was hooked on phonics, okay? The nerves in the small places where my arms bend were trembling. Isaac's lips were hot against the ridge of my collarbone and I felt strands of his hair massaging the soft part of my cheek, as if they were kissing me too. His tongue danced along the ridge of my collarbone like an artist on a high wire; then when he got real comfortable, Isaac began to suck my neck, and my arms gripped his shoulders in a vise. I squeezed, hoping to lock him away in this position . . . forever. The soft hairs on my body stood up in shock as a hot current ran the length of my outstretched arms, down my spine, through my hips, and into the meeting place of my thighs. I noticed that the delicious smell of ourselves was filling the room like wafting spices from two cooking pots. I was sweating in places I didn't know I had.

My breasts were hurting around the nipples because they had gotten so firm. Each time Isaac squeezed them with his hands, I'd get a shock of pain that ended in a burst of soft, real comfort. Isaac then took a journey, moving down the center of my body, marking his trail with soft kisses.

I felt his left forearm slide beneath my upper thigh and slant my hip at an angle and a drop of sweat rolled from the soft part of my hip, down across the top seam of my vagina, and splashed against, against . . . his . . . lips.

Isaac is a hard-working man when he puts his mind to it. I spoke to him in appreciation, my legs singing to his in soft, long strokes. My hands massaged messages of love across his back, butt, and thighs. I was gasping for air, not just through physical satisfaction but because of the tender care that our minds were ordering our bodies to give to one another. We went left together, right together, up together, and down together. Thrusting trust is what we had now together. And in that timeless freedom that thrusting trust gives—fear aside and expectations kicked to the curb—there was a release of roasting sensuality that soaked our bodies and our minds until we were drunk, naw, uh-un, until we were downright tore down with each other.

I was so pleased, y'all, this was how pleased I was. When all was said and done, I put on my own tape. Guess what it was? "Ring My Bell" by Anita Ward, number one with a bullet in '79 and hitting the top of the charts with me and Isaac too.

Sandy

Hooked on phonics! Uh-huh! Bebe thinks she is so tough! She came over to tell me about her night with Isaac and her voice was bouncing off the walls. Hooked on phonics! Bebe said that she was thrilled and so relieved that they got all that settled. She said that she made a mistake the first time but never again. And that was her way of acknowledging that I was right and that she was wrong. That was, oh, about three-four weeks ago, and Bebe has been flying ever since.

Every time I talk to her, she's like "Me and Isaac did this" or "Isaac said that" or "Isaac gave me this." And she giggles. Not an out-loud giggle like a woman would normally do, because Bebe is too cool for that. But her body is giggly. Her eyes are bright and, well, giggly. And her walk is giggly like crazy. That walk, a sashay already, is shaking it to the east and shaking it to the west, and the one she loves the best is Isaac. He gave her a black cameo; the base is made of white ivory and the figure, ebony wood. It's one of the most unique and beautiful things I've ever seen. Bebe found Isaac a first-edition in mint condition album of Stevie Wonder's "Talking Book." She even baked him her famous seven-up cake and took it over to the firehouse. Yes, it's clear to me that it's here. It's arrived. Bebe is finally, head over heels, in love. So, I asked her one evening, "So you ready to admit it or what?"

Bebe

Admit what? I was playing the nutroll and I have to confess, it was kind of funny, us having these reverse roles. Now Sandy was sweating me about my business and usually I'm the one sweating her. Okay? If imitation is the sincerest form of flattery—if it truly is?—I should be tomato red from head to toe, blushing in shame, the way Sandy was grilling me about Isaac.

I teased, "Ain't enough that you know most of my business. You wanna know it all, huh?"

"C'mon now, what's going on? I think it's getting quite serious. I think Isaac is out for the count. What's going on, Be?"

Sandy and I were at my place, in the rockers in my cool-out room. Sandy and I were just a-rocking and drinking strawberry daiquiris.

I told her, "Isaac and I are having fun! We're having the time of our lives, that's all."

"You all are too old to just be having the time of your lives without a commitment. It's time for a permanent situation, if you asked me," Sandy said.

I sat right up in that rocker. Freeze! Strike a pose. Give eyeball and attitude. " 'Cuse me? Who are you calling old?"

Sandy hunched her shoulder and took another sip of her drink. "Must be this daiquiri talking."

I took that drink right out of her hand. "Must be!"

"Aw, Bebe!" Sandy said, reaching for it.

I slapped her hand away twice. "G'on before your drinking and your mouth get you in bad!"

Sandy just smiled and slid back in the rocker. "Okay, but you understand what I'm driving at, don't you?"

I just nodded.

"You're not going to tell me whether or not you love him?" Sandy asked me right out this time.

I didn't say a word.

"You're not going to tell me? Me, your girl?" Sandy said. She got up and walked behind me and started to massage my shoulders, "Loosen up those muscles and those big liver lips!"

I laughed. "You are on some thin ice up in this bad boy tonight!"

"Well, answer the question 'cause I already know!"

I smiled on the outside and on the inside. I knew. Sandy knew. I hoped that Isaac knew. Yes, I loved him. Yes, I was in love. I nodded softly.

"Uh-huh, say it!" Sandy grinned, hugging my shoulders.

I whispered, "I'm in love!"

"Shout it!" Sandy said, hugging my shoulders tighter.

"I'm afraid . . . I'll break it," and I couldn't help but snicker like some little kid or something. I felt silly and happy that that silliness was coursing through my veins, spreading a sustaining joy in my body. "Sandy, I love him. I love Isaac, very much."

I felt her hands hesitate on my shoulders, then she patted my shoulders.

"I'm so happy for you, Be. I really am. And can I say something to you—it's hard but can I say it?"

"Sure," I said, a bit surprised, and I brought her from behind me by gently pulling her hand. "What is it?"

Sandy knelt by my rocker and said, "I know I can say this to you, because we are so very tight, like sisters. I'm happy for you but I'm a little jealous, too. When I hear you talk about Isaac, and I see you guys together, I'm happy for you but I get nervous, afraid almost that something that good might not ever happen to me. And it makes me feel funny inside. So I just wanted to say that, and you know I don't mean any harm. You're my best friend, so don't take it wrong . . ."

Wrong? No! "I'm not going to take it wrong. People have feelings like that all the time. Sometimes, girl, sometimes I'm so jealous of you it's a pity."

"Why?" Sandy said, very surprised.

"Look, you're youngER . . . you are smart and so polished and sophisticated! And until I got my degree, I was jealous of you having one!"

"But," Sandy said thoughtfully, "I never felt that."

"Stop lyin'! Not even a little bit? C'mon now," I said, frowning at her. "I can remember a crack or two that I made that was 'bout as subtle as a g-string bikini."

"Yeah," Sandy said, understanding. "Yeah, I hear you. But I never felt that it was anything bad."

"Oh no, you right. It's not bad. It's not a nasty jealous. It's not envy. Envy to me is nasty, like you don't want that person to have whatever it is. But jealousy, I think, is when you recognize something that is wonderful or good or desirable for someone else and realize what a perfect fit it would be in your life. You not trying to shoplift their good thang. Naw. It's just that you want good things, too—not in place of someone else—but just like them TOO. Girl, what you're feeling is as natural as yawning in the morning after a good night's sleep. Ain't no crime, Sandy. Ain't no crime."

Isaac

Alicia came back in my life.

I never would have thought it. Not in this lifetime would I have thought it, although in previous years I'd wished it.

I was driving down the street, near Midway Airport. I'd been at a wholesale flooring place. I was pricing kitchen tile for Uncle Lucius. The ancient, bronze and white speckled linoleum in his place was dangerously pitching little tents across the floor. Uncle Lucius tripped over one the other day and nearly broke his neck. I'd spotted some good buys on tile but I had to rush out of the store because I was running late.

Out of nowhere, on Cicero Avenue, which always has such heavy traffic, a cab tried to cut in front of me.

I saw the driver's side window and the side door swerve and jerk toward my passenger side.

I swerved to my left and back again.

I glared over at the cabby—dark-haired, perspiring, hunched around the steering wheel, thumbs hooked on for dear life—and my eyes cut back in front of me.

I had to slam on the brakes—then pump, pump, pump. My eyes darted back and I saw her sitting in the back seat before the cab sped away in the other lane.

I nearly rear-ended the Jeep in front of me and I swerved, managing to avoid a serious accident for the second time in what seemed like thirty seconds.

Did I see what I thought I saw? Or was my mind playing tricks? Was I crazy? Or had I just glimpsed the twin everyone is suppose to have? Or was it her?

ALICIA.

I cut over, hearing a chorus of horns cursing my move.

I thought: CATCH THE CAB! CATCH THE CAB!

I hit the accelerator, gunning the engine.

CATCH THE CAB! CATCH THE CAB!

I was three blocks or so behind the cab and I struggled to keep it in view.

ALICIA.

I felt my heart rippling with excitement. Was it her? If it was, what was she doing here in Chicago? Where was she going? I cut in front of a powder-blue Caddie and the sister gave me the finger and I waved my hand to apologize. I felt acid building up in my stomach. The radio was playing. The song was the Temps, "Can't Get Next to You." I looked down and slammed the radio off with my fist.

When I looked back up I was braking for a red light. I felt my shocks shouting, *Damn, man!*

The car lurched to a stop, across the crosswalk, but OUT of traffic. I jerked my head left, then right.

Where'd the cab go?!

Bebe

To heck with this funky butt job! I'm reat ta go!

Have you ever had somewhere fun to go after work and just couldn't wait?

I'm there.

I'm so excited I can hardly wait to get out of this crazy bank! I've been working on CDs all day and the only real CD on my mind is the new one by the O'jays which I've been listening to nonstop since last week.

That's because Isaac and I are going to the concert tonight! It's going to be the bomb! I love live music! I just love it and I ain't talking about that trifling lip-synching kind neither. I mean a real group with a real band. Hey now! Like the O'jays! And Dash—Dash, that chile, said, "Y'all have fun at the *Old'jays'* concert."

I told her we would, *especially without her!*

And my man Isaac got us the bomb seats! Fifth row center, and I like to died when I found out that Jean Carne is opening up too? Whoooooo-weeeee! It's going to be a sho' nuff show time.

Can I stand being up in here, Lord, let me see the clock, Timex says . . . whoa, fifteen minutes?

Got to hold on, got to hold on.

Isaac

Where's . . . the cab?

There it is!

I saw the cab just up ahead turning into the airport. I rolled forward, watching a frantic merry-go-round of cold car colors pass my
front bumper as I anxiously waited for the light to turn green.

Go! My tires screeched when I took off. But when I turned into
the lanes marked for departures, I came to a dead halt. The cars were
backed up as people stopped to let their passengers out. It had been
raining a little bit but now it was starting to come down hard. I hit the
wipers and watched as Alicia got out of the cab several feet in front of
me. I saw her grab a small bag, turn, and run for the terminal door
that was labeled CONTINENTAL.

A car ahead of me began to pull out of an unloading space. I cut
off the driver behind me and bogarted in. I jumped out of my car and
ran for the door leading into Continental's gates. I was running and
breathing hard and suddenly I thought . . . a crazy, silly, simple
thought.

What will I do if I catch her?

Bebe

Where is Isaac? The man must crib in a time warp with *no clocks!* He's always late! Isaac knows doggone well that I can't stand to be kept waiting! And it's starting to rain, too. The bank is closed and I'm waiting here in the enclosed cash station lobby. I thought I'd be waiting for a few minutes. Not half an hour!

Where is Isaac? I started kicking myself, wishing that I hadn't left my struggle buggy at the flat. But Isaac said he would pick me up. Or did he tell me to pick him up?

No, no, no . . . now. I distinctly remember Isaac saying that he would pick me up here. I checked my watch. Shoot, it was creeping up on evening rush hour. Whooo, chile, it's going to be rough ridin' for the posse out to the concert!

It's being held at the Holiday Star Plaza Theater in Merrillville, Indiana. Sounds farther away than it actually is—you know—Illinois to Indiana, but the two states are cross-eyed kissing cousins. Our program is all jacked up now, man, we had hoped to get a jump on the expressway traffic.

Where is Isaac?!

Tardy, tardy. I wondered out loud, "What is on that man's mind?"

Isaac

I ran inside the terminal and thank God it wasn't very crowded. I spotted my ex-wife right off and I ran toward her. When I got close enough I yelled out, "Alicia!"

She turned, stared, and her jaw dropped straight down. I was staring at her so hard that I read her lips when Alicia whispered my name. Have you ever gotten a brain freeze from cold food? That icy pain that stops you in your steps? That's what got this brah, and bad.

I hate to say it, and hate the fact that I thought it, but Alicia looked GOOD. I cleared the metal detectors and I walked up to her. "Hi," I said and felt like a fool. After all these years, years of absence, of pain, of wondering and waiting, hoping and disappointment, of regrets and all other kinds of feelings—I simply said, "Hi." Hi. Like I was talking to the yard man, or the woman at the paper stand, or the clerk at the grocery store.

Alicia was just as nutty to me. She just nodded. Alicia nodded like she was saying 'bye to a grocery store clerk, like she was thanking a driver who let her change lanes. She nodded and I said, "Hi."

Excuse my French, but what a fucked-up mess!

Time can hurt. In the seconds that I stood there my mind played match game. I pictured Alicia back in the late seventies when we were young and in love. I pictured the moonlight attempting, and failing, to trim the panoramic view of her Angela Davis 'fro.

Alicia's eyes got me next; "fluid" is the best way I can describe them, always gleaming like rivers ran through them.

Now move on to her lips. Alicia's lips are big and soft like I liked. I'm a lips and hips man. Always have been, always will be. I used to be crazy about brushing the tips of my fingers across Alicia's lips before kissing her. Right there in the airport, in those hurting long seconds, I pictured the kiss.

Then I matched that up with Alicia now.

Alicia looked thin, but healthy . . . she ditched the radical locks of her 'fro and replaced them with a bouncy bob cut that looked very European. Her demeanor seemed a little different—or was it just the stress of this chance meeting? Finally Alicia spoke.

"Let's, let's go somewhere, please," she finally whispered. "Can you?"

I stood there for a minute. Chivalry wasn't dead in my book—it was just a little shocked and surprised. Honestly, I was frozen solid. What was wrong with me? Here she was, my ex-wife, after all these years. Brah just forgot hisself. And unfortunately I wouldn't realize until later that I also forgot about Bebe.

Bebe

I ain't gonna trip 'cause he's late a-gain. Maybe there was an emergency? Could be. I'd better start calling around, trying to see what's up. I dug down in my purse and found some change. I went to the phone booth around the corner. I called and checked my answering machine first. No messages from the Isaac man. Then I called the fire station. L.A. answered, "Hey, Bebe!" Then he started clowning, "Get on board, Love Train! Love Train!"

"You sound like a train wreck," I told him. "I'm waiting on Isaac. Is he there or has he left yet?"

"Is-eye left a long while back, Bebe. He said he was going to price some kitchen tile, go home and change, then he was going to pick you up later from work. Don't put my boy in the doghouse for being a little late!"

"I'm just trying to figure out if I should wait or what? You know how the expressway gets."

"Straight up, that traffic is a monster, girl."

L.A. said exactly what I was thinking.

"I'll try Isaac at home, thanks." Then I hung up.

I dug out my last bit of change and rang Isaac's line. There was no answer and his machine picked up on the fourth ring. He hadn't made it yet. Cool. I left an important message: Just get dressed, stay put. I'd cab it over there and we could leave from his house.

Isaac

I found out Alicia was an airline stewardess. She took me to a new private lounge for airport personnel. Once we were inside, Alicia called around and found a friend to switch flights with her to give us time to talk.

We decided to go to my place. It was close and it would be more private than anywhere we could possibly find inside Midway Airport.

Can you imagine the silence in the car? I'll never forget it. Alicia and I didn't say anything until we got into the house and she asked, quietly, "Where's Dash?"

My first thought when Alicia asked that was, Like you give a shit, being out of her life for so long. I started to say, She's at the mall with her friends. But what your mind wants, and your mouth does, is not always one and the same. I was beginning to get pissed off, you see, and why not? But I wanted to be cool. This woman had hurt me, rejected me, and I wanted to be cool. Brah wanted to give off that look, the body language of . . . of . . . well, put it like this. I used to have a partner back in the day and girls loved him because he had this way of letting nothing faze him. Whenever anyone used to say, "What's going on, man?" my partner would answer, eyes away from the person speaking, "Everythang is everythang."

That's what I wanted to show Alicia. That everything was fine. She

259

left me. She left our child. I'd been lonely. I'd had doubts. I'd been afraid. I'd been numb and angry. But now, *Everythang is everythang*.

"Dash is at the mall with her friends, one of the girls is having a birthday sleepover. Dash likes that kind of stuff." I'd finally found a civil voice to answer her with.

Alicia smiled. "I always liked parties too."

I thought, And she's pretty like you too.

"Is Dash . . . is she . . ." Alicia choked on her words.

"She's a good kid. Smart. Clean-cut. A real good kid."

"Oh, I'm glad. . . . I had hoped so," Alicia said.

I discovered concern in her voice. Why that made me mad I don't know but it did!

"I'm glad you remembered to at least hope for her." My words were small, which was the only way they could have slipped past my tight lips. I could hear the wall clock banging out every second. *Everythang is everythang*.

Alicia dropped her eyes and her bottom lip drew in as she bit softly down on it. She looked hurt. GOOD!

"You didn't really want to see Dash, did you?" I said, my words bigger, my lips loosened with the challenge of trying to hurt her more.

Alicia looked up and sighed. "Yes, I wanted to see her. Of course, Isaac . . . I'm her mother."

"Biologically speaking, yeah." I let loose a bitter laugh. *Everythang isn't everythang*.

"Isaac," she said, dropping her hands crisscross on her knees, "please."

Oh, now she was begging? Beg me, I thought. I wanted to stop my anger but I couldn't. I still hadn't bent my knees to take a squat. I was standing, defiant in a "Be all you can be" army stance. "Please what? I should be telling you please . . . please get out of my house, away from me and my daughter!"

Alicia's eyes were changing. The fluidness was drying up hard and fast. "I've never seen you like this."

"You haven't been here TO SEE."

Alicia sighed. "I-I-I shouldn't have come."

"Why did you?"

"You chased me down, *again.*"

Damn! That hurt. I sat down in a chair near the window, which was slightly cracked, and the air fluttered softly against my back.

"Isaac, I'm sorry," Alicia said and I saw her hands reaching out to me. Now you wanna touch me? I drew back and folded my arms across my chest.

"No, you're right, Alicia. I chased you down just because I wanted to know why? It's killing me. Just . . . why?"

"It's hard to explain, can't you see that in my eyes? I'm not a monster but I just have to have my freedom and I can't explain it any better than maybe it was because of the way my parents were when I grew up. They stayed together, twisting like vines against one another, growing on top of one another and never, ever reaching the heights that they wanted or being really happy."

"I never tried to . . ."

"You only tried to make me something I didn't want to be but what you thought was best for us. But it wasn't what I wanted or could handle."

She was telling me what I had figured out and felt in my gut but how could she just leave Dash?

"But to leave Dash like that," I said, peeling away and laying out every question I had for her.

Tears began to melt down Alicia's face. "I know. I've had nightmares about it, but I couldn't stay and anchor her down. Dash has spirit. She can fly. I knew that I could fly too, and I wanted to be free in the world of people and places . . . and, Isaac, think, baby, what a crime it would be to stay and be a bad parent who stifles her child. Isn't it *harsh* but yet *right* to leave and allow Dash to grow into her own?"

I wasn't even about to attempt to go there. Instead I switched gears. "What about the postcards?"

"The postcards are to remind her that she is loved by me, that she has love out in the world . . . in exotic spots and places."

"It's a painful way to remind her, I think."

"Is Dash hurt by them?" Alicia asked, drying her tears. "Please tell me she's not."

I started to lie, but why? "No, she cherishes them, I think. But I think she's beginning to realize that you're gone for good."

Alicia nodded and we were silent for a few moments. "Does Dash hate me?"

I laughed, sweetly I laughed. "No, she does not hate you."

"Does she love me?"

"Yes," I said softly, sweeter. "Yes, she does."

"I'll always love her." Alicia smiled for the first time and I felt a warmth down in the pit of my stomach.

"Will you always love me?" I asked her.

"Let me show you," Alicia said and she came over and wrapped her arms around me and gave me a kiss.

Bebe

I can't stand nosy folks that dip in other folks' bizness. But sometimes shit happens, huh?

I'm standing on Isaac's front porch, minding my own business, not dipping in his, but I did an involuntary dip—sorta slipped and dipped—and I saw through the curtains—a woman kissing Isaac.

On the mouth. Wasn't no peck neither.

My scalp started to twitch. My legs started to tingle. I was jealous as a mo'fo and I wanted to bang on the window: "Get your big liver lips off my man! I love him! Stop, thief, trying to rip off my stuff!"

People have always said to me, "Bebe, you sure can go for bad."

I wanted to go for her throat is what I wanted to do. But I calmed my anger down and I tried to figure out where Goodyear Lips had come from and how long this test drive Isaac was doing had been going on. I stepped back and stared at her through the window. She looked familiar but I couldn't place her.

Had I seen her at the bank? At a concert? At an art gallery?

Was she out at the Shark Bar or one of the other restaurants or clubs Isaac and I had chilled out at?

Maybe she was. Yeah, maybe she had slipped him her number and now had come over here trying to be the clean-up woman or something. They gonna be doing some cleaning up on her in the emergency room pretty soon if she don't take her lips off of Isaac. What was this? Who did this hot mama think she was? . . . She-she . . . wait a minute. Stop the bus. Now I remembered where I saw her before! I'd seen pictures in Uncle Lucius's photo album. That's Isaac's ex-wife. I'd secretly nicknamed her "Skipper" 'cause she had run out and left everybody hanging. Now Skipper was back on the scene.

I watched them stare into each other's eyes for a long time. Then Isaac gently but firmly pushed her away. She dropped her eyes and said something. Then he said something. Damn, I wish I had bionic ears!

Whoa . . . I jumped back. Skipper made a call and now Isaac was helping her on with her coat. She was leaving! Good-good-good! Whoa, they were heading for the door, together. I've gotta hide, but where?

Isaac

Alicia and I stood out on the front porch waiting for the cab she'd called. We'd decided to keep this chance reunion just between the two of us. Why tell Dash? It'd be like a second rejection. It'd hurt even more this time, I think. The last thing either one of us wanted to do was hurt Dash.

"I'm glad to see you and Dash here with Uncle Lucius. Say, is he still funny?"

"Yeah, seems like that old man will never get any kind of sense. He's still crazy." I smiled. The rain was still coming down, not as hard, but steady.

"Tell him . . ."

"Tell him what? Remember, you haven't been here," I said sternly. "You still don't exist in our lives."

Alicia dropped her eyes and adjusted her purse. "Well," she said with a fake perkiness, "Chicago weather never changes. It's been cold and rainy for a while now."

"Yeah," I said, looking up at the sky. "You might not be able to fly out of here."

"Well, if not, the company will book us some rooms at the Sheraton and get us out early in the morning. I've been stranded in a lot worse places! But it doesn't bother me." Alicia laughed.

"That's because you don't have anyone at home waiting and worrying about you," and the instant that left my mouth, I regretted that I'd said it.

"That's not true, Isaac. I've got wonderful people in my life—friends and lovers—in exotic places across the globe. They just don't tie me down is all."

Uh-huh, I nodded.

"Isaac, do you have someone special in your life?"

Bebe

I held my breath when girlfriend asked that question. And holding your breath, in the rain, while squeezed up behind the porch gutter trying to hide roller-coaster hips is no easy task. But I did, I did hold my breath. I didn't dare exhale either. I waited and I hoped.

"Yes," Isaac told her, then he smiled and said my name.

Exhale. Man, was that a record for holding breath? Felt like it and I felt warm and satisfied when Isaac, my man Isaac, said my name.

"Is she pretty?"

Ha! I knew the answer to that: *Naw, she fine!*

"Not pretty," Isaac said, "but very attractive and funny."

Fine, Isaac, fine.

"Does she treat Dash well? She doesn't pick on her, does she?"

How anybody gonna pick on Baby Godzilla?

"No," Isaac laughed and leaned back, "in fact Bebe was kind of shy with Dash."

"Oh," Alicia said, "sounds like Bebe is lacking in the confidence area."

Oh no, she not tryin' to front. Please!

"Bebe needs more confidence like dynamite needs a match!" Isaac said.

"Hmmm," Alicia said, "well, does Dash like her or what?"

Now we're cool but the child tried to kill me at first!

"Dash was funky in the beginning, but they've warmed up to each other pretty well, I think."

"Oh," Alicia said.

"Hey, here's your ride," Isaac told her.

I looked up the street and saw the cab waiting at the stoplight at the corner. Good. Time for "Mama was a rolling stone" to get going!

Now Isaac was taking Alicia's hand. He stared right into her eyes. "Alicia. Today was the end. As far as I'm concerned that was a good-bye kiss. Don't yoyo in and out of our lives—"

"Haven't you been listening?" she said.

"I know you want to be free *now,* but freedom *now* still costs later down the road. Don't wait ten years or so when you get tired of those planes and gigolos and want to make an emergency landing here. I'm telling you straight: it ain't going on."

Preach, Isaac.

"Isaac," Alicia said, "I knew you had a nasty temper but you always kept it in check around me."

"Times change," he told her.

The cabby honked the horn.

Alicia said, "Well, this is good-bye."

"AGAIN," Isaac said.

Alicia walked down the steps. "Please, every now and then would you hug Dash for me? A big bear hug, huh?"

Isaac smiled and nodded. Then when she turned, he jerked forward and blurted out, "Alicia, are you happy?"

"Yes, Isaac, I am," she said, turning back around. "I really am."

"Good," Isaac said. "Despite all things, I want you to be happy."

Alicia brought both hands to her lips and blew him a kiss.

And when the cab pulled off he didn't wave. My man Isaac stuffed his hands in his pants pockets and when he did pull them out, after the cab was out of sight, they shook like the wind catching a veil. My man Isaac stayed on the porch for a few minutes more. I waited for him to go inside the house.

First, I stretched because I was a little damp and tired from holding myself so stiff and hearing so much stressful stuff. The two of 'em surely gave me a gray hair or two I ain't have prior. But such is life. Second, I rang the doorbell. When Isaac answered the door he like to died. "Bebe! Awww, I forgot—the concert—I-I—"

"Don't stutter, man, just let me in," I said and gave him a warm smile.

"Where's my head?" he said to himself and grabbed his temple. "I'm sorry, I messed up."

"I left a message on your answering machine."

"I haven't had time to stop and check it," Isaac said. "Listen, honey, I'm sorry but I can't—I'm feeling very stressed out . . ."

"Tell you what," I said, "don't worry about the concert. We couldn't make it now even if we were riding in the space shuttle *Sojourner*. Tell you what. Let me give you a massage, a real good back rub, and then I'll leave you to yourself and your thoughts on whatever it is that's bothering you."

Isaac looked so relieved, and he hunched his eyebrows and gave me a corner smile. "You're wonderful."

I wanted to be, for him.

Isaac

The back rub eased some of my tension. I needed that to relax and I even had a glass of wine, which I don't usually drink. I wanted quiet and Bebe let me have it. I toyed with the idea of telling her about Alicia but decided against it. Why complicate things? No one need know but Alicia and me. After Bebe left, I began thinking.

What is our past? Who knows? I don't pretend to be a wizard, an angel, demon, or psychic. I'm simply a man with man thoughts, man dreams, man ideas, and man . . . regrets.

Time heals all wounds, some-somebody said. Whoever it was assumed that we would all live long enough to heal. What about pain that comes so regular that a hundred years on the planet only dries the tears on the outside?

But I still feel the pain of my regret just a little bit on a regular basis. I think about the level of the heart, the high bar like in the Olympics, that each man is challenged to hurdle. I see my emotional bar and it seems as if, the older I get, the higher the bar gets. The older I get, the harder it is for me to focus and to cross.

I can only be a man who faces these things with a real eye. No shades. No blinders. No fake anything on myself. Just real. Making it real. That's in a song somewhere, isn't it? Jazz or blues? Huh? Making it real. Yeah, that sure is in a song somewhere. I think I need to play it. Umh-huh, yeah, I know I'm going to find it and play it. I'm going to live it, too.

That night I couldn't really sleep. I had something on my mind or rather someone. Bebe. There was something about my run-in with Alicia that made me realize the importance of togetherness. There's something settling about having a oneness with someone, and I know that I love Bebe but I was waiting to tell her, partly because I wanted to be clear and sure that she loved me too. Yes, I saw love in her smile and in her arms when they were around me but maybe I was seeing what I wanted to see. Sometimes that happens. Sometimes you want everything to go your road so you mold it and put your fingerprint on it with your mind and your emotions.

I love Bebe and I wanted to tell her. It was crazy to me why I was going through so many changes emotionally. If I could figure it out, I'd open a 900 line and get rich by helping others out of their emotional mess. The only thing I can reason is that I need stability. That I need anchoring. That I need a oneness of spirit and life and faith. I thought back to the night of our first date. What a big-butt smile spread across my face. That fire truck in the driveway was the trick. Drastic measures call for drastic actions.

Now, I wanted to tell Bebe that I loved her. But I needed something extra with it; some way to seal it in both our minds for all time. I thought . . . and thought . . . and thought . . . and watched the hands on the clock come closer and closer together until they applauded my ability to stay up so late and fret so darn much. Then I got my plan, a brilliant one if I must say so myself, and I do say so with conviction. But first . . . I needed an okay . . . and help . . . from Dash.

Dash

Beat Box:
Boom da-ka boom, da-ka boom-boom-yeah!
Boom da-ka boom, da-ka boom-boom-yeah!

Daddy's in love, wants Bebe to stay,
pulled me aside, to see if it's okay.
Got kind of scared, just a little at first,
didn't know what to say, I thought the worst
But Bebe makes him happy, and that's all good,
happier, I think, then Mama would.
But Mama's gone, and Bebe's right here;
she can be part of the family. I have no fear,
I like her fine, Uncle Lucius does too.
We both told Daddy, "Do what you want to do."
And that made him happy, and that makes me smile.
I hope we'll all be happy together for a long, long while.

Bebe

Aretha is crooning from my stereo:

"Giving him something he can feel."

AND

"Daydreaming and I'm thinkin' of you."

I have something for the Isaac man. I need to reward the brother 'cause he been awful good lately. Give him his just due. Sandy, my girl, she ain't got much on me in ways of life but she does have more on me in the bank when it comes to creative stuff in the bedroom. Sister Sandy told me some of the things she's done—like that body caress she threw on piano man T.J.—and I had to look at my little homette and say, "Well, g'on with ya bad self!" I told Sandy I wanted to sex-up Isaac like that.

She said, "Go ahead. I'll even loan you the stuff, including the blindfold."

I told her no, 'cause some things you just don't borrow.

"Well, what are you going to do?" Sandy said, grinning. "It's got to be unique!"

I rolled my eyes at her. "Is there anyTHANG ordinary 'bout me? I'm going to come up with my own thing, an outrageous Bebefied thing."

"Like what?" Sandy said, all anxious.

"Like something befitting . . ."

"Uh-huh, uh-huh . . ." Sandy said.

"You like that word, befitting? I read that in one of those literary classics when I was in night school. Befitting. Got a sweet little old ring to it. I like new words because—"

"Bebe, who cares! WHAT are you going to do?"

Sandy

Of all the nerve. Bebe would not tell me what she was going to do until AFTERWARD. All she said was that she had to convince her cousin to let her use her apartment because her Cousin Jean had something in her bedroom that few people had.

"What is it?" I asked her.

"It's necessary," Bebe said. "A must gotta!"

Then the only other thing Bebe would say was that she also had to go by the hardware store. "The hardware store!" I said and couldn't help but laugh. "Remember the last time we were in the hardware store together?"

Bebe said, "Yeah, getting the makings for our BIG PAYBACK scheme on T.J.!"

Yeah, our little commando raid was something else. "But, Be," I said, "we're not mad at Isaac. What—" And Bebe cut me off and said, "Don't sweat me! I'll tell you all about it later. Just wish me *love*."

And I did.

Isaac

Brah man is confused! Bebe is acting strange. But she sounds happy. I guess it's some happy strange black woman thang and I just don't understand. But Bebe called me and said that I should meet her at this address she gave me. Meet her, she said, at midnight.

Dudes in the firehouse were like, "Hold up! Hold up! you didn't make her mad or nothin', huh, man?"

At first I said, "No!" Then I was a little less sure of myself and said, "No." Then I thought, I don't think so.

"Dog, careful with them females, it could be something scandalous!" L.A. howled. "Somebody better go with him!"

Then the other guys started joking, throwing in their two cents, saying things like, you're on your own, not me, did you see Angela Bassett blow up that car in *Waiting to Exhale?*

Cliff gave me props when he wolfed, "Isaac knows how to handle himself, jack!"

"Maybe," Bobo said, letting his accent thicken like gravy, "maybe it's one of those sex parties, games with more than one girl, huh, Esee?"

Everybody looked at me at once and said, "I got your back!"

Bebe

And the O'jays sang, "Almighty dollar!"

Cousin Jean gave up her apartment. It was a struggle but she owed me sixty-five dollars, a debt which I erased for the use of her crib for one night.

This sexed-up business ain't cheap. First sixty-five dollars for Jean's flat and another forty-five dollars for the stuff I needed from the hardware and the toy store. Then I was all set. I got to Jean's place carrying all my bags. I checked the clock and it was 10:30 P.M. I went into the bedroom and got to work. I got everything in place, then I got dressed. As my Aunt Corey used to say, I was "reat ta go!" But the question was, where was Isaac?

Isaac

Brah was running a little late. Bebe says I'm going to be late for my own funeral. I was late leaving the firehouse. I got to the address wondering what could Bebe be up to. I was cautiously excited. I didn't want to jump to conclusions and then later get disappointed. I got to the apartment door and it was cracked open. I opened it wider, just enough to stick my head in. "Bebe?"

The living room was dark but right by the door was a partially rolled-up garden hose with a note propped up on it that said, "Follow." Then the hose unraveled like string until it reached a door in the corner of the living room. The door was partly open and I could see a white light flickering on and off, off and on. I kept following the hose, walking over, and I opened the door all the way and said, "Bebe?"

As soon as I said her name, a tape player in the corner came on playing the Ohio Players' cut, "Fire!"

My mouth dropped open. The strobe was throwing light all around the room. There were candles around this huge circular bed.

"Fire!"

I was looking over there at the bed. Suddenly the closet door opened from the other side and out jumped Bebe in a red fireman's hat, a trench coat, red pumps, doing a hip-swinging dance.

The tape was pumping, "The way you walk and talk . . ."

Talk? I was speechless. She came over and ran her hands up and down my body. She started opening her coat and closing it. Girl had nothing on underneath! She led me over to the bed and slowly eased off her coat and let it fall to the floor at my feet. My head was spinning. Now all she had on was the fireman's hat and the red pumps and she straddled my leg and ran her hands around my neck and nibbled at my ear, then stopped and swung back as I reached for her. . . .

"The way you swerve and curve really wrecks my nerves . . ."

The Ohio Players weren't lying! I felt sweat dropping down the back of my neck. Bebe kept dancing and she came back over and unbuttoned my shirt and then my pants. . . . I was throbbing up high in my chest and down low. The song kept playing and she rolled over by the nightstand near the bed and picked up a toy fire truck she had there and the ladder was extended, and on the steps of the ladder were little packages of condoms all in a row!

"Fire!"

I almost fell out. But Bebe grabbed me by the neck and ran her lips across mine, brushing them, but not a peck did she give a brother. Instead Bebe pulled me over to the bed and she took off the hat as the record began to end, and she placed it on my head. And at that last drumbeat, Bebe fell back on the bed and it began to roll—a water bed? I didn't know anybody still had one of those things! I was breathing heavy and she, she was sweating, her body glistening, and she said, "Fire! Now. Put me out."

Sandy

I picked up Bebe to go to the talent show. Her car was on the bonks again and Isaac had to go ahead and help get things ready at the community center, so Bebe caught a ride with me. Bebe was wearing the dress I made her.

"You look fabulous, Be!" I told her. That's all the intro someone like Bebe needs! Vain! That woman is so vain it's a crying shame.

Bebe started parading around the room. "Oh, I'm so fine. Yes, yes, I am! 'Fine' should be my middle name or should it be 'Stunning' or maybe, just maybe, 'Sho' you right'?"

"You know my car is small in the front. We're going to have to toss out that big ego."

"Nah-un! Let go my ego!" Bebe said and kept sashaying and posing. She stopped and reared back.

"Isaac is going to really like that dress," I said.

"He'll like it better off," Bebe said and rolled her left shoulder.

"Fast! Fast! C'mon, hot mama!" I told her and took her by the arm. I didn't want to be late, because I knew Miss Thing had a surprise coming.

The community center was about six blocks away from the firehouse. Isaac had called me and during our conversation told me that the talent show was an annual spring event and so word had gotten around very quickly. He said that the ticket money was used to make repairs at the center or to buy new athletic equipment. We were in the gym, which was very large, and had that musky gym smell to it. But the kids had decorated it very nicely with red, blue, yellow, and orange balloons. There was even a big welcome banner made out of crepe paper tacked onto the wall. The letters were cut out of black construction paper and outlined with gold glitter. The *M* was crooked but the message was warm. The metal folding chairs were all lined up in sections on a slant so everyone could see the performances. As soon as Bebe and I walked through the door, a senior gentleman with a gold tooth in a gray suit, hat, and white-handled cane yelled, "Bebe! I say, I say, come over here—you and your chocolate gurlfriend! I've been waiting on y'all sweet thangs!"

"Don't tell me," I leaned into Bebe and whispered. "That's Uncle Lucius."

"Who else?" was Bebe's answer and we walked over and he gave her a big hug. We were introduced and he gave me a hug too.

We were early and Uncle Lucius was our early entertainment. He kept us laughing, talking about Isaac when he was a kid, himself, and anyone that walked into the room. I was checking my watch, anxious for the show to start, and for Bebe's surprise. She didn't have a clue and I was loving it.

Isaac came out from a back room as the gym started to fill up. He just had on a T-shirt and jeans, wasn't dressed yet for his performance. He came over and gave Bebe a big hug and he kissed me on the cheek. The show was going to start any minute and Dash and her friend were going on first.

It was fun being in the gym. Neighborhood events like this still seemed to draw a crowd like they did in the old days, when I was a kid.

There wasn't an empty seat in the house now. A tall, nice-looking guy, around my age, cute but real skinny, came up to the mike and started talking. He had on a fireman's T-shirt like Isaac's. I leaned over to Bebe, "Say . . ."

"I know where you're going," Bebe concluded and concluded right, "but you don't wanna go there. That's L.A. He gambles too much and likes to get busy too much with too many different sisters."

That was that.

The house lights dimmed. Theater lights came on in back and the stage area was bathed in blue, red, and white light. Then the music came on, the speakers hoisted high in the corners of the room popped a couple of times first, but the music came on and it was a low, sexy beat from "Don't Look Any Further" by the Temptations' lead singer Dennis Edwards. But it wasn't the words, just that smooth funky beat looped over and over again. Dash and Tasha came out, from opposite ends of the stage, doing a slow languid step with just a smidgen of bop to it. They had on black swing dresses, above the knee, sleeveless, with silver sequins around a high neck. They looked chic but not too sexy. They had their braids up in the back, high off the neck, but with strands dangling just along the ear, in front with a twist. As they strutted onto the stage, mikes in one hand, the other on their hips, I heard Bebe say, "Walk, y'all!"

Bebe's mark was all over this choreography. I nudged her with my elbow and she smiled back. "They look great, huh?"

And they did. Dash started singing when they hit center stage; it wasn't the words of the song, just a very gospel-bluesy, scat and rolling of notes up the scale—the girl had range. Tasha then broke out with a rap . . . a slow, sassy rap about love and respect in relationships. They had steps and everything, a bop move here . . . a slow tootsie roll move to a stop . . . hand movements, too. . . . They were bad! Everybody in the whole place was cheering when they finished! They were a hit! Dash and Tasha ate up the applause, then hugged each other and waved as they left the stage.

The other acts were good, some funny, mostly it was kids. One little boy stood in the middle of the stage and was supposed to read a poem but instead said nothing and just scratched his temple, pulled at his tie, and wiped his crying eyes with it. Even his daddy couldn't get a word out of him. But we clapped anyway.

Then Isaac and his crew had their turn. They came out in white suits with white shirts and white ties. White on white! They looked smooth! They lip-synched to the Tavares' "Remember What I Told You to Forget"—it's a slow cut but very gritty. They were jamming. Then there was a hard three-count beat—boom, boom, boom—then the Temptations' "Get Ready" came on. They were running in place and then started doing all the old hand moves and side steps, the works!

After about thirty seconds of that, they slipped behind a makeshift curtain. Then, on cue, the guys came running out and slid one right behind the other to a stop. And they were right in time to that beginning piano riff of the Jackson Five's "I Want You Back!" But now their jackets and ties were off, shirts were open three buttons down, and they had on these big afro wigs! You remember how the Jackson Five used to have those huge afros, especially Jackie?! The guy Bebe said was L.A., he was playing Michael, and he was doing that little skip dance Michael used to do. Well, he started to spin and because he was so skinny it made him look as if he was moving extra fast, like he was going to drill a hole in the stage straight down through the floor. Then all of the guys lined up and did the move that was on the "Motown 25th Special," one step forward, knees bent to a lean, point and bob the head. Bebe was cheering, jumping up dancing! The entire gym was going wild, just like a real concert or something! I was sorry that I was going to miss the rest of it but I had to sneak out. . . . I had to sneak out fast and in a hurry, as Bebe would say, to keep my promise, my part in the big plan.

Isaac

I was dying! My legs were hurting! But we were having a ball! We're going over big! I could see Uncle Lucius nodding and waving his cane in the front row and Bebe was dancing and clapping and the whole crowd was really behind us.

After changing into a loud leopard jacket, we ran back out as the song, "The Bird" by the Time, was playing. My legs were killing me but I was huffing and puffing and sweating but keeping up! I was squawking when I was supposed to and doing the "bird" dance, which was nothing but the penguin from the old schooldays with a little slide on the end. I held the mirror for Bobo, who was Morris Day, rubbing his hand over his slicked-back black hair. The crowd ate it up!

We did the dance all the way back behind the curtain and took off the jackets and put on our fire hats and grabbed a cut-off hose from one of the old trucks for the last number, which was by far the easiest because I was on the back end and all I had to do was walk slow. . . . The Ohio Players, which used to be the Ohio Untouchables first, their cut "Fire!" came on and we started stepping out. Cliff was in front. He broke away and we kept walking, holding the hose, walking in step, only turning our heads left . . . hold—hold . . . turn right as the group grunted, "Fiiiii-re!"

WOW!

Cliff had on a big Afro wig and he had cut it so part of the hair was hanging over his left eye like the Ohio Players' lead singer Leroy "Sugarfoot" Bonner. Cliff looked funny as hell! We finished it on out, I was going to pass out if we did another step or had another change! Thank God it was over! We took a bow and the crowd gave us a standing ovation. Some people, mostly the teenagers, were barking like dogs and pumping their fists in the air, Arsenio Hall style. The noise was deafening. When the curtain closed, we all collapsed on top of each other. We were all hugging each other and then Bobo shook me and said, "Get busy, Esee!"

I went to change quickly. I ran into Dash, Sandy, and Tasha and they were already dressed. I was hurrying as fast as I could. My heart was beating as I hurried down the short hallway. It was time for my personal encore.

Bebe

Heyyyyy now! My baby jammed, he got off! Isaac and them tore up the house! They were great and a lot of fun. But I ain't never lied, Isaac looked like he was about to die at the end there. Whooo, he was a-huffing and a-puffing. Thought I didn't see it, but I saw it. The Be don't miss much INCLUDIN' meals. Yes sir, I'm gonna tease his butt later.

Now . . . where was Sandy? She must have gone to the bathroom and fallen in! L.A. took the mike and said that there was one more act, an added bonus performance. Me and Uncle Lucius fell back in our seats, exhausted because we had just about given ourselves out from watching and cheering for Isaac and 'em.

Where is Sandy?

I got up and Uncle Lucius said, "Where you goin'?"

"To find Sandy," I said, "maybe she got lost or something."

"This ain't no tollway! The gurl can find her own way back! Sit, sit and keep me company so I can keep up my rep as a dirty old man!" he joked.

That made me smile and I patted his knee and sat back down. A couple of minutes later, L.A. came down to the front row and said, "Bebe, can you come backstage and help us for a second? Dash and Tasha are in this last number and need your help."

I got up. "Uncle Lucius?"

"G'on! G'on!" he said and faked like he was mad. "L.A. gotta steal all the women!" And then he scooted us along with his cane.

I hurried with L.A. backstage. I didn't know they had added a number. L.A. flipped back a heavy drape that served as a curtain. He said, "See the table behind our prop curtain? Right next to that stool there? We left all our junk there, wigs and jackets and stuff, and they need that cleaned off right quick so they will have enough room to put their props and stuff out."

Cool. I went behind the table and started folding up the leopard jackets and collecting the mirrors and wigs. Now I'm trying to hurry and I got all this stuff in my arms and all of a sudden I hear the main curtain go back, and the stage lights come on! I'm looking all around, thinking, Wait! Wait! Now I'm dropping stuff, trying to get off the stage when these hands roll away the prop curtain and I'm staring at the audience and they're all staring at me and I just dropped every- thing and the whole place starts laughing! I like ta died! Then I see L.A. standing in the wings with the curtain, waving! I wave back, looking out front, then at him, waving, C'mon! Get back out here, fool! I start walking offstage and my shoe gets caught in the clothes on the floor and comes off, now I'm walking like Hopalong Cassidy! The whole place is laughing! L.A. and the rest of the people crowding around him are yelling, "Stay there!"

"Noooo, Lordy!" I yell back. "For what?"

"For this," Isaac says over the mike system. He's at the other end of the stage in a tuxedo. "Have a seat, lady."

Then I hear this music start playing and it's Barry White's "I'm Never, Never Gonna Give Ya Up!"

I had to sit down on the stove before I fell down. Isaac started dancing, a sexy dance with the hips, and the crowd was up clapping and from the other end of the stage comes . . . Dash, Tasha, and

Sandy! They had on these black miniskirts with black short-sleeve tops and those colorful feather boas around their arms, swinging them and throwing their hips. And Isaac is coming my way lip-synching, "Right on! Right on! Whatever, whatever!"

I had to cover my eyes, I was so shocked! Now the girls were at an angle on the left, two-stepping and dipping, and Isaac was singing to me on the right. Isaac sang that he'd found what he was looking for and that he had hoped and prayed for me. Isaac sang and got on one knee and said he wasn't about to give me up and couldn't live without me!

Isaac was cuttin' up! I was looking through my fingers because I was so excited and tingly all over and I didn't know what to do with my hands or what to do with my face—look cool? Just grin? Laugh? What?! I could feel my legs just shaking because I was so excited and I felt the love that he was giving me and in front of all these people! And Tasha, Dash, and Sandy were over there "do wopping" their butts off, singing, "Go 'head! Go 'head!"

Then the audience jumped in, "Go 'head! Go 'head!"

When the song ended, Isaac was in front of me down on one knee, holding up a red velvet box and he said into the mike, "I love you and I'm never gonna give you up!"

I looked over at the girls and they were just grinning! I looked right at Dash and she winked at me and gave me a nod.

The crowd was quiet, and Isaac said, "You want my arm to fall off?"

He sounded just like Billy Dee Williams in *Lady Sings the Blues,* only *better!* I took the box out of his hand and the gym got quiet. And that's saying something for a roomful of black folks to get that quiet that fast. I opened the box so slowly and I swear I could hear it creak just a bit as I opened it. And right there inside was a girl's best friend—a big ole diamond—sparkling at me. The ring was gorgeous!

Isaac said, "Will you marry me?"

And I whispered in the mike, "Yes!"

And the place went kah-kah! Isaac slid up and filled my arms with his body and my heart with love and he gave me a long, passionate kiss and I curled my toes inside my shoes. I've never been so happy in my life and felt so secure and warm and loved! Dash came over and gave me a hug and I asked her, "This is okay with you?"

She said, "Yeah, would I agree to be a do wop girl if it wasn't?"

Then I cut my eyes at Sandy and she said, "Congratulations, Be. I'm so very happy for you!"

And I gave her a hug and I felt the tears coming and they felt so good and clean and I was happy to let them come. Then from the wings, the song . . . the song that would now be our song . . . the song that we danced to that first night in my apartment began playing. "Betcha By Golly Wow." Isaac wiped away my tears of joy and took my hand and hugged me tight. Then he lifted me off the stool in a whirl and we began to dance. And I felt his hands firm against my back and in one hand he still held the mike. I brought that hand around and snuggled the mike between us and I sang, I sang with all my heart to him. I sang; "Bebe's by golly wow . . . you're the one I've been waiting for forever. . . ." And, y'all, I'm telling you, I felt the most wonderful, all-encompassing love . . . ever.

About the Author

Yolanda Joe is the author of the *Blackboard* bestselling books *He Say, She Say* and *Falling Leaves of Ivy*. A former newswriter for CBS in Chicago, Joe is a graduate of Yale University and the Columbia School of Journalism. She lives in Chicago.